THE PHOENIX BALLROOM

ALSO BY RUTH HOGAN

The Keeper of Lost Things
The Wisdom of Sally Red Shoes
Queenie Malone's Paradise Hotel
The Moon, the Stars, and Madame Burova

THE
PHOENIX
BALLROOM

A Novel

RUTH HOGAN

wm

WILLIAM MORROW
An Imprint of HarperCollins*Publishers*

THE PHOENIX BALLROOM. Copyright © 2024 by Tilbury Bean Books Limited. All rights reserved. Printed in the United States of America. No part of this book may be used or reproduced in any manner whatsoever without written permission except in the case of brief quotations embodied in critical articles and reviews. For information, address HarperCollins Publishers, 195 Broadway, New York, NY 10007.

HarperCollins books may be purchased for educational, business, or sales promotional use. For information, please email the Special Markets Department at SPsales@harpercollins.com.

Originally published in Great Britain in 2024 by Corvus.

FIRST U.S. EDITION

Designed by Diahann Sturge-Campbell
Elegance vintage chandelier illustration © Morphart Creations/Shutterstock

Library of Congress Cataloging-in-Publication Data has been applied for.

ISBN 978-0-06-334874-5 (paperback)
ISBN 978-0-06-338667-9 (hardcover library edition)

24 25 26 27 28 LBC 5 4 3 2 1

To Ancients of Moo Moo

Blessed are the cracked, for they shall let in the light.
—ATTRIBUTED TO GROUCHO MARX

PROLOGUE

Once upon a time ...

The ballroom was a sleeping beauty waiting for the kiss of life. After years of neglect, the floor was velveted with dust that lay undisturbed save for the featherlight tracery fashioned by resident mice. The once bright stars that studded the indigo ceiling were now a ghostly constellation barely visible beneath the dirt, and the art deco chandeliers were choked with cobwebs. Along one wall, tall mirrors hung in a line, but the glass in each was mottled: a metallic leopard print that threw back only a scattered mosaic of imperfect reflections. A dozen or so chairs stood moth-eaten and forlorn around the edges of the room, like wallflowers waiting for an invitation to dance, and the piano in the corner was silent, its keys sticky with damp. Dead flies freckled the sills of the windows where faded curtains still hung, ravaged by moths. But outside, as the sun slipped down behind the rooftops of the town, its fiery light caught crystal from a chandelier and ricocheted a rainbow across the ballroom floor.

Up on the roof, Crow watched ribbons of gold and purple light bleed into blackness and the moon swap shifts with the sun.

CHAPTER 1

Venetia Hamilton Hargreaves wondered whether sandwiches and sausage rolls might have been a better choice than canapés as she waited for her husband's corpse outside Saint Paul's Church. It would soon be lunchtime, and surely people would prefer something more substantial than a sliver of smoked salmon on a cracker smeared with cream cheese? Well, it was hard cheese now. Too late to change. The air was heavy and humid, and a heat haze shimmered off the gleaming black paintwork of the hearse. A storm was forecast. The coffin was crowned with an elaborate spray of lilies and ivy, and the blooms trembled with every step the pallbearers took as Venetia followed them down the aisle—the same aisle that she had walked as a bride, carrying freesias and lilies of the valley on the arm of her handsome groom almost fifty years before. A sad but somehow satisfying symmetry. This time she had her son at her side. It had been her son, Heron, who had insisted on canapés, specified the champagne, and booked the hotel where both were to be served after the service. Venetia's suggestions had been swatted aside because Heron had assured her that he "knew best." He had even chosen her outfit, and she had let him have his way. For now. He took his place beside her in the front pew as the coffin was set down on trestles before the altar. His face was red with the effort of containing his emotions, and he clutched a meticulously folded handkerchief in his fist in case eventually he should fail. Heron was an unfortunately comic misnomer for one so deficient in stature and grace, but his grandfather had been a keen amateur ornithologist. He had named his children Hawk, Osprey, Nightingale, and Swan, and his sons had continued the practice with their own offspring. With his scarlet cheeks and tubby torso, poor Heron looked more like a crotchety Christmas card robin. Venetia placed her hand on his arm and gave it a gentle squeeze. She felt him tense at her touch and returned her hand to her lap. In contrast to her son's discomfort, Venetia was surprisingly sanguine for her public debut as a widow. She would miss her husband—of course she would—but in the way that one misses a comfortable cardigan that has shrunk in the wash and become too tight to wear.

The church was almost full. Hawk Hamilton Hargreaves had been a popular and well-respected man, and he would have been gratified to see such an impressive turnout for his last hurrah. He had chosen the order of service himself, and Venetia was grateful. It had saved her the worry, and she was glad for him that he was getting exactly what he wanted. After welcoming the congregation with respectful solemnity, the vicar announced the first hymn, and as they stood to sing "Jerusalem," the small boy beside Venetia clattered to his feet, dramatically brandishing his hymnbook in both hands. Kite was Venetia's ten-year-old grandson, and this was his first funeral. He was clearly enjoying the occasion immensely and sang with gusto, his dark curls bouncing as he nodded vigorously in time to the music. A growl of thunder added an impromptu percussion accompaniment to the organ, and Kite's eyes widened with delight. The front-pew lineup was completed by his mother, Monica, who was a born-again atheist and had made it clear that she was there only to keep up appearances. When the congregation sang "Bring me my spear, O clouds, unfold," their command was seemingly obeyed as a bolt of lightning flashed and forked behind the largest of the stained-glass windows, showering its rainbow colors onto the altar.

The rest of the service was conducted in competition with the storm and was, at times, all the better for it. Heron's eulogy to his father—touching and sincere in sentiment but a little dull in its delivery—was much enlivened by cracks and booms from the heavens above. Swan, sister of the deceased, wearing a velvet opera coat and a black net veil attached to a jeweled headband, recited the Henry Scott Holland poem about death being nothing at all and the person having only slipped into the next room. Having forgotten to replace the batteries in her hearing aids, Swan spoke at a volume that not only could be clearly heard above the thunder, but was probably audible in the next street. Kite struggled valiantly to suppress his giggles until Monica silenced him with a scowl. Venetia caught his eye and winked at him consolingly. Prayers were said, "Abide with Me" was sung, but it wasn't until the final piece of music began to play that tears blurred Venetia's eyes. Hawk had chosen Edward Elgar's "Nimrod" to mark his farewell. Of course he had. Dignified, tasteful, British. Achingly conventional. Exactly like himself. A decent, kind, respectable, slightly pompous man who had guarded his conventionality with his life. Literally. And Venetia couldn't help wondering how things might have been if he hadn't. But he had been the best husband to Venetia that it was possible for him to have been, and for that she would be forever grateful.

Before leaving the church, Venetia approached the coffin and brushed her fingertips across the polished oak.

"Goodbye, Hawk," she whispered. "Time to face the music." She hoped sincerely that he would dance.

Kite hovered behind her uncertainly. "Can I touch it?" he asked.

"Of course," Venetia replied.

Kite slapped both hands down on the lid of the coffin with a resounding thud. "Bon voyage, Grandpa! And don't forget you said I could have your chess set!"

Outside, the storm had passed, and the air was clean and fresh. Sunlight glistened on the wet pavement. It was only a short distance to the hotel, and although Heron would have preferred them to travel in the limousine, Venetia insisted on walking.

"The arrangement was that we should take the car," he chided her, clearly irritated at the deviation from his meticulously planned program for the day. But Venetia held firm. She took Kite's hand to cross the busy main road and set off toward the town's Victorian embankment in her smart but sensible low-heeled, much-hated black court shoes. Within minutes they had reached the hotel and were met by a member of the staff who told them that she was "very sorry for their loss" and showed them through to a function room overlooking the river where the wake was to be held. A waiter offered Venetia a glass of champagne, which she accepted gratefully, and she took a large sip. Heron frowned.

"Best take it easy with that, Mother," he warned. "We have a lot of guests to greet"—the first of whom arrived before Venetia had a chance to reply. There followed almost half an hour of thanking people for coming and accepting their condolences, during which time the waiter discreetly refilled Venetia's glass as necessary. It struck her once again that this was a strange echo of their wedding—the stream of guests and perfunctory exchanges with people ranging from family and friends through to acquaintances and even some, to Venetia at any rate, complete strangers. The last mourners to enter the room were two men whom she had never seen before. Heron thanked them for coming and excused himself before they could reply, his priggish sense of propriety finally exhausted, or perhaps simply usurped by the desire for a drink. But Venetia was curious. They certainly didn't look like former colleagues of Hawk's from the legal profession, nor did they resemble his usual brand of cronies who wore corduroys and had season tickets at Twickenham and Lord's and holiday homes in Scotland or Norfolk. The first of the two, a man of about Venetia's age with gray hair and pale green eyes, took her hand and, instead of shaking it, simply held it between his own.

"You must be Venetia," he said. "We were old friends of Hawk's. We lost touch with him some years ago, but we thought of him often. I'm so very sorry."

His sincere and concise expression of sympathy was spoken quietly, but with warmth and confidence, and Venetia was touched. Before she had time to respond, Kite appeared wearing a pained expression and waving a canapé, and the two men moved away toward a waiter serving champagne.

"Nisha, what *is* this?" Kite asked in a stage whisper, sniffing the canapé with exaggerated suspicion. "Why isn't there any proper food?"

"Nisha" had been his earliest attempt at pronouncing her name and had somehow stuck.

"It's smoked salmon and cream cheese."

Kite was unimpressed. "It's all slimy. Aren't there any sandwiches? I'm starving." He was still whispering, having been warned by his father to be on his best behavior, but his grandmother was always his chosen ally.

Venetia smiled. "I'll see if we can rustle up a bag of crisps." She spoke to one of the waiters, and Kite was soon tucking in to his favorite salt and vinegar snack.

"Now that I've got you some crisps," she told him, "you can return the favor."

He immediately offered her the packet. She shook her head.

"No, I want you to come with me and chat to your great-aunts. I need a wingman."

"What's a wingman?"

"Someone who helps out in tricky situations. Someone you can trust."

Kite grinned. "Well, that's definitely me. I'm your wingman. Mum says Nightingale and Swan are as mad as a box of frogs."

Venetia glanced over to the window where her husband's sisters were sitting surveying their fellow guests and downing as much champagne as they could.

"That may be true, but they're also family."

"I like them," Kite replied. "I like frogs too. But not to eat."

Nightingale saw them approaching and waved them over. "How are you bearing up, my dear?" she asked Venetia.

Venetia shrugged, hoping that that would suffice as the answer to an impossible question, but one that everyone kept asking her. She had no idea how she was. Her husband had died, and she had just attended his funeral. How was she supposed to be?

"And how's my great-nephew? Let me have a proper look at you."

Kite stepped forward gamely, waiting for the inevitable "Haven't you grown?"

"Haven't you grown? You look exactly like your father did at your age."

Kite didn't appear to be flattered by the comparison, but remembering his role as wingman, he offered Nightingale a crisp. She declined—to his obvious relief.

"It's lovely to see you both. How was your journey?" Venetia wondered how many platitudes they could exchange before Swan interjected.

"Bloody awful!" bellowed Swan. She had lifted the black veil away from her face and swept it back over her hair. She looked like a Halloween bride.

"Oh dear! Was it the trains?"

"No, not that! I'm not talking about that. I'm talking about dying! Bloody awful thing to happen!"

"Grandpa was *very* old," ventured Kite.

"*I'm* very old!" Swan replied. "But I don't want to bloody die!"

Kite offered her his crisps and she took a handful.

"Now don't upset yourself, dear. You're years younger than Hawk was." Nightingale grabbed another two glasses of champagne and handed one to her sister. Swan swigged from her glass.

"I'm not upset! I'm bloody furious! It'll be us next."

Venetia's wingman stepped up once again. "It's an empirical fact that women live longer than men," Kite announced. "So, it's more likely that Great-Uncle Osprey will die first."

Great-Uncle Osprey was standing at the bar looking perfectly well and drinking a whisky and soda. Meanwhile, Heron had joined them, anxious to find out what all the shouting was about and equally anxious to put a stop to it.

"Is everything all right?"

"No, it bloody well isn't!" boomed Swan. "We're all going to die!"

"But Great-Uncle Osprey's going first," added Kite helpfully.

THAT EVENING, ALONE in her bedroom, Venetia stood at the window watching a pair of swans glide beneath the elegant arch of the suspension bridge. She recalled that swans mate for life (except her sister-in-law, who had never shown any inclination to mate with anyone), and Venetia too had pledged "till death do us part." She had kept her promise. But what now? It had been a long day and she was exhausted. She kicked off her shoes and sat down on the bed where she had laid Hawk's dressing gown on top of the covers on *his* side. They had their own rooms, largely due to their conflicting nocturnal habits. Hawk had snored like thunder and would fall asleep as soon as his head hit the pillow, and Venetia liked to read or watch old films until past midnight. But they had still occasionally shared a bed, and it had been comforting and companiable. Sometimes one would read aloud to the other, or they would attempt a crossword together. Sometimes they would simply hold hands and say nothing until they drifted off to sleep.

Catching sight of herself in the full-length mirror beside her wardrobe, she shook her head in disbelief. How had she allowed herself to become this old woman? At eighty-four, Hawk had been ten years her senior. He *had* been old, and perhaps it had rubbed off on her like rust. But she wasn't ready for that yet. She wasn't ready to be old. She studied her reflection in dismay. Her gray hair was styled in a neat but unflattering bob, and the black crepe de chine dress that Heron had chosen for her was little better than an expensive sack. He had wanted her to stay with them for a few days. "It isn't right that you should be on your own at a time like this," he had told her, but she had insisted that she would be fine. He had eventually relented but told her that he would be around first thing in the morning to check on her. Poor Heron. He always tried so hard to get things *right*. But right for whom? He worried far too much about what other people thought instead of thinking for himself. It had been hard for him today—Hawk hadn't just been his father, he had been his hero. Venetia had told him that the day had been perfect, that his father would have been very proud of him. Heron had broken down and sobbed in her arms. He had spent his whole life trying to live up to his father's example, but Venetia hoped that now he might discover that he could be his own man.

She drew the curtains and got undressed, folding the black sack and leaving it on the back of a chair. There was no point returning it to her wardrobe because she had no intention of ever wearing it again. The shoes were going in the bin. Suddenly she wasn't tired anymore. She pulled on Hawk's dressing gown. The faint scent of Acqua di Parma, the cologne that he had always worn, still clung to the fabric. Downstairs in the kitchen, she took a bottle of wine from the fridge and poured herself a glass. It was getting dark, and stars were beginning to prick the evening sky. She raised her glass in a silent, affectionate toast to the man who had died, and vowed that her life was about to begin anew.

CHAPTER 2

Heron arrived too early the following morning, apparently keen to get something off his chest.

"I'm arranging a live-in companion-cum-housekeeper for you," he announced, his tone clearly implying that his mother should be pleased. Venetia was appalled.

"I don't want a companion-cum-housekeeper! I can manage perfectly well on my own."

Heron sighed. "Now, Mother, we can't have you rattling around in this big house all alone. What if you were to have a fall?"

"I'm perfectly fit and healthy. Why on earth should I have a fall? I'm not a toddler!"

"Exactly! You're an elderly lady who simply needs a little help around the house and someone to keep you company on outings— visits to the theater and cinema and the like . . ."

The word "elderly" stung like a nettle.

"For heaven's sake, Heron! You sound like one of those advertisements for domestic staff in *The Lady*. I don't need any help, and I already have company for visits to the theater and cinema and the like. They're called friends!"

Heron flushed a little. "It's completely understandable that you want to keep your independence, and surely this is the best way? Better than moving into some dreadful retirement village."

Venetia laughed out loud in disbelief but was saved from saying precisely what she thought by the breathless arrival of Kite, who had been distracted on his way in, checking for ripe strawberries in the garden. The red stains on his fingers revealed that he had found some.

"Did Dad tell you that he's getting you a granny nanny?"

There was an awkward silence that Heron hurriedly filled.

"I didn't say that at all! I said that we were going to get Nisha someone to . . ." He struggled to find an appropriately placatory phrase and eventually settled on "to help her out with . . . things."

"Mum definitely said that you were getting Nisha a granny nanny. I remember because I didn't know that grannies had nannies."

"They don't," Venetia replied pointedly.

"I found some strawberries," Kite informed her. "Did Dad tell you that he and Mum are going to France and that I'm going to start as a boarder at school next term?"

"No, he didn't. But I'm sure he was just getting round to it." Venetia looked at Heron and raised her eyebrows expectantly. "Would anyone like tea?"

Kite's face lit up. "If you've got any dead-fly biscuits then I would, please."

Venetia smiled. "I think there's some in the pantry. You go and have a look, and I'll put the kettle on. And then your father can tell me all about his defection to France."

As they sat around the table, Kite dunked Garibaldi biscuits into his mug, and Venetia watched her tea grow cold while Heron explained that he and Monica were opening a new office in the South of France and that they needed to be there for eighteen months or so to oversee the start-up. They ran a lucrative business selling holiday properties—Monica did the selling and Heron the conveyancing.

"I appreciate that the timing isn't ideal so soon after . . ." Heron let his sentence tail away, unable to bring himself to say the words "Dad" and "died" in such painful proximity.

Kite was fishing around with his finger for half a biscuit that was floating in his tea. Venetia passed him a teaspoon. Having regrouped, Heron continued.

"I'm afraid it can't be helped. We have to be in France by the beginning of September, which is why I want to make sure that you are safe and well looked after before we leave."

Venetia was tempted to remind him that she was the parent and he was the offspring in their relationship, and that she was neither old nor infirm enough to warrant a role reversal just yet. But now, at any rate, his motivation was clear. The appointment of a companion-housekeeper hybrid would enable him to depart to France with a clear conscience that he had fulfilled his filial obligations, despite his physical absence.

"And what about you, Kite? How do you feel about boarding?"

Kite shrugged.

"It'll be fun! He'll love it!"

Heron proclaimed it as fact rather than opinion, but Venetia knew that he genuinely believed it. Heron himself had been at boarding school from the age of eleven (against Venetia's wishes, but she had been overruled by both her husband and her son) and had thrived, finding comfort and confidence within the confines of routine and conformity, just as Hawk had before him. He had enjoyed the camaraderie of the cricket and rugby teams, the rough-and-tumble of dormitory pranks, the swagger and zeal of the debating society, and the sense of pride and achievement at prize-givings. His school days had confirmed rather than formed who he was. He had belonged. But Kite was different—in so many ways. Venetia worried that too many rules and expectations might bruise and chafe a boy whose character was still unfixed, and stifle his ability to choose his own place in the world.

"He doesn't have to board," Venetia offered. "He could live here

with me and be a day pupil." She saw a glimmer of hope flicker in
Kite's eyes, only to be immediately extinguished by his father.

"Nonsense! It'll be good for him!" Heron replied with that irritating jollity that parents employ to win over reluctant children.

Kite said nothing, but Venetia could see that he was unconvinced.
She wanted to fight his corner and insist that he stay with her while
Monica and Heron were in France, but they were his parents, and
while she could offer her opinion, only they had the right to make decisions concerning their own child. But she had thought of something
that might make Kite smile.

"I think we ought to go and fetch Grandpa's chess set," she told him.
"It belongs to you now."

Heron had some "errands to run" in town that would be completed
more speedily without his son in tow, so he excused himself and departed, leaving a delighted Kite in the company of his beloved grandmother. The chess set was in Hawk's study, a small room lined with
bookshelves that led off the square entrance hall of the house. Venetia
opened the door, and she and Kite paused for just a moment in reverent silence before going in. This was the room where Hawk had died,
dozing in his chair after a light lunch of Welsh rarebit followed by a
small whisky and soda. *The Times* had been spread across his knees
when Venetia found him, the crossword almost completed in his confident black scrawl. His fountain pen had fallen from his fingers and
stabbed an ink stain into the carpet. The only unsolved clue had been
5 down: "Endgame," nine letters. This had been the mundane minutiae of Hawk's death. Later that evening before going to bed, Venetia
had completed the crossword for him: *checkmate*.

"It still smells like Grandpa," whispered Kite. Venetia drew back
the half-closed curtains to let in the sunlight, startling glittering dust
motes into the musty air. Her husband's leather chair still bore the
vestiges of his presence: indentations in the cushion where he had sat
for so many hours, and patches on the arms polished to a shine where

his sleeves had rested. This was the chair where a younger Kite had perched on his grandfather's knee and listened to the adventures of Beatrix Potter's Peter Rabbit and the exploits of Richmal Crompton's Just William. The chess set sat on Hawk's battered mahogany desk in a small wooden box. It was a travel set made in the 1930s that had originally belonged to Hawk's father. The pieces themselves were cherry-red and butterscotch-yellow Bakelite, and Kite had loved to play with them long before he had learned the rules of the game. His grandfather had taught him the rudiments when he was eight, and Kite had been addicted ever since. Venetia handed the box to Kite, who hugged it to his chest.

"But who will I play with now?" he asked, his eyes suddenly filling with tears.

"Perhaps one of your new friends at school?" Venetia suggested.

"But what if I don't make any new friends?"

"Why wouldn't you?"

Kite sniffed and rubbed his eyes with the back of his hand. "Because I'm not very good at that stuff. I don't know the rules. I don't know how to get people to like me."

Venetia wrapped her arm around his shoulders. "Making friends isn't like chess, sweetheart. There aren't any rules, and you can't make people like you. But I do know that anyone would be very lucky to have you as their friend."

"Or their wingman?"

"Absolutely! You are an excellent wingman. And if you can't find anyone else to play chess with you, then you can teach me how, and I will. Now, is there anything else of Grandpa's that you would like to remember him by?"

"Yes please," Kite replied. "Can I have his bow ties?"

Heron returned at lunchtime to collect his son and present Venetia with the book of condolences that had been signed by guests at the wake.

"I thought that perhaps you could write to the people who came and thank them. It might be good to have something to keep you occupied and take your mind off things," he said as he handed it to her.

Kite squeezed her hard in a hug and thanked her for the chess set, but his shoulders drooped as he followed his father out to the car.

Later that afternoon, Venetia sat in the garden watching the bees dipping in and out of the honeysuckle, their legs fuzzy with orange pollen. Her head buzzed with irritation at Heron's revelations. Her first concern was for Kite. He was clearly unhappy at the prospect of becoming a boarder, but his father was far too engrossed in his fancy French business plans to notice. Kite had a quick mind, a kind heart, and a couple of friends, but no reliable internal map when it came to navigating the ways of the world. For the most part, he lived on his own private planet. But at least Venetia would be his designated guardian as far as the school was concerned while his parents were abroad. She would be able to intervene if it became necessary. And as for the "granny nanny"—what a damn cheek! Heron had actually called her "elderly." At only seventy-four, she was younger than Cher! She couldn't imagine anyone having the nerve to call Cher "elderly." But she had to concede that, in a way, it was her own fault. She had allowed herself to become subsumed by her marriage. She had finished up *being* the character she had, at the start, only played. She had become the supporting actor, never the lead—the directed, never the director. And that was how her son saw her and so assumed that she would be unable to cope on her own. What he failed to understand is that support requires strength. As a supportive wife, *she* had been the cornerstone of the marriage, the buttress that had kept their family solid. Hawk had been a traditional, head-of-the-household husband, but he couldn't have managed that without her. She didn't need a carer or a chaperone, but perhaps it might be useful to have some help around the house. After all, it was a big place for her to manage on her own. She knew that it would ease Heron's conscience, and it would certainly give her more time to pursue new interests and make the changes to her life that were long overdue. She wasn't sure exactly what they would be yet, but she was pretty sure that Heron wouldn't approve of them. But then Heron would be in France. And perhaps the granny nanny could write the thank-you notes to the funeral guests.

CHAPTER 3

Liberty Bell watched her mother's coffin disappear behind the not-quite-velvet curtains of the municipal crematorium while the Edwin Hawkins singers belted out "Oh Happy Day." Some of her mother's friends from church were joining in. Some were even dancing. The rest of the mourners looked on with affectionate smiles. A few brushed away tears, but from the expressions on their faces they could just as easily have been attending a wedding rather than a funeral. Liberty felt hopelessly detached from everything that was happening around her—a spectator rather than a participant. She couldn't quite believe that her mother had been in that box. Bernadette Bell had been a Technicolor tornado of a woman who had lived this life gleefully, vigorously, and splendidly. And she had had no intention of going quietly into the next. She had chosen her own funeral director, left him with precise instructions, and prepaid the bill. The arrival of her coffin had been accompanied by Shirley Bassey singing "Get the Party Started." They had, to Liberty's relief, also sung the more traditional "All Things Bright and Beautiful" and said a few prayers before Liberty had delivered a dignified and loving eulogy to her mother. This was followed by a flash mob from the pews performing "This Is Me" from *The Greatest Showman*—but without the waving of sparklers that Bernadette had requested. The crematorium had had to draw the line somewhere.

Outside, in brilliant sunshine, Liberty stood by a profusion of floral tributes, leaden with grief. A lone gray figure in a kaleidoscope of color. Bernadette had specified "No black," but gray was as far as Liberty could permit herself to stray from the confines of convention. She allowed herself to be hugged and consoled by a handful of relatives and a seemingly endless stream of her mother's friends. She smiled and nodded, agreed that the service had been exactly what her mother would have wanted, and yes—they'd been lucky with the weather, and yes—the flowers were beautiful. But what she really wanted to do was to tell them all to bugger off so that she could go home, down an obscene quantity of gin, eat her own body weight in chips, and cry herself to sleep. She desperately needed the release of tears, but so far, they had resolutely refused to fall. She had inherited none of her mother's carefree spirit and hoped that spirit of a different kind might help to unlock her frozen emotions.

"Are you ready to make a move, darlin'?"

She felt someone take her elbow and turned to find her mother's oldest friend, Evangeline, beside her. Evangeline guided her toward a waiting black limousine and climbed in after her.

The wake was held in a local pub just around the corner from the house that Liberty had shared with her mother. Bernadette had paid for a substantial tab at the bar, and there were a great many increasingly rowdy toasts proposed and drunk in her memory. Liberty sat at a table in a corner nursing a large gin and tonic and a growing sense of grievance that she was incapable of truly participating in this glorious celebration of her mother's life. Evangeline arrived at the table with a plate piled high with food from the buffet and sat down opposite her.

"Have something to eat, sweetheart. You don't want to be drinking on an empty stomach," she said, sipping from a tall glass of rum and Coke.

Liberty selected a sausage roll and bit into it without enthusiasm.

"She'll be missed at church, you know," Evangeline declared, and helped herself to a cheese and pickle sandwich from the plate. "But at least she's with your father again now."

And several other boyfriends who came after him but went before her, Liberty thought, wondering how that might work in the afterlife, if there was such a thing.

Evangeline interrupted her musings. "What are you going to do now? Your mother told me that you'd lost your job before she died. And no bad thing it is either! That man was never going to walk you down the aisle, girl! You're worth a lot better than him." Evangeline kissed her teeth to emphasize her point.

Liberty chewed morosely and wondered how many more details of her personal life her mother had shared with her friend.

"You sold yourself short with that married man," Evangeline continued, warming to her theme. "You're a fine-looking lady and clever too. You can get yourself another job and a proper gentleman friend in no time." She raised her glass toward Liberty and then took a serious swig. "You just need to loosen up a little."

That evening Liberty sat in her mother's courtyard garden, surrounded by wind chimes and Moroccan lanterns, sipping more gin and wondering how she had ended up with so little to show for her forty-six years on the planet. By the same age, her mother had enjoyed numerous interesting jobs, including working as a croupier in Cannes, a nanny to the children of a famous British actor, a driver for a viscount and viscountess in London, and a personal assistant to a bestselling crime novelist. She had also clocked up several lovers, one husband, one daughter, a public disorder offense at an anti-apartheid march, and a beach hut in Brighton. Liberty had loved that beach hut, but her mother had swapped it on a whim one summer for a VW camper van. Bernadette had truly been a bohemian soul, and she had also been a loving wife and mother. But when her husband, Liberty's father, had died five years previously, she had grieved and then she had gotten on with life. For the last twenty or so years, she had worked as an antiques dealer, traveling to fairs all over the country and selling items online. She had flatly refused to retire, even when she was told that she was dying. Her defiant response to her doctor, her daughter, and her friends had been "I intend to live right up to the moment when I bloody well die." And she had, propped up in bed in the local hospice wearing her favorite silk dressing gown and listening to Dolly Parton on her headphones.

Liberty drained her glass and leaned back in her chair to watch a pair of pigeons fussing and fluffing their feathers on the wall at the bottom of the garden. Without warning, tears began to trickle down her face. Her mother's greatest gift had been her capacity to find happiness. Liberty hadn't the first idea where to look.

CHAPTER 4

Geoffrey Court glanced down at the paperwork on the desk in front of him and straightened it unnecessarily. He pulled off his glasses, smiled at Liberty, and then parked them back on his nose. A more diligent observer might have deduced his discomfort, but Liberty considered this visit to her mother's solicitor to hear the terms of her last will and testament to be a mere formality. She was an only child and next of kin, so naturally she assumed that everything would come to her. Mr. Court loosened his tie a fraction and cleared his throat.

"As you are no doubt aware, Miss Bell, I drew up your mother's will at her request and undertook to share its contents with you when the time came. Sadly, that time has now come."

Liberty nodded encouragingly, hoping that it might speed things along. After a moment's pause, the solicitor finally took the plunge.

"I'm afraid it may not be the news that you were hoping for. Well, not hoping," he hurriedly corrected himself, "but expecting— perhaps that's a better word."

Now he had Liberty's full attention.

"Your mother's last wishes were somewhat unusual. Perhaps the easiest way to begin is if you take a look at her will for yourself."

Liberty felt a prickle of unease as he passed the relevant document across the desk. Mr. Court watched her face crumple into a perplexed frown as she began to read. She understood the meaning of each word in isolation, but together they mutated into unnerving nonsense. This couldn't be right.

"I'm sorry, Mr. Court, there must be some mistake."

"I'm afraid not, Miss Bell. Your mother was very clear in her intentions."

"But according to this, she left me nothing. Absolutely nothing at all."

Mr. Court pulled off his glasses once more and set them down on the desk. "Well, that's not strictly the case. You may take whatever you wish from the contents of the house and its garden before they are sold."

Liberty couldn't believe what she was hearing. Her mother had left her without a penny and soon to be homeless. It was completely unfathomable. And cruel. What on earth could she have done to deserve it?

"She couldn't have been in her right mind," Liberty protested, somewhat desperately.

Mr. Court sighed. "I think we both know that she was," he replied gently.

"Well, who gets it, then—the money, the house, the antiques?" Liberty's disbelief was distilling into anger as the implications of her mother's will began to sink in.

"I'm afraid I'm not at liberty to disclose that. Your mother made me the sole executor of her will, and she instructed me to keep the details of the beneficiaries confidential."

Liberty leaned back in her chair and took a deep breath. She felt sick.

"Would you like a glass of water?" Mr. Court inquired.

Liberty shook her head. A neat gin might be more helpful.

"I realize that this might have come as a bit of a shock, but if you turn over to the second page you will see that your mother did, in fact, make some provision for you in her will."

Liberty looked up at him, her expression full of suspicion, and then down again at the page he had directed her to. She read the words but was none the wiser for doing so. "What on earth does that mean?"

Mr. Court cleared his throat again. "Mrs. Bell left something in trust for you, but at present, I'm unable to divulge any specifics."

Liberty was sorely tempted to reach across the desk and throttle him with her bare hands to squeeze some answers out of him. "At present!" she exploded. "Well, if not now, then when? *When* the sodding hell will you be able to tell me *what* the buggering hell is going on?!"

It was unlike Liberty to swear—particularly in public—but these were unprecedented times. Mr. Court raised his eyebrows in response to her expletives.

"The inheritance from your mother is dependent on you fulfilling certain conditions. I am not able to tell you what they are, but I am to judge on your mother's behalf whether or not her criteria have been met."

Liberty felt like screaming. At first, she had been shocked, but now she was beginning to recognize her mother's idiosyncratic stamp on these maddening machinations. "So let me get this straight. My mother has left me something, conditional on something else, and you can't tell me what either of these somethings are?"

Mr. Court nodded. "That's exactly right. I was also instructed to give you this," he added, handing her a shopping bag from behind his desk. Liberty snatched the bag from him and got up to leave. She'd had enough. But then something struck her.

"How will you know when the conditions have been met?"

Mr. Court stood up to see her out. "You are to meet me for lunch at regular intervals, and I will . . . assess the situation."

Liberty shook her head in disbelief. "Well, I hope you're paying!"

BACK HOME, SHE flung the shopping bag onto the kitchen table, sloshed some gin into a tumbler, and took a bottle of tonic water from the fridge. When she looked inside the bag she found a small photo album and the latest copy of *The Lady*.

CHAPTER 5

The interviews for the granny nanny were being held in Venetia's sitting room, which made Heron's suggestion that Venetia should "leave it all to him" and take no part in the final selection process herself all the more preposterous.

"Of course I'm going to be there," she had told him. "I'm the one they're supposed to be 'assisting,' and it's my home they'll be living in while you're swanning around in the South of France." She would also be paying their wages, she thought ruefully. The successful candidate, should they manage to find one, would actually be living in the garden, in the studio flat above the former coach house that now served as a garage. Some years ago, Heron had persuaded his father to consent to the flat conversion on the grounds that it would make a profitable Airbnb, but once the work had been completed, Hawk had demurred, preferring instead to seek a "respectable, long-term tenant." But he had never got around to it. Instead, it had been used occasionally as guest accommodation at Christmas when Hawk's relatives had come to stay.

Heron and Venetia had eventually managed to whittle down a motley assortment of applicants to a short list of three. The CVs had made interesting reading. Venetia had immediately discounted the ex-headteacher of a girls' school—"She can't possibly need the money. She just wants someone else to boss about now that she's retired"—and a Nordic walking enthusiast—"She'll be forever trying to get me to walk with those silly sticks!" Heron had vetoed an army veteran aged sixty-three, who described himself as having "excellent organizational and interpersonal skills, a cheerful disposition, and all my own teeth." Heron declared that facile humor had no place on a professional job application and that, in all probability, the man was a gold digger. Venetia was a little disappointed. She thought that he sounded quite fun.

The first interviewee was a Miss Stella Stoney. She arrived promptly, and Heron met her at the front door and showed her through to the sitting room. She was dressed in a no-nonsense navy pleated skirt and matching cardigan over a white blouse and flat Mary Jane shoes with Velcro straps. Her gray-streaked beige hair was pulled back into a doughnut-shaped bun. Venetia's heart sank.

"This is my mother, Venetia Hamilton Hargreaves."

Miss Stoney looked Venetia up and down appraisingly and offered her a hand to shake. "Good morning, Mrs. Hamilton Hargreaves—or may I call you Venetia? I'm sure we shall get along famously."

I'll be the judge of that, thought Venetia.

"Please take a seat, Miss Stoney—or may I call you Stella?" Heron permitted himself a wry smile, which was quickly wiped from his face by her reply as she sat down with her legs spread and placed her hands firmly on her knees.

"I'd prefer to keep things on a professional basis, if you don't mind, so I think we'll stick with Miss Stoney."

Heron sat down beside his mother and consulted his clipboard. "Right, then, Miss Stoney, perhaps you'd like to tell us why you think you'd be suitable for the job?"

Miss Stoney flashed a confident, perilously-close-to-smug smile. "Well, I have over thirty years of nursing experience, eleven of those on geriatric wards and four in a nursing home for the elderly."

Venetia flinched—that damn word again!

"So you can be sure that any medical needs your mother has would be taken care of. Other than that, I'm punctual, well organized, and have excellent interpersonal skills."

Venetia begged to differ. The wretched woman was completely ignoring her and addressing all her answers to Heron, who appeared to be favorably impressed. He consulted his notes again.

"And it says here that you have a clean driving license and are au fait with online shopping."

"Absolutely. I've never had so much as a parking ticket, and I have an Amazon Prime account and I'm a long-term Ocado customer."

"And you're a competent cook?"

"Oh, more than competent. I'm a great believer in good, plain, wholesome food cooked from scratch. Much better for an elderly digestive system than too much rich food and alcohol. Although I wouldn't want you to think I'm a killjoy—there's no harm in the occasional glass of wine on special occasions."

Venetia had had enough. She'd sooner run naked down the high street during rush hour than have this woman set foot in her house again. But she couldn't resist making a little mischief before ending the interview.

"Miss Stoney, what's your favorite musical?"

Miss Stoney looked surprised, as though she had forgotten that Venetia was in the room. She glanced at Heron as though expecting him to intervene, but when he didn't, she turned her attention back to Venetia.

"Well, I'm not sure how relevant that is," she replied slowly and softly, as though speaking to a small child. "I'd have to give it some thought."

"It's relevant because my son is keen to find me a companion to accompany me on outings—I believe it said as much in the advertisement—and I love musical theater. I'm also a fan of opera—what about you?"

Miss Stoney looked relieved. "Oh yes—Oprah! Oprah Winfrey. Well, she's certainly an interesting woman."

Venetia smiled sweetly. "No, no, I'm afraid you've misunderstood.

O-pe-ra," she continued slowly, adopting Miss Stoney's earlier tone. "Puccini's *La bohème* and Bizet's *Carmen*—that sort of thing."

Miss Stoney refused to be ruffled. "I can't pretend to be an expert, but I'm sure I'll get the hang of it."

Heron made a note on his clipboard. "Now, Miss Stoney, are there any questions you would like to ask?"

Miss Stoney shook her head. "I don't have any questions, but there are a few things I should like to clarify. Firstly, I will need to see my accommodation."

"Of course."

"I should also point out that I don't do cleaning, I don't do personal care—assistance with washing, toileting, et cetera—and I don't do dog walking."

"My mother doesn't have a dog," Heron replied, clearly keen to get away from the topic of toileting.

"But I'm thinking of getting one now," Venetia added. She didn't know whether to laugh or cry. The interview had been a farce as far as she was concerned. She would never consent to having Miss Stoney under her roof. But it had also been a stark and distressing reminder of her own mortality. A warning that she had passed the halfway point long ago and was now facing, if not the final furlong, then certainly the closing stages of the race, with all the frailties and indignities that it might entail. And it did seem now as though her life had raced away from her like a runaway horse. Was this truly all that was left to look forward to—infirmity, insanity, and incontinence? While Heron showed Miss Stoney the studio flat, Venetia went through to the kitchen to fix herself a medicinal gin and tonic. As she went to the fridge for ice, she caught sight of a note that Kite had given her a few days after he had taken the chess set home.

You're the best, Nisha! Love you lots! From your wingman, Kite xxx

The thought of her grandson banished her gloom. What had she been thinking? Old age might be coming for her, but she wasn't going

down without a fight. Kite needed her as his protector and potential chess partner, and now that Hawk was gone, she could have a
whole new life if she wanted. And she did want. She took a large swig
from her glass and checked her watch. Heron would be mortified if he
caught her drinking before six P.M. on a weekday. There were twenty
minutes before the next candidate arrived, and this time, Venetia was
going to take charge of the interview. She watched as Heron accompanied Miss Stoney back through the garden and down the side of the
house out to the street, where her car was parked.

Good riddance! she thought.

CHAPTER 6

Liberty assessed her appearance critically in the mirror and wondered whether a swipe of nude lipstick would be too much. She applied some sparingly, deciding that it would make her look more polished. She was wearing the same gray suit that she had bought for her mother's funeral. She remembered noting at the time that it would come in handy for job interviews and had then immediately felt guilty for having such a callous thought. For fifteen years she had been tethered to a position that neither stretched her intellect nor swelled her savings account, but then she had been "let go" by her previous employer only a couple of weeks before Bernadette had died. "Let go" made her sound like a balloon whose string had been released, sending it up into an infinite sky, or a boat untied from its mooring and cast adrift on open water. That was exactly how she felt, and the sudden freedom was unwelcome and terrifying.

Liberty had seen the job advertisement in the copy of *The Lady* that Geoffrey Court had given her. At first she couldn't fathom why her mother had wanted her to have it, but then she remembered Bernadette telling her that the magazine was where she had found some of her own amazing jobs. Liberty had flicked despondently through the pages, not really expecting to find anything suitable. But the realization suddenly hit her like a stubbed toe that she could no longer afford the luxury of "suitable" as a criterion. Desperation had reduced her options to "doable." The advertisement had caught her eye for two reasons. First, the position was local, and second, it came with accommodation. A For Sale sign outside her mother's house taunted her each time she passed through the front door, and the estate agent had already arranged an open house for viewings that coming weekend. Liberty checked in her bag to make sure she had put in a copy of her references. She had emailed them along with her CV in her original application, but she wanted to have them on hand, just in case she was asked for a paper copy as well. It had been so long since her last job interview, and she was nervous. She had tried to prepare herself as best she could, making a list of her strengths and making up a couple of minor weaknesses so as not to appear arrogant if that question were to be asked. The interview was for the position of live-in companion—housekeeper to a recently widowed lady in her seventies. How hard could it be looking after an old lady? Liberty had reasoned. After all, she had looked after her mother in the last months of her life. Even so, she had still been a little surprised when she had been short-listed. Perhaps she was just a little surprised that somebody thought she was still good for something. She checked her watch. It was time for her to leave. The walk would take around fifteen minutes, which gave her ten minutes contingency should any unforeseen delay or obstacle waylay her en route.

The house was a beautiful and rather grand Victorian property in what local estate agents liked to call one of Bedford's premier residential areas. It stood in a prime position on the town's embankment, facing the well-kept public gardens and, beyond them, the green-and-cream suspension bridge that spanned the Great Ouse. To the front of the house was a neat lawn bordered by rose trees and topiaried privet bushes. With exactly ten minutes to spare, Liberty climbed the arc of the bridge until she reached its apex, where she turned and stood, looking down at the water flowing beneath her.

"Not gonna jump, I hope, love?" A sprightly old chap grinned and winked at her as he crossed the bridge, accompanied by his Jack

Russell terrier, who was pulling on the lead to get to the grass on the other side.

"Not today, at any rate," she replied with a smile. She checked her watch again. It was time.

The door was answered by a short, stocky man who looked uncomfortably stuffed into his expensive linen suit. He introduced himself as Heron Hamilton Hargreaves. Liberty followed him into the hallway, wondering if she had misheard him, but was too nervous to check in case she hadn't. He led her through to a pleasant, light-filled room where a woman whom she presumed to be the widow was waiting. On first impression the woman was a puzzling paradox. Her appearance was old-fashioned, dowdy even. But her expression was lively and inquisitive, and her voice confident and youthful. She stood up as they entered, her posture elegant and her movements graceful. She offered Liberty her hand.

"Good afternoon. I'm Venetia Hamilton Hargreaves. You must be Miss Bell. Please take a seat."

Liberty sat.

"Now, perhaps you'd like to tell me why you left your previous employment?" the woman asked her.

The question winded Liberty, and she felt her cheeks redden. She had hoped for something a little more benign to start with—a warm-up question or two, or a chat about the weather—before they got to the business end of things. The man consulted his clipboard.

"It says on your CV that you worked as a personal assistant to a partner in an accountancy firm until recently. Did you leave, or were you pushed?" He smiled as he said it, but Liberty wasn't sure if he was joking or not.

"I decided that it was time for a change," Liberty replied, choosing her words carefully.

"And you left before finding another job?" The woman's tone implied only idle curiosity, but her steady gaze made it clear that an explanation was required. This was a question that Liberty had anticipated, and she was ready with her well-practiced answer.

"My mother was unwell. I wanted to help care for her." It was true. That she had been having an affair with her married boss for the past fourteen years until it ended recently, painfully, and messily was also true, but probably not helpful to mention here.

"I'm sorry about your mother's illness. Has she recovered now?"

"No. She's dead." The words were out before Liberty could translate them into something softer.

"My sincere condolences," the woman replied calmly. "As you know, my husband died recently. It's hard to lose someone you love." She reached across and lightly touched Liberty's hand. "But now you think that you're ready to return to work?"

Ready or not, thought Liberty, *I don't have much choice.*

"Yes, I feel ready for a new challenge." It seemed like a good thing to say in an interview.

"Well, hopefully you won't find my mother too much of a challenge," the man replied with a forced grin. "So long as you don't kill her off as well!"

Liberty was sure this time that it was a joke, and in very poor taste, but instead of feeling angry, she felt a little sorry for him. She sensed his awkwardness and sympathized. After all, he was a short, chubby man called Heron. The woman was clearly accustomed to her son's maladroit manner and smoothly moved things along.

"Now, Miss Bell, would you like to tell me why you want this job and what makes you think you'd be good at it?"

When Liberty emerged into the sunshine thirty-five minutes later, she had no idea whether the interview had gone well or not. She had answered all their questions and asked a few of her own. She had been shown the accommodation that came with the job and told that they would be in touch. They had one more candidate to see, and they would be making their decision the next day. And what about Liberty? Did *she* want the job? She wanted the flat—it was perfect. The woman seemed nice enough but wasn't at all what she had been expecting, and the son was off to France and so she wouldn't be having anything to do with him—which was perhaps just as well! She strolled along beside the river under the dappled shade of trees. The public gardens were ablaze with flowers whose colors shimmered in the sunlight, and the old chap whom she had seen earlier was sitting on a wooden seat admiring the view and sharing an ice cream with his dog. In truth, it didn't really matter what Liberty thought. Beggars can't be choosers. If they offered her the job, she would take it.

CHAPTER 7

The third candidate was a no-show. She telephoned to say that she had entered the wrong day into her phone diary, and would it be possible to rearrange? Heron told her that it wouldn't be necessary because they had already filled the position. Venetia prepared to fight her corner.

"Let's have some tea," she told Heron, heading off toward the kitchen, "and then we can discuss the interviewees."

Heron trotted along behind her, clutching his clipboard. "Well, I'm not sure there's much to discuss," he replied, sounding rather pleased with himself. "The choice is obvious."

"I agree." Venetia took mugs from the cupboard and clicked the kettle on.

"Miss Stoney is perfect for the job!" Heron declared.

"I'm sure that Miss Stoney is perfect for *some* job—a prison guard or a traffic warden, perhaps. But not this one."

"You didn't like her?" Heron seemed genuinely surprised.

"She made Mrs. Danvers look like Mary Poppins!" The comparison was lost on Heron. Venetia sighed. "She was overbearing and insensitive. She spoke to me—and about me—as though I was completely gaga, and she was fully intent on feeding me tasteless mush and policing my alcohol intake. Her shoes were dreadful, and she doesn't like dogs."

"But you haven't got a dog."

"That's not the point. There's something very dubious about people who don't like dogs."

"So, you preferred the other one—Miss . . . ?" Heron consulted his clipboard.

"Bell. Liberty Bell. Yes, I did. She seemed like a perfectly pleasant, sensible, and competent woman."

"She seemed nervous to me," Heron replied a little sulkily.

"Hardly surprising considering you accused her of killing off her own mother."

"I was joking! I was trying to put her at ease."

Venetia had no doubt that he was telling the truth. Heron was proficient enough with procedures and paperwork, but he found people much more perplexing.

"Well, I think you're being a little hard on Miss Stoney. She's obviously very efficient, and her references were excellent."

Probably because her former employers couldn't wait to see the back of her, thought Venetia.

"And I couldn't see anything wrong with her shoes."

Venetia couldn't help but smile, remembering the awful dress that Heron had chosen for her to wear at Hawk's funeral. "Be that as it may, Miss Bell is my choice. She will do very nicely."

If she was forced to have a granny nanny, Venetia wanted one who was pleasant and compliant. And there was something about Liberty Bell that intrigued her. Something more to her than met the eye, like the secret compartment of a puzzle box.

"Very well," Heron reluctantly conceded. "If you're absolutely sure? Would you like me to call her and give her the good news?"

Venetia shook her head. "No, I'll do that. You can contact Miss Stoney and let her know my decision. Oh, and, Heron . . ."

He looked up from his clipboard where he had noted Stella Stoney's number. His mother winked at him mischievously.

"Let her down gently!"

Before Venetia had a chance to telephone Miss Bell, a van pulled up on the gravel at the front of the house. Heron had arranged for a local firm to install several motion-activated lights and a CCTV camera for additional security, now that his mother was living alone in the house. Venetia had agreed, but only to keep the peace. She didn't really understand how the absence of an eighty-four-year-old man with arthritic knees, a dodgy ticker, and debilitating lumbago had increased her vulnerability to intruders. She only hoped that the house didn't light up like a Las Vegas casino every time a cat wandered through the garden. She answered the door to a lugubrious-looking man whose fleshy jowls and downturned eyes put her in mind of a bloodhound. He introduced himself as Trevor in an apologetic tone and went off to set up his ladders. But before he could unload them from the van, he was intercepted by Heron, whose car was now blocked in. Venetia went inside and left them to motor-vehicle musical chairs. Once Heron had gone and she could hear the clatter of ladders being propped against brickwork, Venetia ventured outside again to offer Trevor some tea. He declined. She was about to return to the house when a thought struck her.

"Would you prefer coffee?"

Trevor's face finally cracked into a smile. "That would be great, if it's not too much trouble."

Venetia was unexpectedly moved and felt tears prick her eyes. That such a small, simple thing could raise a smile. She blinked hard. Hawk had always expected his own and his family's feelings—or at least any evidence of them—to be constrained by his notions of propriety. But now that he was dead, Venetia's emotions were much less biddable, and she found it strangely exhilarating.

"How do you take it?"

Trevor was positively beaming now. "Milk, no sugar, please—but

I don't suppose you've got any biscuits, have you? To keep my energy levels up?"

Venetia brought him a tray with a mug of coffee and a plate of chocolate digestives. "For energy!" she told him.

As Trevor tucked in, he gestured, biscuit in hand, toward one of the lights he had already installed.

"You know, these things are all well and good, but I reckon the best deterrent is a bloody great big dog."

Three mugs of coffee and half a packet of biscuits later, the job was done, and Trevor and his ladders were gone.

While Trevor had been upgrading her security, Venetia had rung Miss Bell. Between them they had agreed on a start date and that Liberty could move her things into the flat the weekend prior to that. She had sounded relieved rather than pleased when Venetia had offered her the job. Venetia couldn't shake the feeling that Miss Bell was burdened by something more than grief for her mother. Although, God knows, that was enough. Still, she was entitled to her secrets. Venetia had plenty of her own. She was just considering whether to take the newspaper into the garden and start the crossword or go for a stroll beside the river, when the march from *Raiders of the Lost Ark* interrupted her indecision. It was the ringtone that Kite had selected for her mobile phone. Venetia took the call. It was Beverley, her friend from book club. And she had a favor to ask.

CHAPTER 8

The enormous German shepherd lay on Beverley's kitchen floor with his head on his paws. One of his ears was flopped over at half-mast, and his eyes, which were the color of treacle toffee, reflected a resignation with the world that was unbearably sad.

"I'd happily keep him myself," Beverley told Venetia, "but Ant and Dec are making his life hell. They've already tried playing tug-of-war with his tail, and Dec keeps biffing him in the face as soon as my back's turned. The poor soul has been trying to squeeze himself behind the sofa to get away from them." Ant and Dec were Beverley's murderous cats who had a fearsome reputation for killing rodents and terrorizing the neighbor's cockapoo.

Venetia sat down close to the dog, and he eyed her warily.

"Where did he come from?"

"Lee brought him home." Lee was Beverley's son and a detective sergeant in the local Criminal Investigation Department. "They raided a house in one of those roads near the park that are all named after saints. The ones where all the yummy mummies and London commuters live. They'd had a tip-off that it was a cannabis factory, and, lo and behold, the whole place was full of plants—even the loft! They'd bypassed the electricity meter and there were special lamps and heaters everywhere. Lee said it was a real result for them. It just goes to show that you never know what your neighbors are up to even if you've got a premium postcode. The people who lived next door were mortified—they hadn't suspected a thing!"

Venetia smiled. Beverley loved to tell a story.

"There's probably all sorts of funny business going on round there behind those stained-glass front doors with their potted bay trees and perfectly cut logs stored in the porch."

"Be careful what you say," Venetia said, laughing. "Some of our book club members live in those streets."

Beverley grimaced. "God, I can't imagine Rowena getting involved in anything dodgy—but then I suppose you can never tell!"

Rowena was one of the more serious members of their book club. Without fail, she chose very worthy books that had been nominated for some literary prize or another or had been reviewed in one of the broadsheets. When Rowena hosted their meetings, the wine trickled rather than flowed, the nibbles were unappetizingly healthy, and she always had a printed list of preprepared topics for discussion, which made it feel like some kind of test.

The dog sighed heavily, redirecting them both to his part in the story.

"So where does this handsome chap fit in?" Venetia gently offered the back of her hand for the dog to sniff. He raised his head a little and his nose twitched.

"The police found him in the house. They think he was supposed to be a guard dog, but he just let them in. When they broke down the door, he was cowering in a corner."

"Does he have a name?"

"He was wearing one of those hideous studded collars, and the nameplate on it said 'Terminator.'"

"He doesn't look much like a Terminator."

"He isn't. He's as soft as anything. He just needs someone to love him." Beverley's tone was wheedling now. Venetia was already in love. But she was determined not to be bulldozed by Beverley.

"It's a big commitment. We don't know what he's like to walk or how he is with other dogs. I might not be able to cope with him."

"Nonsense! You're brilliant with dogs. You used to volunteer at that rescue place for years, and whenever we're out anywhere and we see a dog, you always have to stroke it. And he'll be company for you now that you're on your own."

Venetia rolled her eyes. "Don't you start as well! It's bad enough with Heron fussing around me. And besides, the granny nanny will be starting soon."

"Ah, yes—I'd forgotten about the granny nanny!" Beverley grinned. "Well, the dog can protect you from the granny nanny."

"I'll need a couple of days to think about it."

By that, Venetia meant that she would need a couple of days to buy everything that would make the dog comfortable in his new home, register him with a vet, organize pet insurance, and wave Heron and Monica off to France. Heron wasn't really a dog person.

"But you know you want him," Beverley coaxed.

It was true. When she was a girl, her family had always kept dogs, and when she and Hawk first married, he had had a brace of black Labradors. But when Heron came along, the dogs were in their dotage, and when they died there were no more dogs. The only pets that Heron was ever interested in were stick insects.

"He'll have to have a new name. You can't be yelling 'Terminator' across the park when you take him for a walk." Beverley was clearly certain that the deal was done.

Venetia reached down and gently stroked the dog's head. His ears flicked at her touch, but he didn't move away, and he held her in the gaze of his mournful brown eyes.

"I think he has a look of Colin Firth about him," Beverley suggested. "That sort of noble but worried expression he had in that film *The King's Speech*, when he was addressing the nation on the outbreak of war. He's a handsome devil too," she added.

Venetia smiled. Only Beverley could be that random. But oddly, she was also right.

"Colin Firth it is, then," she conceded.

Driving home, she remembered Trevor's advice. Colin was, indeed, a bloody great big dog.

CHAPTER 9

Liberty loaded the last box of her belongings into the car and slammed the boot shut. Her entire life was now crammed into her Toyota. It hadn't taken long to pack, and that in itself seemed a bit sad—that all her worldly possessions should amount to so little. The new flat was already furnished, so the contents of her mother's home, save for a few bits and pieces that Liberty had kept for sentimental reasons, had been collected to be sold by the local auction house. It would have been nice to have someone—a friend—to help her move out and move into her new place. Liberty used to have friends, but one by one they had deserted her like leaves falling from a tree in autumn. It had been her own fault, she supposed. Once she had begun her affair with Graham, her social life had evaporated in the white heat of her infatuation. She had refused endless invitations just in case Graham was able to get away for a couple of hours. Too many evenings and weekends were spent drinking wine and watching TV—and the window. Listening for the trill of the phone or the sound of a car pulling up outside. Too many evenings and weekends were spent teetering on that cruel knife edge between excitement and disappointment, and all that time Liberty was held hostage by hope. Occasionally he would turn up at her flat unannounced, with champagne and flowers in his arms and lust in his eyes. They would fall into bed where she would make love and he would have sex, and that became the convention of their coupling. Sadly for Liberty, it took too many years for her to realize what had always been this painful and humiliating truth.

She closed the front door to her mother's house and pushed the keys through the letterbox. And now she was at the mercy of strangers. She kicked the wooden post of the Sold sign in passing. "Thanks for nothing, Mum!" she muttered, then got into her car and drove away.

Only minutes later she pulled onto the gravel drive of the splendid house on the town's embankment. At least she would have a pretty smart address now, even if she was, strictly speaking, living in the servants' quarters. The elegant woman who answered the door was almost unrecognizable as the Mrs. Hamilton Hargreaves who had interviewed her just a couple of weeks previously. Her drab steel-gray hair was now a chic blond bob, and she was wearing beautifully cut palazzo pants and a silk duster coat with a dramatic peacock print. By her side stood an enormous German shepherd. Liberty swallowed hard. She wasn't really a dog person. Seeing her apprehension, Mrs. Hamilton Hargreaves smiled.

"Don't worry, he's friendly. Now, would you like some tea, or would you prefer to unpack first?"

The dog looked worryingly like a wolf to Liberty. No one had mentioned a dog at the interview. She hoped she wouldn't have to walk it. Or feed it. Or have anything to do with it really. She declined the tea, saying that she'd like to get settled in. Mrs. Hamilton Hargreaves handed her the keys.

"You can drive right up to the old coach house. Have you brought anyone with you to help out?" she asked, looking past Liberty toward her car. "Would you like me to give you a hand?"

Her offer only served to magnify Liberty's embarrassing aloneness. Liberty shook her head. "Thank you, but no. I'll be fine."

Her new employer looked at her quizzically but said nothing more than "Well, pop in and see me once you've unpacked. Just let yourself in the back door. It'll be open."

The studio flat was homely and full of light, and there was a vase of fresh flowers on a small table. There were tea bags and coffee in the kitchen area, and milk and a bottle of prosecco in the fridge. Someone had gone to the trouble of trying to make her feel welcome. Liberty sat down on the bed, which was already made up and smelled of laundry dried outside on a sunny day. The windows in the flat all looked out over the large back garden of the house, and when Liberty lay back on the bed to test it out, she could see treetops floodlit by summer sun and, between the leaves, glimpses of clear blue sky. Perhaps she *could* be happy here.

An hour later she presented herself at the back door. She was about to knock when she remembered that she had been told to go straight in. On the other side of the door lay the wolf dog in the middle of the kitchen floor. Seeing Liberty, he sat bolt upright with his ears pricked and his eyes fixed on hers. She froze.

"Good dog." Her voice was tentative, and the upward inflection betrayed her words as a query rather than a placatory statement. She took one step into the room. The dog stood up. She retreated. The dog sat down. They repeated the sequence three times with no advance being made on either side, like a series of futile chess moves resulting in stalemate. Liberty considered going around to the front door and ringing the bell, but she couldn't face the humiliation. She needed to up her game. She squatted awkwardly. The dog tipped his head to one side but remained sitting.

"Look—I'm Liberty," she told him, feeling utterly ridiculous but sufficiently desperate to dispense with her dignity. "I work here now. It's okay to let me in."

The dog's tail began to wag, not because they had now been properly introduced, but because his mistress had walked into the room. Liberty stood up and smoothed nonexistent wrinkles from her skirt. "He wouldn't let me in," she said, nodding toward the dog.

"Did he growl at you?" Mrs. Hamilton Hargreaves sounded concerned.

"No. But he stood up."

"Did he approach you?"

"No. But he . . . he looked menacing."

Mrs. Hamilton Hargreaves smiled as she stroked the dog's ears. "You're not really a dog person, are you, my dear?"

Liberty shook her head.

"Never mind. I'm sure my boy will win you over."

If he doesn't eat me first, thought Liberty.

"You must call me Venetia."

Venetia pulled out one of the chairs from around the table and indicated to Liberty that she should sit. Liberty crept warily around the dog and perched on the edge of her seat.

"And I shall call you Liberty. Now, shall we have a drink to toast new beginnings? What would you like?"

Liberty was about to suggest tea, but Venetia was plinking ice cubes into glasses.

"Is a gin and tonic okay?" Without waiting for an answer, Venetia fixed their drinks and sat down opposite her. The dog followed her every move and then rested his head in her lap.

"Cheers!" Venetia raised her glass. "I hope that you'll be very happy here."

Liberty took a small sip from her glass. She couldn't decide if she had already started work or if this was merely a social occasion. She had a feeling that in this job, the line might often be blurred and that she would need to be on her guard so as not to overstep it. Fortunately, on this occasion Venetia made it clear.

"I realize that you don't start work until Monday, and I shan't bother you again until then. But I just wanted to check that you understand exactly what your role will be—whatever my son might have said."

Liberty shifted nervously in her chair. Oh God—surely she hadn't missed something about dog-walking duties? Had he said something

when she hadn't been paying proper attention—perhaps when he'd
been showing her the flat? It was possible. She had been so pleased
with the accommodation when she'd seen it, and he had talked end-
lessly. Perhaps she had switched off for a moment. Venetia continued.

"I am fit and healthy, and fully compos mentis. I have no need of a
granny nanny. My son seems to think that I am a frail old lady, but as
you can see, I am nothing of the sort. What I need is some amiable,
practical help around the house and not someone who is paid to be my
minder and my 'friend.'"

Liberty was hugely relieved. Practical she could do, whereas her
record on friendship wasn't great. But there was one more thing she
wanted to check.

"I don't have to walk the dog, do I?"

"His name is Colin Firth. And no, you don't have to walk him. But
hopefully there may come a day when you want to."

CHAPTER 10

Crow sat on the black-painted steps of the ballroom's metal fire escape, as high as the neighboring treetops, savoring the warmth of the late-afternoon sun on his crippled leg. Sometimes heat helped to alleviate the pain. Far below him, the Embankment bustled. Geese grazed on the verges, and gulls scavenged in the bins. People strolled beside the river, holding ice creams, holding dog leads, holding hands. Swans and ducks swam in parallel to the promenaders, hoping to be fed. Occasionally an individual caught his eye—a little boy riding a shiny red bike, then an elegant woman in a straw hat walking a German shepherd—but for the most part he gazed without focus, and all those individual beings blurred into a single stream of color and movement beneath him. His own life was often a daily struggle simply to survive, but here on his lofty perch he could rest for a while in solitude and peace.

CHAPTER 11

Liberty sat at the kitchen table with Hawk's address book in front of her. Venetia was out shopping with a friend and had asked Liberty to write and thank everyone who had offered their condolences at Hawk's funeral. She had provided a list of recipients and specified that the thank-yous be handwritten in the notecards that she had bought for the purpose. The cards depicted a series of five bird illustrations, and Liberty wondered idly where this family's ornithological obsession originated. The first card she selected portrayed a heron taking flight from a riverbank at sunrise—a magnificent creature sweeping heavenward, backlit by a flame-brindled sky. Liberty's handwriting was small and neat as she carefully copied the words that Venetia had dictated. She remembered her first encounter with the human Heron and was grateful that she had managed to stifle the snigger that had threatened her composure when she had first heard his name. She probably wouldn't be sitting here now, she thought, had she succumbed to such immature behavior. She closed the card and pushed it into the stiff cream envelope. According to Venetia, he was in France now with his wife on business. Liberty was curious about the kind of woman who, despite his bluster and pomposity, would want him for her husband. But she had sensed in Heron a vague vulnerability, so perhaps he had hidden depths.

The next hour or so passed very pleasantly. The pile of cards grew smaller, and the pile of sealed envelopes grew taller. Liberty enjoyed this type of methodical, repetitive task. It was both satisfying and soothing, and the perfect start to her first day in her new job, quelling the anxiety that was almost always tapping on her shoulder.

Suddenly the back door burst open and a small boy in a school uniform charged in, followed by the dog, who had been banished to the garden while Venetia was out. On seeing Liberty, the boy stopped in his tracks.

"Who are you?" he asked with polite but enthusiastic curiosity.

Liberty eyed both the boy and the dog warily. "My name is Liberty Bell, and I work for Mrs. Hamilton Hargreaves," she replied, a little frostily.

The boy grinned broadly. "You're the granny nanny!" he exclaimed delightedly. He thrust his hand toward her. "I'm Kite. Pleased to meet you!"

Liberty didn't know quite how to respond. She stood up and shook his fingertips briefly and awkwardly. The dog took a step forward, and Liberty hastily sat back down.

"I'm Mrs. Hamilton Hargreaves's personal assistant," she said, attempting to regain control of the situation. "And who are you?"

The boy bent over and threw his arms around the dog affectionately.

"I told you," he replied patiently. "I'm Kite. And you're definitely the granny nanny."

It occurred to Liberty that with a name like "Kite," the boy was likely to be one of the family. Meanwhile, he had gone to the fridge and was rummaging through its contents.

"I didn't know Nisha had a dog," he said, feeding the dog a chunk of cheese that he had broken off. "What's he called?"

Liberty's mind went blank. Since she had arrived, she had made every effort possible to avoid the dog. All she could remember was that he was named after an actor she had recognized from the film *Love Actually*.

"Hugh Grant?" she hazarded doubtfully.

The boy shook his head in disapproval. "Nisha can't call him that! He doesn't look a bit like Hugh Grant."

Liberty was conscious that she still hadn't confirmed who this boy in Venetia's kitchen was and what he was doing here. "Is Mrs. Hamilton Hargreaves expecting you?"

The boy laughed out loud. "I shouldn't think so!"

"Well, what are you doing here?"

"I've run away from school."

The boy wandered around the table and picked up one of the cards. "That's a heron," he said, pointing to the picture on the front. "My dad's called Heron."

Thank God for that! At least now Liberty knew who he was. "So you're Venetia's grandson?"

The boy nodded and smiled at her kindly, as though she were a small child who had just managed to spell a simple word correctly.

"Who are the cards for?" he asked, picking up another and inspecting the illustration of a blackbird.

"They are for the people who came to your grandfather's funeral—to say thank you."

"They should be saying thank you to Nisha for letting them come. Grandpa's funeral was excellent! There was thunder and lightning that almost smashed through the church window, and Swan shouted her poem because she's deaf and mad as a box of frogs, and then she got drunk and was swearing at the party afterwards and telling everyone they were going to die."

Liberty checked her list for the madwoman. "Who's Swan?" she asked.

"She's my great-aunt and I do like her, but she ate too many of my crisps. You see, the food at the party was rubbish and so Nisha got me some crisps, and I was being her wingman and I offered one to Swan to calm her down when she was shouting, but she took a whole handful." The boy shook his head in disgust.

Liberty shook her head in bewilderment.

"Have you ever been to a funeral?" the boy asked her.

"Yes. I went to my mother's a few weeks ago."

"Was it any good?"

"It was . . . different."

"What was the food like at the party?"

"Sausage rolls and sandwiches."

"I wish we'd had sausage rolls at Grandpa's," the boy replied wistfully.

Liberty could see from the badge on his blazer that he was a pupil at the local private school.

"Won't you be in trouble for running away from school?" she asked him. "Won't your grandmother be cross?"

The boy considered for a moment before answering, and as Liberty watched him, she could see in his expression a faint resemblance to his father.

"I won't be in trouble yet because it's still lunch break and no one will have noticed that I've gone. And I don't think Nisha will be cross because she didn't want me to be a boarder anyway. She wanted me to live here with her."

Liberty wondered if childminding might have been one of her duties, had Venetia got her wish. It was bad enough that there was now a resident dog for her to contend with, let alone a small boy. The tranquility of her first morning had been swept away by these two unexpected intruders, and she had not a clue how to deal with either of them.

"What time will Nisha be back?"

Soon, Liberty hoped, but "I'm not really sure" was her honest answer.

The boy seemed undecided about what to do. His initial exuberance, excited by the anticipation of seeing his grandmother, had abated in the light of her absence. He sighed. "Well, I suppose I'd better go back to school."

Liberty was delighted to hear it, but the disappointment in his face snagged her conscience like a bramble caught on her sleeve.

"Would you like me to make you a sandwich to take with you now that you've missed your lunch?" she offered.

The boy smiled in recognition of a kindness. "Thanks, but there's no time. I'll be late for Latin. But can I take some dead-fly biscuits? Nisha usually has some in the pantry."

Liberty nodded, having absolutely no idea what he was talking about. He returned from the pantry with his pocket bulging and his mouth full. As he headed for the door, the dog got up and followed him. He had almost closed the door behind them when he reappeared.

"I'm sorry your mum died."

Liberty was touched.

"But I expect she *was* very old."

CHAPTER 12

It wasn't long after Kite's departure that Venetia clattered through the front door and threw her keys onto the hall table. Several glossy paper shopping bags hung from her forearms containing the spoils of that morning's shopping spree. Venetia deposited the bags at the bottom of the staircase and went through to the kitchen, where Liberty had finished the last of the cards and was eating her lunch.

"Have you had a good morning?" Venetia asked, going straight to the back door to let in Colin Firth, who greeted her with an affectionate headbutt and a furiously wagging tail. She filled his bowl with fresh water and set it down on the floor.

"Your grandson came," Liberty replied. "He said that he'd run away from school."

Venetia seemed neither surprised nor unduly concerned. "Is he still here?"

"No. When I told him that you were out, he went back to school. I offered to make him a sandwich, but he took some biscuits instead."

Venetia smiled. "Dead-fly biscuits."

"Yes. That's what *he* called them."

"Did he say why he'd run away from school?"

"No. I assumed he'd just come to see you. I think he was joking about running away. It was the lunch break."

Venetia wasn't convinced. She knew her grandson very well. Better, perhaps, than anyone else. She also knew that boys as young as Kite were not permitted to leave the school grounds during the day without permission and had to be accompanied by an adult. But it was only a week into the new term. She would give Kite a little longer to settle in before raising it with him or speaking to someone at the school.

"The cards are all done except for these two," Liberty told her, pointing to the only names on the list that hadn't been crossed through. "I couldn't find addresses for them."

Francis Taylor and Torin McGuire. They were both unknown to Venetia.

"Never mind," she told Liberty. "I'll ask some of Hawk's friends and ex-colleagues. Perhaps one of them will know where we can find them."

"I could search online if you like?" Liberty offered. "They may be on Facebook or have business profiles of some sort."

Venetia smiled at the thought of any of Hawk's cronies engaging with Facebook, but she was impressed by Liberty's keenness.

"That would be very helpful, but please do finish your lunch first. And then perhaps you can take the cards that are ready to the post-box."

Venetia left Liberty in the kitchen and took her bags upstairs, closely followed by Colin Firth. The shopping had been fun while it lasted, but now, as she dumped her purchases on the floor and sat down on the bed, she felt somehow deflated and horribly guilty at having spent so much money on new things that she didn't really need. She already had two wardrobes full of dull, sensible, perfectly serviceable clothes. Perhaps she was being foolish, even selfish, trying to reinvent herself now that Hawk was gone. Perhaps the desire for pretty things—and to look pretty—was ridiculous in a woman of her age. She had become so accustomed to putting the needs of others before her own that now that she was finally free to put herself first, she couldn't enjoy it. Couldn't *allow* herself to enjoy it. After all the years spent being a good wife and mother, she had forgotten how to be just Venetia—a woman in her own right, independent of any role that she had taken on. In fact, she had all but forgotten who the real Venetia was. But perhaps that no longer mattered. It was who she might become that was important now. Circumstances had presented her with the precious gift of possibility, but was she brave enough to take it? Could she resurrect the person she might have been in a different life?

"Do you think I'm ridiculous?" she asked the dog, who was sniffing curiously at her shopping bags. He looked up, and in one leap he joined her on the bed and rolled onto his back, snorting joyfully with his legs flailing in the air. She watched him having fun messing up the bedcovers. Having fun—surely she was entitled to have a little fun too, rather than wasting whatever time she might have left in widow's weeds? Colin righted himself and sat next to her, dropping his head onto her shoulder. Venetia studied their reflection in the dressing-table mirror. He was a handsome dog, and in the short time that he had been with her, his confidence had grown, and his playful side was slowly revealing itself. She had taken him on, and she was determined not to let him down. He deserved more than a timid, dowdy old lady. Had she forgotten that she was younger than Cher?! Cher wouldn't be seen dead wearing any of the clothes in Venetia's wardrobes, but she might be more tempted by those in the bags on the floor.

An hour later, Venetia's new clothes were hanging in the wardrobes and her old ones had been neatly folded into black bin bags ready to go to the charity shop—with the exception of one of the ugly black shoes Venetia had worn to Hawk's funeral, which Colin had purloined as a plaything and was now tossing up into the air and catching with such enthusiasm that it brought Liberty rushing up the stairs to check that nothing was amiss. Venetia reassured her that everything was fine. "It's just this big, goofy chap having a game."

The dog paused briefly to look at Liberty before shaking the shoe violently from side to side to make quite sure that it was dead.

"Would you mind taking these clothes to the charity shop at some point? I'll start going through Hawk's things tomorrow, so there'll be a few more bags to add to these."

Liberty nodded. "I've had a quick search online, but so far I haven't been able to find anything on Mr. Taylor and Mr. McGuire. I'm assuming that they came to the funeral together because their message of condolence was from both of them."

Venetia cast her mind back to the funeral. There had been so many people.

"Not to worry. I'll take a look in my husband's study and see if I can find anything amongst his papers that helps."

She sighed at the enormity of the task that lay ahead of her—the legacy of a death. Hawk's corporeal remains had been simple enough to deal with, but his worldly possessions and the ephemera of his life were more problematic. Some objects embody emotions and memories, endowing them with a sentimental value far greater than their intrinsic worth. But how much could she—should she—keep, to remember and respect the man, without remaining shackled to the past?

Hawk's study was still exactly as he had left it, save for the chess set that was now in Kite's dormitory at school. The imprint of his body was still visible in his chair, as though his ghost sat there now, and the ink stain on the carpet had grown stiff and dry.

"Who on earth were Francis Taylor and Torin McGuire?" Venetia asked herself out loud. And if Hawk's ghost was in his chair, he didn't answer. Venetia opened the drawers in Hawk's desk and riffled through old bills and receipts. One drawer was full of old appointment diaries—perhaps they might contain some addresses too. Venetia piled them on top of the desk, but as she reached to the back of the drawer her fingers closed on a different sort of book. It was a paperback edition of *The Lion, the Witch and the Wardrobe*. It was tatty—or perhaps much-loved—and the pages well thumbed. Venetia opened the cover, and on the title page there was a handwritten inscription.

When I became a man, I put away childish things, including the fear of childishness and the desire to be very grown up.

Beneath it were the initials A. F.

CHAPTER 13

The next morning Venetia decided to take Colin for a stroll along the Embankment before sorting through Hawk's clothes. It was pure procrastination. She was worried that it might be too soon, too callous, too brutal—that the physical, practical elements of letting Hawk go should be undertaken incrementally. But then what difference did it make how or when she did it? It *was* a brutal thing to consign his beloved tweed jackets, his dinner suit, his handmade shoes, and his Charles Tyrwhitt shirts to a bin or a charity shop, depending on their condition. But it was also necessary. She couldn't keep them all, and some of his things might do someone who needed them a good turn. When the clothes themselves were gone, she would still have the memories of him wearing them. One or two of his sweaters were patched and threadbare, but he had refused to part with them, insisting that they were perfectly good for pottering about in the garden. She could picture him now in his ancient racing-green Aran jumper with a hole in the armpit, deadheading the dahlias, and tears pooled in her eyes as she bent over to clip Colin's lead to his collar. And what about his socks and underwear? she thought. Was it appropriate to donate those? The ones without holes, of course.

Outside, the sky was forget-me-not blue, and the sun cast everything in a soft golden light that filtered through the leaves on the trees and scattered mottled shade onto the pavement beneath them. It was still warm enough for Venetia to venture out coatless, but the air had taken on that freshness and faint earthy tang that augurs autumn waiting in the wings. Colin had turned out to be surprisingly easy to walk. He didn't pull on his lead and was happy to trot along at Venetia's side, greeting other dogs and humans with polite interest, and gazing with rapt attention at the balletic antics of squirrels that swung and leaped among the branches above them. They crossed the suspension bridge, and Venetia unleashed him. He set off across the grass toward the newly painted bandstand, nose to the ground, pausing every now and then to sniff or greet another dog. He made his way over to a wooden bench where a woman sat alone drinking a takeaway coffee. Venetia followed, ready to retrieve him should the woman not welcome his overtures, however friendly they might be. But by the time she reached them, the woman was stroking his head and telling him what a handsome boy he was.

"I hope he isn't bothering you," Venetia said. "It's unlike him to be so bold. He's normally quite shy with new people."

The woman smiled. "Of course he isn't! He's just saying hello. Perhaps he knew that I needed cheering up," she added, almost to herself.

Venetia studied her more closely. She was a handsome woman who radiated an energy and vigor that was both attractive and imposing. But behind her smile, her eyes bore something of the sadness that Venetia saw in her own when she looked in the mirror.

"Oh dear. I'm sorry to hear that." She didn't know what else to say.

The dog sat down beside the woman with a contented sigh, clearly enjoying the fuss she was making of him. "His ears are so soft," the woman marveled. "Just like velvet!"

Venetia joined her on the bench. "Don't be fooled by that butter-wouldn't-melt expression of his," she warned. "He's full of mischief when the mood takes him!"

"What's his name?"

"Colin Firth."

The woman laughed. "I wouldn't mind getting up to some mischief with *him*! By the way, I'm Evangeline."

"Venetia. It's very nice to meet you."

"Likewise. You two have put a smile on my face for the first time today."

"What took it off to begin with? You don't have to tell me, of course, if you'd prefer not to. But you know what they say about a problem shared . . ."

"I do, but I'm not sure I believe it. It only really helps if the person you share it with can do anything about it."

"Try me!" Venetia dared.

Evangeline held up her hands in mock surrender. "Okay. Okay. But only because I like your dog," she joked. She looked away for a moment, gazing at an untidy column of ducks drifting down the river, and her face became serious. "Do you have faith, Venetia?"

Venetia considered for a moment. "Do I believe in God, do you mean? Well, I'm not a regular churchgoer, but yes, I suppose in my own way, I do believe in a god of some sort. Or at least, I hope that one exists."

Evangeline nodded. "My church is my life. I've been running it for nearly twenty years, and now someone is trying to take it away from me."

"Are you a vicar . . . or a minister?"

Evangeline smiled. "No, not exactly. It's not that kind of church—we don't have many rules. Yes, we say prayers and sing hymns, but we also have evenings of healing and clairvoyance."

Venetia's face must have betrayed her surprise, and Evangeline laughed.

"Don't look at me like that! It's not a cult or anything spooky. And everyone is welcome, man, woman, child—or dog," she added, nodding at Colin. "Some people come to our services, others just come for a cup of tea and a chat. Maybe they're lonely or have troubles and need someone to talk to. Most of them have tried other churches but have found them too . . . stick-in-the-mud, too stuck-up, or just plain scary. We are there for those people and anyone else who cares to join us. Our doors are open for as many hours as we can manage, but now someone is trying to close them for good."

"So, you're a spiritualist church, then?" Venetia had heard of such things and always dismissed them as being a relatively harmless whimsicality. She imagined them to be frequented largely by the grieving and the gullible, and run by well-intentioned but deluded and decidedly flaky old ladies. But there appeared to be nothing flaky about Evangeline, who couldn't have been any older than in her early fifties.

"Some people might call it that, but we don't like labels. They invite too many preconceptions and prejudices."

Venetia colored slightly, as though she had been caught out. "But clairvoyance—do you really believe that you can communicate with the dead?"

Evangeline sighed. It was clearly a question she had been asked too many times. "Tell me, Venetia, have you ever lost anyone close to you?"

Venetia nodded.

"And have you never caught yourself talking to that person even though you know that they are dead and buried or burnt to a cinder?"

Venetia nodded again, remembering how many times she had spoken to Hawk since he had died, alone in her empty house. "But I don't expect an answer and I never get one."

Evangeline raised her eyebrows. "Perhaps you do, but you just don't realize it."

Venetia didn't want to think about this now. She had to go back and sort out Hawk's clothes, and she couldn't bear the idea of him as a spectral spectator while she did it. She turned the conversation back to Evangeline's problem. "So, who is trying to take your church away?"

"The owners of the building where we meet. We've been renting the ground floor since we started. We had a twenty-year lease, but it's about to expire and the new owners won't renew it. They've applied for residential planning permission to convert the whole building into luxury apartments."

"Can't you find another place to meet?"

"The good Lord knows we've been trying, but it's not that easy. You'd be surprised how many landlords get the jitters at the notion of leasing to a church."

Venetia wasn't overly surprised, considering what kind of church it was.

"Where is it that you meet?"

Evangeline pointed across the river toward town. "Over there—the building in front of the castle mound."

Venetia didn't need to look. She knew it well. "Whatever happened to the old ballroom on the first floor?"

"It's still there," Evangeline replied. "But it's been empty for years. The previous owner hung on to it because he had some sort of sentimental attachment to it, but when he died, his sons inherited it, and they wasted no time putting it on the market. They don't give a damn about the ballroom or my church, and they have no qualms about throwing us out on the street. They only care about the money!"

She kissed her teeth in disgust.

"They already have a potential buyer, and they're just waiting for their planning application to be heard."

"And is it likely to be successful?"

Evangeline shrugged. "Nothing's certain. But the estate agent thinks they stand a good chance."

"Well, I'll keep my fingers crossed for you!"

Venetia was conscious that her voice had a forced brightness to it that sounded as hollow as her optimistic offer of help had turned out to be. She stood up to continue her walk with Colin, who clambered reluctantly to his feet.

"It was nice talking to you," she added, somewhat lamely. Evangeline smiled but said nothing.

Venetia continued their walk up past the boathouse and crossed back over the river on the white town bridge, keeping the dog on her inside to shield him from the busy stream of traffic that shared the bridge with pedestrians. She would never usually bring him this way, but it meant that their return route took them past Evangeline's church. Venetia gazed up at the grimy panes of glass that glinted in the elegant windows of the abandoned ballroom. The ballroom where she had met Hawk for the first time and where she had taught him to dance.

CHAPTER 14

1971

Venetia wriggled into her coat and checked her lipstick in the hall mirror. She tied a silk headscarf over her newly blow-dried hair and grabbed her keys from the drawer in the hall table.

"Bye, Mum!" She opened the front door to pouring rain.

Damn! Her hair would be ruined by the time she got to the bus stop. She snatched an umbrella from the coat stand.

"Bye, love!" her mother called from the kitchen. "Be careful!"

It was her mother's constant refrain whenever she left the house, no matter that Venetia was now a grown woman of twenty-three.

"I will. See you later." Venetia slammed the door behind her and hurried off down the street, splashing her tights as she ran through puddles on the pavement. When she turned the corner, her bus was just pulling up. She waved her umbrella wildly and sprinted toward it.

"Made it by the skin of your teeth!" The bus conductor winked at her as she clambered on and closed her dripping umbrella.

Half an hour later, having changed her sodden shoes for the spare pair that she kept in her locker, Venetia stood by the piano at which Dorothy, the ballroom's resident accompanist, was seated and watched as her new class of adult beginners filed in. Venetia preferred to use a pianist with her beginners, as Dorothy was easier to stop and start than a record player. Venetia's colleague was greeting people at the door and ticking off their names on the list attached to his clipboard.

With his thick, dark hair, dancer's physique, and irresistible smile, Brendan Kelly was particularly popular with the female students. But his dealings with them never strayed beyond the professional, and his sharp wit and quick tongue soon put them in their place if ever they overstepped the mark with him. Venetia was secretly glad. She adored Brendan. He had taken her under his wing when she had started work as an instructor at the ballroom almost five years ago now, and she often taught classes with him. They had become close friends and had even talked about one day opening a dance school together. Venetia occasionally went so far as to allow herself to imagine a future where they were more than just close friends and business partners. They made a glamorous duo as they demonstrated a breakdown of the steps and then partnered the students in turn.

Today's class was a real assortment: several couples, a group of young women who had clearly come together, three middle-aged ladies who appeared to be friends and were chatting in excited whispers, a spritely old chap in a dapper bow tie, and two men whom Venetia judged to be in their early thirties. One of them was grinning broadly and seemingly joking with his companion, who looked more serious and a little apprehensive. Once Brendan had confirmed that everyone was present and correct, Venetia introduced herself, Brendan, and Dorothy and asked the beginners to arrange themselves into three rows in front of her.

"We're going to start with a waltz," she told them. "Brendan and I will show you the first step sequence a few times, and then each of you can find a partner and join in."

There were a few nervous whispers and giggles. Venetia smiled.

"Don't worry—we'll take it very slowly. The most important thing is to relax and enjoy it!"

Venetia nodded at Dorothy, and then she and Brendan began to dance, Venetia calling out the steps above the melody of "Moon River." Before long, nine couples were moving to the music. Some were almost waltzing, while others were counting as they clumped out the steps, staring at their feet. Venetia and Brendan worked their way around the room, encouraging those who were dancing and assisting those who were floundering. Stanley in the bow tie turned out to be a nimble-footed natural, guiding Sheila, who had come with her two friends, firmly and fluently around the floor. Sheila's friends, May and June, were giving it their best shot together, and clearly enjoying themselves immensely.

"A little more rise and fall, ladies!" Brendan coached them. "Remember to use the balls of your feet."

May, who was generously proportioned fore and aft, and a little out of breath from her exertions, fanned her heaving bosom. "I reckon there's plenty of rise and fall going on here already," she joked with June.

"I heard that!" Brendan called over his shoulder with a grin, as he moved on to another couple.

The two men who had come together were dancing with a couple of the younger women. The more somber of the two had ended up with a frizzy-haired, flat-footed girl called Deirdre who wore owl-like spectacles and clearly thought that the whole thing was an absolute hoot. Her lack of concentration—and rhythm—were seriously impeding their progress, and Venetia could see that the man was growing irritated but trying valiantly to conceal the fact. She took pity on him and intervened.

"Perhaps you can show me how you're getting on while Brendan helps Deirdre find her feet, so to speak." Venetia shot Brendan a glance that clearly said, "And good luck with that!" and he rolled his eyes at her in reply.

The man looked relieved as Venetia took him to one side.

"I'm sorry—I didn't catch your name?"

"Hawk Hamilton Hargreaves."

Venetia smiled. "That's quite an alliteration you have there."

She took his right hand and placed it on her left shoulder blade, then rested her left hand on his upper arm. Up close, she noted that he was fastidiously turned out. His sandy hair and well-cut clothes were conservative in style but immaculate, and he smelled of expensive soap with a trace of citrus cologne. His natural posture was strong and upright, but Venetia could feel the tension in his touch.

"Relax!" she told him. "It's supposed to be fun."

He smiled for the first time, briefly and somewhat apologetically.

"I'm afraid I have an ulterior motive," he confessed. "I'm not a huge fan of all this, but I need to learn some basics. My job requires that I attend formal events—balls and the like—and I don't want to look like a complete fool." He spoke brusquely but not rudely.

"And what about your friend?" Venetia gestured toward the man he had arrived with.

"Andrew? He only came to keep me company. He's got two left feet, I'm afraid, but he doesn't let it hold him back. He's got enough charm to get away with pretty much anything."

Venetia couldn't tell if Hawk's tone was one of envy or approbation. Andrew's partner certainly appeared to be enjoying his company, despite the fact that he had trodden on her toes more than once and they had just collided with another couple. As Venetia guided Hawk through the steps, she discovered that he was a keen pupil and a fast learner. But his intense concentration on the mechanics of the dance made his movements a little robotic. Venetia brought them to a halt.

"That's good, Hawk. You've learned the steps really well," she told him. "But remember it's a dance, and one of the most romantic. You need to surrender yourself to the music and let it carry you—a bit like a leaf being swept along by the wind."

Hawk nodded but looked uncomfortable. He didn't seem like a man who would willingly surrender himself to anything. His cheeks had colored a little, and he couldn't meet her gaze. Venetia wondered if the mention of romance had flustered him. She could tell that Hawk was unsettled by their physical intimacy, by her hand in his and the proximity of their torsos. It was, Venetia suspected, something that perhaps he had desired more than he had experienced. Perhaps he hoped that his ulterior motive of "balls and the like" would also provide the opportunity for meeting prospective girlfriends. Venetia was willing to bet that he had probably attended an all-boys private school, then university with his sights firmly fixed on his career before the distraction of any romantic entanglements, which might account for his apparent inexperience when it came to the opposite sex. But now maybe he had both the time and inclination for a relationship, and something about Hawk's dogged determination despite his embarrassment moved her.

"Take a deep breath," she told him, "and look at me, rather than at your feet."

With some reluctance, Hawk raised his cool blue eyes, and Venetia dazzled him with her brightest smile. "Shall we dance?"

CHAPTER 15

Liberty lugged the last of the black bin bags from the boot of her car and into the Greenfields Animal Sanctuary shop. Castle Road boasted three charity shops supporting an ever-changing choice of worthy causes, and Liberty had donated two bags of Venetia's things to each for the sake of impartiality. It had been over a week since her employer had cleared out her wardrobes, but she still hadn't managed to tackle her husband's and Liberty was reluctant to prompt her. The memory of sorting through her mother's things was still raw, and she thought how much harder it must be to relinquish the relics of a husband with whom you had shared most of your life. Venetia had told her that she and Hawk had been married for almost fifty years—longer than Liberty had been alive! Her longest relationship to date had been with Graham, but to call it a relationship now seemed to be an overstatement. She was finally able to admit, if only to herself, that their affair had been little more than an arrangement where he had taken what he wanted, and she had allowed him to. And with that admission came the inevitable and humiliating recognition that she had been a first-class bloody fool. In fact, if being a fool had been an Olympic event, she would undoubtedly have won a gold medal. She was embarrassed even thinking about it, even more so because a part of her—a part that she despised—still missed him.

Having distributed her bin bags, Liberty decided on impulse to treat herself to a coffee and a pain au chocolat. She chose a café where she could sit outside and enjoy the autumn sunshine, and as she sipped her hazelnut latte, she marveled at her own decadence. She never did this. She used to meet friends for coffee or lunch—in the days when she still had friends—and occasionally her mother. She and Graham had never been out together in broad daylight in case they were seen. Graham had deemed it to be too risky. Their clandestine outings had been confined to dimly lit dinners in out-of-town restaurants. Back then, she had thought it exciting and romantic. Now, hindsight had extended her a cruel but clear perspective, and those secretive dinners seemed depressingly sleazy. But she had never been in the habit of visiting a café on her own. It simply wouldn't have occurred to her to treat herself with such indulgence, however trivial. She would usually wait until she got home and then make do with a cup of instant and maybe a biscuit. Nothing fancy—a rich tea or a digestive. But how much better did this coffee taste, topped with froth, laced with syrup, and served with a smile? Liberty sat and watched the passersby in a state of unfamiliar contentment. But she couldn't help keeping an eye on her watch to make sure that it didn't last too long. She was, after all, "at work." The job seemed to be going well so far and she loved her new accommodation. Venetia was friendly, but not too friendly, and kept her busy. Liberty was even becoming accustomed to the dog. At least her mother had done her a good turn by leaving her the copy of that magazine. She was wearing her mother's wedding ring on the middle finger of her right hand, and now she twisted it around and around as she thought about the photo album that had accompanied the magazine. The album contained a series of seemingly random photographs from when Liberty was a toddler through to when she went to university. Liberty had been unable to fathom any significance in their selection. But then perhaps there wasn't any. Perhaps it was simply her mother's idea of a joke. As she drained her cup and got up to go, she recognized a familiar figure walking purposefully toward her. *Oh God, no,* she thought, but there was nowhere for her to hide.

"Liberty? I thought it was you. How are you? I was sorry to hear about your poor mother."

I bet you were, Liberty thought as she did her best to muster a tight smile. The woman in front of her was an attractive, well-dressed brunette in her midfifties with sharp features and an astringent edge to her plummy voice. Imogen Snyder was the office manager at the accountancy firm in Milton Keynes where Liberty had worked previously with Graham. She layered her self-importance with a mist of Chanel No. 5, both of which caused Liberty to recoil slightly as Imogen leaned in and patted her arm. Liberty thanked her more politely than her insincerity deserved.

"It must have been so dreadful for you, particularly after you . . ." Imogen paused briefly. ". . . decided to leave us so suddenly."

Liberty could feel her cheeks reddening. "But that was why I left—to look after my mother."

When Graham had told her—after almost fifteen years!—that he was "letting her go" because he owed it to his wife to try to "reinvest emotionally" in his marriage, she had no choice but to resign. She could no longer bear the sight of him. He would have been a constant reminder of her own stupidity.

"Ah, yes. I remember now. You mentioned it in your letter of resignation. Have you managed to find yourself another job yet?"

"Yes, I have actually. I'm working as a personal assistant to a recently widowed lady. It's something completely different for me, and I'm really enjoying it."

Imogen was clearly only half listening. She checked her watch. "I must dash. I'm seeing the chap in the antiquarian bookshop down the road about selling some books that my great-uncle left me. Anyway, it's lovely to see you. I'm glad you've managed to find something else—and if your boss is an old lady, you should be able to keep out of mischief this time!" she added with a conspiratorial wink.

Liberty was stunned and, for a moment, speechless. Imogen arched an eyebrow in amusement.

"You surely didn't think that it was a secret? *Everyone* knew." And with a smug smile, Imogen turned and walked away.

"Oh, why don't you just bugger off!" Liberty muttered under her breath. But then something snapped. She grabbed her bag and car keys and stood up. Imogen was still only yards away, waiting to cross the road.

"Imogen!" Liberty yelled.

She turned.

"Why don't you just bugger off!"

BACK AT THE house, Venetia was in Hawk's study, reading through the appointment diaries she had discovered.

"I've still had no luck finding any mention of our two mystery gentlemen from the funeral," she told Liberty, when she put her head around the door to let Venetia know that she had returned. Venetia had already asked several of Hawk's friends and former colleagues but had so far drawn a blank. She rubbed her eyes. She looked tired.

"Would you like me to take a look?" Liberty asked, gesturing toward the diaries.

Venetia shook her head. "No, it's fine. They may just have to go without their thank-you notes."

Liberty was determined that they would not. She hated loose ends.

"But there is something I'd like you to do," Venetia continued. "Would you please find out which estate agent is dealing with the sale of that building in front of the castle mound?"

"You mean the church?"

"Yes. It's a church on the ground floor. Do you know it?"

"It's the church my mother used to go to."

"Did she know a woman called Evangeline?"

Liberty smiled. "Evangeline was her best friend. Do *you* know her too?"

"Not really. I just happened to meet her last week when I was walking Colin, and she told me that the building was being sold."

"I didn't know. Evangeline must be devastated."

Venetia nodded thoughtfully. "She was. But it seems there's nothing she can do about it. There's no sale board outside, but I wondered if you could search online?"

"Of course. But why do you want to know? You're not thinking of buying it, are you?" Liberty knew it was none of her business, but the words were out before she could stop them.

Venetia laughed. "What on earth would I do with it? Apparently it's going to be converted into luxury apartments. I'm just curious, that's all. On the first floor, there's a ballroom where, many years ago, I used to dance. I've love to take a final look before it's gone for good."

CHAPTER 16

Change rippled in the air like vibrations on a track when a train is approaching. Crow could sense it. He lifted his head and watched clouds the color of Carrara marble scudding across a bleached sky. The wind had grown sharp enough to redden cheeks and chill fingertips. It whipped swirling eddies of fallen leaves into a capricious waltz along the pavement and ruffled the feathers of the ducks and swans that bobbed upon the river's rumpled surface. The change of season was expected, accepted, as part of the natural order. But from his perch on the fire escape, Crow had seen signs of other changes that unsettled him and made him wary. This had long been his safe place where he could spend time unnoticed, where no one bothered him. But through the window he had seen men in the ballroom with their phones and their notebooks, making footprints in the dust and disturbing the cobwebs. He had heard them tapping on the walls and the floor and talking in loud voices. The ballroom had been silent and asleep for so long.

Would its rude awakening be a dream or a nightmare?

CHAPTER 17

Over a week had passed since her conversation with Evangeline before Venetia finally forced herself to go up to Hawk's room and begin sorting out his clothes. But she was readily distracted by the collection of photographs that stood on top of his chest of drawers. There was one of Hawk's beloved black Labradors, Gilbert and Sullivan; one of Heron as a teenager in his cricket whites; and another of Hawk in their garden playing football with Kite when he was very young. But the largest, in an art deco silver frame, was of Hawk and Venetia in evening dress, dancing together at Claridge's. It had been taken at a dinner and dance hosted by Hawk's chambers soon after he had proposed and presented her with his grandmother's emerald-and-diamond engagement ring. She picked up the photograph and studied it. Her dress had been made of deep red satin and cut off the shoulders, and her hair was swept up into an elegant chignon. She was smiling, but Hawk's expression betrayed his concentration. He had been a competent rather than natural dancer, but he had looked extremely dashing nonetheless.

"Bless you, my darling," Venetia murmured. "You always tried so hard."

The shrill peal of the telephone interrupted her musings. It rang only twice before it was picked up, and Venetia moved onto the landing to listen in case she was needed. Almost immediately

Liberty called her. She made her way downstairs, and Liberty handed her the phone. She looked worried.

"It's Kite's school. He's gone missing."

Mr. Howard, Kite's housemaster, was an avuncular-looking man in his late forties. He turned up at Venetia's door around half an hour after the telephone call.

"I thought it best to come in person," he explained as Venetia took him through to the kitchen where Liberty was boiling the kettle. *Because that's what we British do in a crisis*, thought Venetia—*we make tea*.

"Would you like tea?" Liberty asked, right on cue.

"Yes, please. Milk and two sugars. Now . . ." He turned to Venetia. "We've informed the police, but purely as a precautionary measure at this stage. The school and grounds are still being searched. As I'm sure you understand, there are a great many potential hiding places for a small boy if he doesn't want to be found, and although we're moving as fast as we can, it could take some time to cover everywhere."

Venetia appreciated his honesty and the fact that he hadn't patronized her by telling her not to worry. She was, of course, desperately worried but trying her best not to let panic overwhelm her. A cool, calm head was what she needed now, and she was somewhat reassured by Mr. Howard's sensible, pragmatic manner.

"When was Kite last seen?" she asked.

"Last lesson before lunch. Apparently, he asked to be excused to use the toilet and didn't come back to the classroom. His teacher assumed that he had gone straight to the dining hall, but no one remembers seeing him over the lunch break, and he didn't turn up for his first lesson this afternoon."

"He came here once in his lunch break," Liberty blurted out, before catching herself. "I'm sorry—I didn't mean to interfere, Venetia."

Venetia shook her head. "No, you're quite right to bring it up. He did," she said, turning to Mr. Howard. "But it was only a flying visit and right at the start of term. Kite was a little . . . uncertain about boarding, and I think he just needed to see a familiar face. I hoped that he would settle into it after a few weeks, which is why I didn't contact the school at the time. But it seems I was wrong."

Venetia was struggling to keep her voice steady. What a fool she had been not to take Kite's concerns more seriously! Particularly after he had turned up to see her and she hadn't been there for him. She had spoken to him on the phone since then, but he had seemed fine. Or maybe that was what she had wanted to believe. She had heard his words but perhaps not truly listened. Passive not active—as she had been for so many years of her life.

"Has anything happened recently at school that might have upset him?" she asked Mr. Howard.

"I was just coming to that," he replied. "There was an incident this morning in the boardinghouse between Kite and an older boy. I wasn't there myself, but another member of staff had cause to intervene when things got physical. Neither boy was really hurt, but the school takes these things very seriously, and I was going to speak to both boys this evening. I must say, I was rather surprised when I heard about it. From what I know of him, it isn't like Kite at all to get involved in a scrap."

Venetia bit her lip. "It's completely out of character. I can tell you that as his grandmother. Kite is a gentle soul through and through. But then I would say that—because I *am* his grandmother. I suppose most people can be provoked to behave badly, given the right circumstances. Do you know what the argument was about?"

"It was something to do with a chess set."

Venetia's heart sank.

"Have you contacted his parents yet?"

"No. You are the school's named first contact. I understand his parents are abroad?"

"In France—yes. I'm not sure if it's worth worrying them yet. He's only been missing a couple of hours, and it's not as though they can do anything other than fly home. By the time they get here, Kite will, most likely, have been found. I think we should give it a little longer before I phone them."

Venetia knew that she was trying to convince herself as much as anyone.

"Would it be worth searching the garden and the garage—and maybe the coach house?" Liberty offered. "He may be hiding out there if he thinks he's in trouble."

"It's worth a try," Venetia agreed, while hating the thought that Kite would rather hide than come to her with his troubles. But then he'd tried that already, she thought bitterly, and she'd let her wingman down. "We'll take Colin. If Kite's out there, he'll find him."

The dog rose from his place at Venetia's feet and followed her to the back door.

A little over fifteen minutes later, their fruitless search was over, and they were back in the kitchen.

"I must get back to the school," Mr. Howard told her apologetically, "but obviously I'll keep in touch. I expect if there's no news, the police will want to talk to you next."

"But I need to go out and look for him."

Mr. Howard smiled sympathetically. "I completely understand that you want to *do* something other than sit and wait, but what if Kite turns up here? Wouldn't it be better if you were at home? And try to think of anywhere else he might go. I'm sure the police will find it really helpful, should it come to that."

Venetia saw him to the front door and watched him walk away. Daylight was fading into dusk and the temperature had dropped, turning her breath into mist as she whispered into the air: "Where are you, Kite?"

Back inside, she reluctantly conceded to herself that she ought to ring Heron. She began to search for her mobile, before remembering that she had left it to charge in her bedroom. She rarely used it in the house, preferring the landline, but Heron's number was stored in its memory. A blue light was winking on the screen, indicating that she had received a voicemail.

"Nisha, I think I'm in trouble. Can you ring me back please?"

With shaking fingers, Venetia pressed redial and held the phone hard against her ear.

"This person's phone is switched off. Please try again later."

CHAPTER 18

Kite had spent the afternoon hiding out at the lawn bowling pavilion in the park. Its veranda at one end was shrouded by bushes and gave him plenty of cover. He had decided that it would be best to keep out of sight during school hours to avoid raising any suspicions about what he might be doing if anyone spotted him. He had passed the time quite happily reading a book called *The Silver Chair* that Nisha had loaned him from Grandpa's study, but now his legs were stiff and fizzing with pins and needles from sitting with his knees tucked up, and it was getting cold. He stood up and hopped from one leg to the other until the numbness and prickling had worn off, and then he checked in his pocket for his phone to see what the time was. It wasn't there. He rummaged in the small backpack that he had brought with him, but he still couldn't find it. The last time he had used it had been to ring Nisha that morning before lessons had begun.

Kite hadn't had much time to plan his escape, but he had managed to sneak back into his boardinghouse during the lunch break, get rid of his tie, swap his blazer for a dark hoodie, and throw a few things—but, most important, his chess set—into his rucksack. He had switched off his phone then because the battery was low and he wanted to save some charge in case of an emergency. Besides, Nisha had had plenty of time by then to call him back if she was going to. But she hadn't. On his way out, he was nearly caught by Mrs. How-ard answering the door to a delivery driver, but he had ducked into the common room and climbed out a window into the garden. Perhaps that was when he had dropped his phone.

He hoped that he would be less conspicuous out of school uniform and had eventually made his way to the park close to Nisha's home. He had been tempted to go straight to his grandmother's, but he had been worried that his absence would have been noticed by now and that the school might have sent someone to see Nisha. Or maybe even the police would be there, either because he was missing or because of what he had done. After all, Ollie Vane-Percy's father was a school governor. Kite went over that morning's events in his head to see what he could have done differently to rescue his chess set, but he couldn't think of anything that would have worked quite as well as karate-kicking Ollie Vane-Percy on the kneecap. It was actually quite lucky, he thought, that it had been his grandpa who had shown him how to do it in the first place. He had been teaching Kite the self-defense moves he had learned in the army, and Kite had been able to use his grandpa's lesson to defend his chess set. It was definitely fate, Kite decided.

He really needed to speak to Nisha, which was why he had rung her. But she hadn't answered, and she hadn't called him back. She must be angry with him. He couldn't bear the thought that he, her wingman, had let her down. All he wanted to do right now was to find her and explain his side of the story. But what if she was out walking Colin Firth and the police were keeping the place under surveillance, ready to arrest him if he turned up? He could picture them parked outside in an unmarked car drinking takeaway coffees and watching the house through binoculars. They would probably put him in handcuffs as soon as he set foot on the drive.

He pulled a beanie down low onto his head, threaded his arms through the straps on his rucksack and hoisted it onto his shoulders. Where could he go now? He said a quick prayer because it couldn't hurt, could it? Kite enjoyed attending chapel at school, but that had more to do with the building itself than the presence of the Almighty. He found the candles, the organ music, the light diffused through colored glass, and the cavernous echoes when anyone spoke or sang soothing. But he hadn't fully decided where he stood on God himself. He wasn't surprised at his mother's certainty that there was no such being. She had very definite views about most things, coupled with an unshakable belief that she was right. He also couldn't help but feel that dismissing God altogether might be a bit unwise. After all, no one could prove that he didn't exist. But Kite wasn't hopeful of an answer to his prayer, because he couldn't bring himself to say sorry or even *feel* sorry about the karate kick. In fact, he was pretty proud of it. But he was fairly sure that it wasn't something God would approve of, even in defense of a chess set. He wondered what Grandpa would say.

"Get walking, lad. A moving target is always harder to hit!" The words arrived in Kite's head almost immediately. Whether they were sent by Grandpa, God, or Google, Kite didn't care. They made perfect sense.

At first, his escape from school had felt like an adventure. But that had been in broad and bright daylight, when he was still fueled by excitement and the biscuits he had eaten at break time. Now, long dark fingers of shadow cast by trees and lampposts were creeping farther across the grass and his stomach churned. He was hungry, he told himself. He set off across the park toward the fish-and-chips shop. He kept his head down as he passed a man walking an elderly chocolate Labrador with a graying muzzle and a woman pushing a little boy in a buggy. Along the edges of the park, windows in the houses turned into rectangles of warm yellow light, and chimneys puffed woodsmoke as families arrived home from school and work and began settling in for the evening. Kite reached the street where, farther down, a queue curled out of the fish-and-chips shop. Just ahead of him, a car pulled up in front of a house and a woman emerged from the driver's seat, and from the back, three children spilled out, laughing and shouting, dragging coats and schoolbags.

"What's for tea, Mum?" one of them asked.

"Fish fingers," the woman replied, and her answer was greeted with whoops of delight.

They filed up the path, and a cat jumped down from the garden wall and wound itself between their legs, darting through the front door as soon as it was open. Kite watched as the woman and her children followed the cat inside. He suddenly felt very alone.

He bought himself a bag of chips and smothered them in salt, vinegar, and ketchup, then ate them with a little wooden fork while walking up and down the side streets that bordered the park. He tried to walk purposefully, so that anyone who saw him would think he was going somewhere rather than just hanging around, but it was tricky while he was concentrating on eating. He hadn't realized quite how hungry he was and wolfed the chips, mopping up the last of the ketchup with his fingers. He scrunched the paper into a ball and found a bin to put it in. Now he could think properly about what to do next. He briefly considered trying to climb over the wall at the back of Nisha's house so that he could spend the night in the shed, or maybe the garage if it was unlocked. But then he remembered the security lights that had been fitted. And there was also the possibility that Colin Firth might sniff him out when he made his final inspection of the garden before bed. There was even an outside chance that the police might have someone staking out the garden with one of their own dogs. Colin Firth definitely wouldn't be happy about that.

Kite decided that if he stayed out all night, perhaps everyone would be worried about him—Nisha in particular—and that when he turned up again, they would be so relieved that they would forget to be angry. He also hoped that it would make Nisha realize just how unhappy he was being a boarder and that she might persuade his father to let him live with her after all. It wasn't much of a plan, but it was all he had. He still couldn't understand why Nisha hadn't rung him back. She was the one person he had hoped would be on his side.

It was getting dark, and Kite headed up Castle Road toward town. The shops and cafés had closed and there weren't many people about, except outside the pub and one or two waiting for their takeaways. Kite knew that now the sight of a small boy alone on the streets was more likely to attract attention. He needed to find somewhere to stay for the night. It dawned on him that although he couldn't hide at Nisha's, he might be able to get into the garden of one of the other houses on the street and find a shed or outbuilding that was unlocked. There was one house in particular that Kite remembered as being a bit scruffier than the others. Its front was caged in scaffolding, and there was a Sold sign in the front garden and a dumpster full of rubble. If the house was empty, he might even be able to get inside. He knew that if he kept walking, he would reach a pair of alleyways that would keep him off the streets and take him back onto the Embankment. The final alley came out conveniently close to the house that was now his destination. The straps of his rucksack had begun to dig into his shoulders, and he stopped for a moment to adjust them.

It was then that he noticed the man on the street behind him. Kite couldn't really see the man's face, but he was tall and broad and wore a long, dark coat with the collar turned up. The coat was unbuttoned and flapped behind him—like Batman's cape, Kite thought. Or Dracula's. Kite began to walk a little faster, glancing behind him every now and then. The man moved strangely but matched Kite's pace, keeping up but never closing the distance between them. Kite made a diversion down a side street, walking halfway down and then crossing over and doubling back on himself. The man followed. Kite took a deep breath, trying to stay calm, but as he exhaled his chest juddered and his heart fluttered like the wings of a butterfly beating against a pane of glass. Turning back onto Castle Road, Kite willed his tired legs to keep moving. The entrance to the alley was in sight, and he ducked into the passageway before the man turned the corner from the side street, before the police patrol car that was searching for a missing boy drove past.

The alley was streaked with sinister shadows, but Kite could make out the glow from a streetlamp ahead of him. He half ran, half stumbled and emerged briefly to cross another road, risking a quick glance behind him before entering the second alley. There was no one following him, but ahead he could see the silhouette of a figure leaning against a lamppost. He pressed on, but more cautiously now, trying to make out who it was that he would have to face to get to the other end. He was ashamed of the tears that filled his eyes and blinked them back furiously. He thought of his grandpa, sniffed hard, and straightened his back.

"Hey, mate! Lend us ya phone."

The silhouette belonged to a young man dressed in filthy jogging bottoms and a baggy hoodie. He wore a baseball cap with a hood pulled over the top of it so that his face was barely visible. Between his cracked lips he held a thin cigarette. The end glowed in the dark as he chugged on it and blew sweet-smelling smoke into the night air.

"Ya phone!" he snarled, leaning in closer, revealing brown and broken rodent teeth. He pushed Kite back against the wall, pressing his body hard against him and reaching for the straps of his rucksack.

"Please . . . I don't have a phone." Kite's voice was high and scared, and any thoughts of defending himself with a karate kick were long gone.

"Of course you do, posh boy!" The words were a vicious, drawn-out sneer. "Now hand it over, ya little fucker!"

Kite could feel the warmth of fetid breath on his face. His stomach contracted and vomit rose in his throat. A fist landed hard into his gut, and as he crumpled in pain, he regurgitated undigested chips over his assailant. Kite crouched on the ground, wrapping his arms over his head and in front of his face in readiness for the next blow. But none came. Instead, there was the sound of a scuffle, a groan, and then footsteps running away. When he looked up, the man in the coat was standing over him, his dark eyes full of concern. He reached down and offered Kite his hand.

CHAPTER 19

Venetia sat staring at the house phone and clutching her mobile, willing either or both to ring. But they remained obstinately silent. She had rung Heron and Monica, but neither had answered. She had left messages for them both, but they had yet to return her calls.

What is the point of having a damn phone to start with if you're not going to answer it? she thought furiously. But then she remembered the plaintive message left by Kite on her own mobile and bit her lip hard enough to taste blood. She hadn't told Heron or Monica. It wasn't the sort of news that you could break to a parent in a voicemail: "Your child is missing. Your ten-year-old son is out there somewhere in the dark, alone and most likely afraid, because he asked for my help, and I failed him. I didn't answer my phone. Just like you're not answering yours. Pick up the damn phone!"

No, it wouldn't do at all. So she had simply asked them to call her back as soon as they could. And in the meantime, all she could do was wait. But waiting wasn't *doing*, and it was activity that she required to suppress the panic that threatened to overwhelm her. With little else to occupy it, her mind had been hijacked by her imagination, which was taunting her relentlessly with unspeakable fates for her grandson. Venetia was so wired with fear, frustration, and guilt that she felt as though she might physically explode. Her hands were tightly clasped in her lap, and beneath the pale skin of one wrist she could see a purple vein throbbing as her heart pumped blood too fast around her body.

Liberty sat opposite her at the kitchen table, tapping on the keyboard of her laptop.

"There!" she said finally, and turned the screen around so that Venetia could see the photo of Kite that Liberty had uploaded to Facebook, along with details of his disappearance and a plea for people to look out for him and report any sightings.

"But do you think it will actually help?"

Liberty reached across and touched Venetia's arm, a little awkwardly. "Of course it will! He can't have got far, and the police are looking for him now. Someone will find him."

Venetia pressed her palms down hard onto the table and cursed under her breath. She stood up, and Colin was immediately by her side.

"I have to go out," she said. "I can't sit here any longer. I'll go mad. I'll just take Colin for a quick walk. I won't go far—I'll stay in sight of the house. I've got my mobile so you can contact me if you need to."

Out in the hallway, she pulled on her coat, clipped the dog to his lead, and stepped out into the night.

KITE LOOKED UP at the man who was standing over him. "I'm not supposed to talk to strangers."

The man gave a wry grin. "But wandering the streets alone in the dark is okay?"

"I wasn't wandering. I was going somewhere. Why were you following me?"

"I wasn't. I just happened to be going in the same direction." The man offered his hand again. "My name is Lukasz."

"I'm Kite." He took the man's hand and stood up gingerly, clutching his stomach.

"Are you hurt?"

Kite shook his head despite the pain. He was hurt, he was scared, and he was embarrassed. "I wasn't very brave," he said, as angry tears spilled down his cheeks. "I should have fought back!"

The man looked at him thoughtfully for a moment, and then he took Kite's face in his big hands and gently brushed the tears away with his thumbs. "Sometimes to fight back with your fists is not the right choice. Sometimes you have to find a different way. A smarter way."

Kite thought about the fight that had gotten him into this mess in the first place and wondered if there might have been a smarter way to deal with it. There probably was, but even now, it still felt *almost* worth it to have seen the look of shock on Ollie Vane-Percy's face when Kite had kicked him. Ollie Vane-Percy, who was two years older and a good foot taller than him.

"We should go," the man told him. "I'm sure there's someone somewhere who's worried about you."

Kite hoped so. But he was sorry too. He didn't like to think of Nisha being upset, even though she hadn't rung him back. They walked hand in hand out of the alley and onto the windswept street. Across the road, the decorative lights looped between the trees swung back and forth, and beyond them the choppy surface of the river flashed curling slabs of reflected light.

"Tell me where you live, and I'll take you home."

Kite shook his head. "There's no point. There's no one in."

"Where are your parents?"

"In France. They left me here—like in *Home Alone*."

The man looked puzzled. He'd clearly never seen the film.

"I'm only joking." Kite grinned weakly. "They sent me to boarding school, but I've run away."

"Well, I can't leave you on the streets by yourself. I'll have to take you back there."

Kite backed away. "You can't make me. I hate it! And I'm in trouble. I can't go back there."

"Okay, okay. Isn't there anywhere else you can go? Anyone you can speak to?"

"I tried to speak to Nisha, but she didn't answer her phone and now I've lost mine."

"Who's Nisha? Where does she live? I could take you there."

Kite shook his head. "I have to speak to her first. Can't I borrow your phone?"

The man pulled a cheap pay-as-you-go phone from his pocket. "Do you know the number?"

"I know five numbers off by heart in case of emergencies: mine, Nisha's, Mum's, Dad's, and Papa Luigi's Pizza Place."

"Impressive!" the man replied with a smile, and handed Kite his phone. Kite tapped in the number and waited. An automated voice informed him that the phone had no credit remaining.

"It needs topping up."

Kite passed it back to the man, who didn't look surprised and shoved it into his pocket.

"I have an idea," he told Kite. "I know somewhere I can take you where you'll be safe. The people there will know what to do, and they'll help you get in touch with Nisha."

"I'm not going to the police station!" Kite began to back away again, but the man grabbed his arm and held it tight.

"I wouldn't take you *there*," he said. The scorn in his voice implied that he shared Kite's reluctance to tangle with the law. "Come on. Come with me. I'll make sure you're okay. It isn't far."

Somewhat reassured and ever curious, Kite relaxed and followed the man down the Embankment back toward town.

ACROSS THE RIVER, having walked only as far as the bandstand, Venetia and Colin were heading back over the suspension bridge. Venetia paused for a moment and looked down at the dark water flowing fast beneath them. She shuddered.

"Where *are* you, Kite?"

She didn't whisper it this time but spoke the words out loud. The dog stood to attention, his ears pricked and his nose twitching in the night air. Suddenly he whined and pulled at his lead.

"I know—you're right." Venetia reached down and touched his head. "We should get back."

But once they reached the front gate, the dog seemed reluctant to follow Venetia in. He kept staring down the shadowy street, his head held high and very still. Inside the house, the phone rang, and Venetia started, breaking the dog's apparent trance. They were met at the door by Liberty.

"Mr. Howard just rang. They've found Kite's phone."

THE MAN LED Kite out of the chilly night into the foyer of the building and through to a set of double doors with glass panels. The room on the other side was warmly lit, and a few people sat at tables drinking tea and eating biscuits. There was a buzz of quiet chatter, the clink of cups on saucers, and the oddly comforting sound of music being played on a slightly out-of-tune piano.

"You see that lady there?" The man pointed toward a woman who was refilling cups from a striped teapot. Kite nodded. "Go and speak to her. She's a good woman and she'll look after you."

"Aren't you coming in with me?"

The man shook his head. "I have to go."

"Will I see you again?"

The man didn't answer. Kite looked up at him, studying him properly for the first time. He had a kind face, but there was something about his eyes that made Kite think that he was keeping a secret. Nisha had once told him that someone's eyes were the windows to their soul, which meant that you could tell what someone was thinking or feeling by looking into their eyes. Kite didn't know if it was true, but if it was, the man's windows were tinted like the ones in his dad's BMW. Kite couldn't see into his soul. And he acted differently from most grown-ups, which made him interesting.

"You didn't ask me what kind of trouble I was in." This had puzzled Kite. It was the first thing most grown-ups he knew would have asked.

"It's none of my business. Besides, if you'd wanted me to know, you would have told me."

Kite felt that he owed it to him to tell him now. After all, the man had rescued him and brought him somewhere safe. He hadn't handed him over to the police even though he had no idea what Kite had done. The man had listened to what he had said and trusted him. He had given Kite a voice. People rarely did.

"I karate-kicked Ollie Vane-Percy on the knee because he was messing about with my chess set—the one that Grandpa left me when he died. He broke the king's head off."

The man whistled softly through his teeth. "Really? His name is *really* Ollie Vane-Percy?" And then he smiled—a proper smile that reached his dark eyes and made them sparkle for just a moment before his face became serious once again. "You go in now," he told Kite. "Speak to the lady I showed you."

Kite didn't want him to leave. He had known him for only a little while, but he felt somehow that they could be friends. He wanted to give him a hug, but instead he just stood there feeling sad and awkward.

"Thank you, Lu . . ."

"Lukasz," the man reminded him gently.

"Thank you for looking after me and for not taking me to the police station or back to school."

"You're welcome." The man turned to leave, but before he reached the door, he called over his shoulder, "Maybe I'll see you around."

I hope so, thought Kite as he watched the man go.

COLIN WAS SITTING by the front door, where he had taken up a sentinel post since they had returned from their brief walk, occasionally scraping his claws down the paintwork and whining.

"You're not helping, you know!" Liberty hissed at him, having failed to lure him away with a chunk of cheese. She had remembered Kite feeding him cheese when he'd made his impromptu lunchtime visit, and hoped that it might persuade the dog to return to Venetia's side and stop making such an irritating noise. But he had eyed the cheese with disgust and fixed her with a stare hard enough to make her retreat a swift one. She went back to the kitchen where Venetia was pacing the floor. A police family liaison officer was sitting at the table, and Venetia was helping her to compile a list of Kite's friends. It was heartbreakingly short and a sharp reminder of how isolated and lonely Kite must be feeling. His phone had been found in the garden of his boardinghouse, so now there was no way that she could contact him. The nausea of guilt bloomed once again in Venetia's stomach as she realized how badly she had let him down. Liberty checked her laptop for the umpteenth time, scrolling through the responses to her post on Facebook. It had precipitated an outpouring of sympathy and support, but so far, no credible sightings. One woman was convinced that she had seen him in her local McDonald's just over an hour ago, but that was unlikely given that she lived in Wisconsin. The stirring introduction of "The Raiders March" cracked open the brittle silence, and all eyes flicked toward the table where Venetia's mobile was flashing. She snatched up the phone. According to the screen, the caller was "unknown."

"Hello?"

"Hello. Is that Nisha?"

"Yes. Who's this?"

"My name's Evangeline. I have your grandson with me, and he'd like to speak to you."

CHAPTER 20

They found Kite handing around biscuits and chatting cheerily with the waifs and strays who had come to Evangeline's church for some warmth, a bit of company, and a little light refreshment. Liberty had driven Venetia the short distance from her house, and on seeing her grandson, Venetia wept with relief. Once Evangeline had recovered from the surprise of seeing Liberty, she handed Venetia a tissue and flapped away her thanks with the tea towel she was holding.

"Now don't you go upsetting yourself. That boy is just fine! Look at him."

Kite certainly looked fine. In fact, he seemed to be enjoying himself. Having established in their brief phone call that Nisha was not angry with him, nor was he going to be arrested, he had set about making himself useful while he waited for her to come and collect him. He wandered over to them, munching on a chocolate digestive. Venetia bent down and threw her arms around him, and Kite hugged her back, holding one arm aloft to save his biscuit from being crushed in their embrace.

"Oh, Kite!" Venetia exclaimed, when she finally released him. "You gave me such a scare!"

Kite shoved the rest of the biscuit into his mouth and chewed furiously before answering. He was starving. "I'm sorry, Nisha. I did try to call you, but you didn't answer, and then I lost my phone. Mum and Dad will be furious."

Venetia suddenly remembered that she still hadn't spoken to Heron or Monica.

"You don't need to worry about your phone," Liberty reassured him. "Someone at your school found it in the garden of your boardinghouse. You must have dropped it."

Kite's face plummeted into a fixed frown and his eyes filled with tears, which he scrubbed away furiously with the back of his hand. "I'm not going back," he said quietly, but with absolute determination.

Liberty immediately regretted saying anything. Instead of making him feel better, which had been her intention, she had made him cry. Evangeline offered Kite another biscuit and a diversion from the tricky topic of school.

"Well, young man, I think you've had quite enough excitement for one day. It's time you took your grandmother home. She looks exhausted!" She winked at Venetia before continuing. "I expect you could all do with a good night's sleep, and then you can tell her all about your adventures in the morning."

She took Liberty's arm and squeezed it. "It's good to see you, Liberty. It's a small world, isn't it? Don't be a stranger—especially now you're only down the street. Maybe I can help you find a decent man for a change." She whispered the last sentence, but plenty loud enough for Venetia and Kite to hear. Kite's frown disappeared, and he looked at Liberty with renewed interest.

"Do you know Nisha's granny nanny?" he asked Evangeline in astonishment.

She let out a rich, throaty laugh. "God bless you, child! Is that what you call her? Yes, I know Miss Liberty Bell. Her mother was my best friend."

"But she died, didn't she?" Kite added helpfully. "At least *she* had sausage rolls and sandwiches at her funeral party."

Evangeline looked toward Venetia for enlightenment. Venetia

shook her head with a smile. "It's a long story and one for another day. Come on, Kite, let's get you home."

"Can I come back?" Kite asked Evangeline. "To help with the teas?"

"Of course you can, darlin'! Any time—so long as your grandmother doesn't mind. And bring Liberty with you."

Kite nodded. "I will."

IT WAS PAST eleven by the time Liberty returned to her flat. When they had gotten Kite home, exhaustion felled him, and Venetia had tucked him up in bed with a mug of hot chocolate and Colin for company. Meanwhile Liberty had spoken to the police and Mr. Howard, who said that he wouldn't expect Kite to be in school the following morning but would wait to hear from Venetia. Once Kite was in bed, Venetia rang Heron and gave him a rather simplified and restrained version of events. Liberty was somewhat surprised that she omitted altogether that Kite had been missing. She told him only that they would need to have a proper discussion the following day about some issues that Kite was having at school, but that there was nothing to worry about. Liberty had offered to make Venetia some supper—she'd hardly eaten anything all day—but Venetia had said that she was too tired now and all she wanted was a relaxing soak in the bath and then bed.

Liberty took a bottle of white wine from the fridge, poured herself a large glass, and slumped onto the sofa. As she sat staring at the moon through the open curtains, she wondered—and worried—if the job that she was just beginning to settle into was about to change. Change had always made Liberty uneasy. The greater the change, the greater her unease. And God knows she'd had to face plenty of changes in the last few months. But she had survived, she reminded herself. So far. She was sure that Kite was serious about not going back to his boardinghouse. And if she was honest, Liberty didn't blame him. It would have been her idea of hell too. The lack of privacy would have been agony. But if he didn't go back, then surely he would stay here and she would have to look after him—at least some of the time?

Liberty had never been one of those women for whom motherhood had been a principal life goal. It had been more of an optional side order—something to be decided upon when the time was right. But there had never been a right time while she had been with Graham, and by the time she was without him, the possibility had expired along with her fertility, and there was no longer a choice to be made. She thought about Kite and how she had reduced him to tears with her clumsy attempt at consolation. She had little experience with children and clearly wasn't a natural. But perhaps she could learn the basics at least. Kite seemed to be a nice enough little boy, and very good with the dog. Maybe he could help her to reach an amicable truce with Colin.

VENETIA CLOSED HER eyes and inhaled the scent of vetiver that rose in the steam from the hot water of her bath. What a day it had been. She had been flung from complacency through a maelstrom of fear, frustration, guilt, and desperation before finally emerging into an oasis of euphoria and relief. And now she was shattered—emotionally and physically. She had learned her lesson the hard way, but she knew now that her grandson—her wingman—would not be returning to school as a boarder. Not on her watch.

KITE WOKE IN a cold sweat to the warmth of Colin's body pressed against his own and the sound of his sonorous snoring. In Kite's dream he had been back in the alley, and the youth in the hoodie had lifted his face up to the light, revealing that he was Ollie Vane-Percy. As Kite had crouched on the ground clutching his stomach after the blow had been landed, he had seen the smashed pieces of his grandpa's chess set scattered around him, but when he had reached out to gather them up, Vane-Percy had stamped on his hands. At that moment, a dark shadow had fallen over them, and a figure in a black cloak had swept Vane-Percy away into the night.

Kite pulled the duvet up under his chin and wondered where the man was now.

CHAPTER 21

The next morning Kite appeared to have recovered fully from the previous day's events. He bounced into the kitchen with the dog at his side and announced that he was so hungry he could eat at least five rounds of toast and a gallon of tea. Liberty began feeding slices of bread into the toaster while Venetia sat at the table sipping a cup of milky coffee.

"Well, let's start with one round and see how you get on, shall we?" she said, smiling.

"I need at least two, because one is for Colin Firth."

The dog wagged his tail enthusiastically at the mention of his name. It was tempting to accede to Kite's every wish that day, now that he was home and safe, but Venetia knew that if she were to fulfill her intended in loco parentis role properly, she would need to be fair and firm with her grandson rather than spoil him. She had yet to elicit the details of the boardinghouse incident, and no matter how unlikely she felt it might be, it was always possible that Kite had behaved badly and would need to be held accountable.

"Colin has his own food," she replied, "but as a special treat because he did such a good job as your hot-water bottle last night, he can have a single slice of toast with a smidgen of butter. But no jam!"

After breakfast Venetia invited Kite into Hawk's study. She wanted to find out exactly what had been going on, and she hoped that the use of that room would bestow appropriate gravitas on the conversation. Kite needed very little prompting to come clean. He told her everything. He revealed what Ollie Vane-Percy had said and done, and what his own response had been. He told her how he had gone back to the boardinghouse, changed his clothes, packed his rucksack, and sneaked out through the window. He related how he had spent the afternoon hunkered down beside the bowling pavilion, bought and eaten chips, been followed by one stranger, mugged by a second, and then rescued by the first, who had taken him to Evangeline. He peppered his account with dramatic gestures and sound effects as though the whole thing had been a thrilling escapade rather than a dangerous narrow escape that was clearly prompted by something more serious than a damaged chess piece. He must have been scared out of his wits, but he wasn't about to admit it. Venetia wondered whom he was trying to protect from the distress of the whole truth— her or himself. When he had finished, Venetia allowed the silence between them to grow heavy and uncomfortably expectant, hoping that it might encourage him to say more. Eventually, he added a single comment.

"I'm not going back."

Venetia studied her grandson. His bravado had burnt itself out like a spent sparkler, and she saw in front of her a small boy whose pale face was tired and drawn, with anxious eyes that refused to meet her gaze. He looked like a cornered animal that had been kicked and fully expected to be kicked again. He wore the same expression as Colin Firth had when she had seen him for the first time in Beverley's kitchen. She had failed Kite badly, but now she was going to do something about it. Her overwhelming instinct was to protect him from whatever or whoever had hurt him, but she knew that she would serve him better if she could help her grandson to face his demons and equip him to take them on himself. She took both of his hands in hers and squeezed them tight.

"I promise that I will do anything I can to help you, but you must talk to Mr. Howard, and you must tell him what happened with Ollie.

And you have to apologize for the karate kick. I know you were angry, but that's no excuse," Venetia told him gently. "You should have found a different way to deal with it. You're smarter than that."

"Well, what would you have done?"

Venetia grinned mischievously. "Put salt in his tea—or maybe worms in his bed."

"Or itching powder in his pants," Kite suggested, smiling weakly.

"Now you're getting the idea!" Venetia joked. Her tone became serious again. "You know that you can tell me anything, don't you, Kite?"

He nodded but kept his head down.

"I need you to tell me what's wrong. Not this business with the chess set and Ollie the Pain-Percy. I want you to tell me what's really wrong. Running away was a very dangerous thing to do. Heaven only knows what might have happened to you if that man hadn't turned up. Why don't you want to go back to school? You always liked school before. *Is* it school, or is it just boarding?"

Kite shrugged and dragged the toe of his shoe back and forth across the carpet. Venetia waited . . . and waited, allowing the silence to draw out the answers.

"Just boarding, I suppose," Kite offered eventually.

"But why?"

More silence and more resistance from Kite to avoid filling it.

Venetia was careful to portray a patience that she certainly didn't feel. "It's really important that you tell me, Kite. I can't help you if I don't know what's wrong."

"You wouldn't understand."

"Try me."

Kite sighed. "I don't fit in. I don't like the same things as the other boys. I don't know the right things to say, the right music, the right things to wear—except for the school uniform—and the harder I try to get things right, the worse I get them wrong. They either laugh at me or ignore me. They think I'm a weirdo. And because I live there, I can't get away from them. And even when they're ignoring me, I can *feel* them ignoring me. Before I was a boarder, I had a friend called Ravi at school. But now we're not in the same class and we only see each other at break time. We used to walk home together and do stuff on weekends, but now he's friends with another boy in his class."

How different he is from his father, Venetia thought, *but how similar too*. She sometimes believed that Heron's sole mission in life was to "get things right." But he had been blessed with a natural ability to conform and was happy to follow the tried-and-trusted blueprint for life laid down by so many others before him. Kite's problem was that he was chasing a "right" that was completely wrong for him. She only hoped that she could help him see that.

"Have you ever thought that those boys don't know how to be with you?"

Kite frowned. "I don't know what you mean."

"Well, you say that you're different from them. You don't know how to join in with them because you don't like the same things. Maybe they feel the same way about you. It's not that they don't like you, they just don't know how to *be* with you."

"But why are they mean to me? Why did Ollie Vane-Percy call me names and break Grandpa's chess piece?"

"I don't know, Kite. Sometimes people behave badly when they don't know how else to behave. Sometimes people are even a little scared of people who aren't like them."

Kite's face brightened momentarily. "I bet Ollie's scared of me now!"

Venetia tried not to smile. "But kicking him didn't solve the problem, did it?"

"No, but I didn't have any worms or itching powder." He sighed. "Sometimes I just wish I *was* like everyone else."

"Well, I'm very pleased that you're not. I love you very much exactly as you are—and so did your grandpa."

"But you don't understand, Nisha. *Everyone* likes you."

"But I do understand, Kite. I know exactly how it feels to be different. And I know how hard it is to pretend to be someone else just to fit in. I've been doing it for years."

Kite looked at her in astonishment. Venetia couldn't quite believe that she was going to tell him. She felt hot and a little giddy, but she needed Kite to believe that she truly did understand what he was going through and that he could trust her. It was a terrifying risk for her to take, but for the sake of her grandson it was worth it.

"Can you keep a secret?" she asked him.

"Cross my heart and hope to die."

"I have something to show you."

Venetia led Kite upstairs and Colin followed behind them. Once they were all inside Venetia's bedroom, she closed the door and sat down on a stool facing the mirrors on her dressing table. She took a deep breath and pulled off her hair. The immaculate blond bob was a wig, and beneath it, Venetia was completely bald.

"Nisha!" Kite gasped. "Where's your hair gone?"

"Something happened, a very long time ago. A bad man hurt me, and afterwards my hair just . . . fell out. It never grew back."

Venetia stared at the reflection that was so familiar to her, but unrecognizable to everyone who knew her.

"It made me feel so ugly," she continued, "and I thought that no one would like me if they knew—that they would think I was strange or sick—and so I kept it a secret from everyone. You see, I do understand what it feels like to be different."

Kite reached out and very gently stroked her head. "I don't think you're ugly, Nisha. I think you're beautiful—even without any hair."

Venetia smiled. "I know perfectly well that I look a bit like Gollum from *The Hobbit* without my wig, but thank you for saying so."

Kite studied her critically. "Your teeth are much nicer than Gollum's, and your ears don't stick out like his do—but you *have* both got blue eyes," he conceded. "Did Grandpa know you were bald?"

"Yes, he did."

"But he didn't mind?"

"He was a very good man. A very decent man."

"Does Dad know?"

"No, Kite. No one else knows—except you. I told you because I trust you and because I knew you'd understand."

Kite threw his arms around her neck and planted a loud kiss on the top of her head. "I won't tell anyone, ever—even if they torture me."

"Well, hopefully it won't come to that," Venetia replied as she replaced her wig and tidied a couple of wayward strands back into place. "Now, what are we going to do about you?"

BY THE TIME they came back downstairs, it was almost lunchtime and an agreement had been successfully brokered.

"So, if I speak to your parents and to Mr. Howard and they agree, you'll go back to school as a day pupil and live here with me during term time?"

Kite's slightly awkward fist pump was all the confirmation she needed.

"And can Colin Firth sleep on my bed every night?"

"We'll see. Everyone needs to agree about school first. Shall we find out what's for lunch?"

Over tomato soup and crusty rolls, Kite had one more question: "Nisha, does Amazon sell itching powder?"

CHAPTER 22

It was still dark outside, but Liberty had showered and dressed and was enjoying a mug of tea in the peace and quiet of her flat before going up to the house to supervise Kite's breakfast. He insisted on making it himself, but with boiling water and electrical equipment involved, both Venetia and Liberty felt it was wise to keep an eye on him without overtly supervising, which might dent his growing self-confidence. It was December 1, and Liberty had an advent calendar for Kite. Her mother had always bought one for her every year, even when she was an adult. But not this year. Its absence was just another chafe on that raw patch that grief always scoured somewhere onto even the thickest of skins. Liberty had hesitated before buying it, worried that it might overstep the boundary that she assumed, as an employee, she should maintain even though she was still unsure of its exact location. But then she had ignored her doubts and bought it anyway.

In the short time that Kite had been staying with Venetia, Liberty had grown quite fond of him—although she would have been unlikely to admit it, even to herself. He was, in some ways, a very unchildlike child who seemed to be more comfortable in the company of adults, while retaining an innocence and occasional eccentricity that made him vulnerable—a little like a baby crab, with a soft outer shell that made him ripe for the pecking by predators like Ollie Vane-Percy. Her conversations with Kite were always interesting, if sometimes a little unexpected. Last week he had spent a good twenty minutes telling her about a village in Indonesia where people keep the mummified remains of dead relatives in their houses, before moving on to explain in detail the construction of a coracle.

All things considered, Liberty now found herself to be surprisingly contented. Between them, she and Venetia were still finding out, by trial and error, what worked best for them both. Venetia was a very easygoing boss, which should have made Liberty relaxed but sometimes had the opposite effect, making her worry alternately that she wasn't doing enough to earn her keep and then that she was invading Venetia's privacy by being too much in the house. Although she valued her own space, Liberty found herself drawn to Venetia's lively company—and now Kite's too. He had an exuberant curiosity about life and the world in which he lived that she found refreshing and stimulating, like a splash of cold water in the face. He was showing her the universe through different eyes and from some quite peculiar angles, but time spent with Kite was never dull.

Liberty had worked for Venetia for almost three months now, and as she sipped her tea, she appraised her own performance to see if it passed muster. She managed the day-to-day tasks well enough and had helped Venetia to clear Hawk's wardrobes and cull her own. She had organized the food shopping online to save herself and Venetia trips to the supermarket, and was beginning to learn what Venetia and Kite liked to eat and how to cook it when requested. More often than not, Venetia would invite her to eat with them, and increasingly Liberty accepted. It seemed foolish to cook for them and then go home and cook for herself and eat alone. There were, to date, only two things that she had failed to achieve. She was still searching for the elusive Francis Taylor and Torin McGuire. The last of the thank-you notes to the funeral attendees had been sent months ago, and Hawk's papers had yielded no clues to their identities so far, but Liberty was determined to discover who they were. She had also been unable to get Venetia access to the disused ballroom.

She had contacted the estate agent who was dealing with the sale and had spoken to an oleaginous individual called Kyle, who had informed her that as the property was sold subject to contract, they weren't allowing any more viewings. She had tried to persuade him by suggesting that it might be to their advantage to have a reserve buyer should the current one withdraw for any reason. Kyle had assured her that their buyer was "rock solid" and that there was no need whatsoever for a reserve. Liberty had thanked him for his "help" through gritted teeth and then wished him sudden erectile dysfunction during some crucial and passionate interlude in his future. After she had hung up.

It was Saturday, and when breakfast was finished, they all headed out to walk along the Embankment to Evangeline's church. Kite had cajoled Liberty into accompanying him there several times since he had first met Evangeline. Saturdays were always busy at the church's drop-in center, and Kite very much enjoyed helping with the refreshments and chatting with the people who wandered in. Some of them were regulars, but others appeared and disappeared at random. All were made welcome, and Kite spoke to each of them with equal enthusiasm. For a child who had such difficulty engaging with his peers, he had a remarkable ability to elicit a response and often a smile from the most reticent of strangers, particularly when he was accompanied by Colin, as was often the case. Today was a special day, which was why Venetia was included in their party. Today they were helping Evangeline put up the Christmas decorations in the church and the reception room. Venetia and Liberty both carried bags of holly and ivy freshly cut from the garden, and Kite had tied tinsel to Colin's collar in honor of the occasion.

Evangeline welcomed them at the door with a beaming smile. She bent down and hugged the dog, planting a firm kiss on top of his head. "I don't need any mistletoe to kiss my favorite Colin!" she announced before vigorously embracing the rest of them.

"You're very cheerful today," Liberty said, putting down her bag of greenery and shrugging off her coat.

Evangeline turned her palms upward and raised her hands toward the ceiling. "That's because Lord Jesus, my fairy godmother, Santa Claus, or maybe all three have shone a light into my little corner and shooed away the shadows—at least for now."

Liberty shook her head in bewilderment. "Have you been putting rum in your tea?"

"You did put it in Tommy's tea once, didn't you?" Kite reminded her.

"Yes, darlin', I did. But that's because he'd been sleeping in the park all night and was chilled to the bone. I've only had milk and sugar in mine today, but I've had some news that's made me as giddy as a goat on a windy day."

"Well, for heaven's sake, put us out of our misery and tell us what it is," Liberty replied.

"The sale of the building has fallen through!" Evangeline told them gleefully. "The council refused planning permission for it to be turned into flats, and so the buyer has dropped out."

"Well, I understand how that will buy you some time, but surely they'll just put it on the market again? And wasn't your lease about to expire?"

Evangeline wagged her finger at Liberty. "You need to see the sun peeping out from behind the clouds, instead of always looking for the rain. It's a sign! A sign that someone somewhere"—she pointed upward with her index finger and winked knowingly—"is on our side. They've renewed our lease for six months because they'd rather have some money coming in while they try to sell the building, which is going to be more difficult now that an application for change of use has been denied. We have another six months to find a way to save our church."

"Well, I wish you luck. But it sounds like you need a miracle," Liberty replied.

Evangeline smiled. "Stranger things have happened."

And Liberty *had* spotted a silver lining to this particular cloud in that the loss of the buyer for the building meant the loss of commission for Kyle. Served him right. It also meant that viewings would begin again, and she would now be able to achieve one of her outstanding tasks.

Venetia had been listening carefully to Evangeline's revelations while trying to subdue the conflicting emotions that they had ignited within her. She needed a distraction.

"Where would you like us to start, Evangeline?" she asked.

Evangeline took them through to where the services were held. At the front of the room there was a simple altar covered in a white-and-gold embroidered cloth, on top of which stood a large brass crucifix, candles in ornate candelabras, and two splendid vases of silk roses and gladioli. To the left of the altar there was an ancient-looking pump organ, and facing it, rows of wooden pews. The seats of the pews were topped with cushions covered in fabrics of every hue and pattern, a glorious mismatch of color and design. Along one side of the room, the silvery light of a winter's day flooded in through six large leaded windows, the sill of each crammed with what looked like the contents of a mad magpie's cabinet of curiosities. Among them were several snow globes, paperweights, china ornaments, a beaded pin cushion stuck with hat pins, a pair of opera glasses, a trinket box covered with shells, and a few sets of rosary beads. A diamanté brooch in the shape of a horseshoe nestled next to a doll dressed as a fairy who had lost one leg and a silver acorn egg cup with a tiny leaf-handled spoon. There were numerous feathers, including one that had clearly come from a peacock's tail; a selection of buttons and glass marbles; a rusty tin of fishing flies; and two gold teeth. Kite stared at the collection in astonishment.

"Where did you get all these things?" he asked, moving closer to the windows to take a better look.

"They're gifts," Evangeline replied. "From people the church has helped in one way or another—through healing, prayers, mediumship . . . or just tea and sympathy. We never collect money at our services. Some of the people who come here don't have a penny to spare. But these things mean something to them— something important. These are their treasures, so when they bring them to us, we treasure them."

Evangeline produced a box of tinsel and paper chains and a nativity scene for the altar, and they set to work. They wove ivy and sprigs of holly around the ends of the pews and between the curios on the windowsills, while Colin twirled and chased a paper chain that he had stolen across the floor. Soon the church was thoroughly dressed in festive cheer, and they returned to the reception room where Norma and Norman were setting up the tea table. The couple were long-standing members of the church's congregation and regular helpers at the drop-in center.

"Good morning, young Kite. You're here early today," Norman greeted him, while Norma slipped Colin a ginger biscuit from one of the plates.

"We're helping Evangeline put up the Christmas decorations."

"Aha! So, you've abandoned your post as tea boy?" Norma teased.

"No," replied Kite earnestly. "I'll be back as soon as we've finished. I can stay, can't I, Nisha?"

Nisha nodded. "I'm Venetia, by the way," she introduced herself. "Kite's grandmother."

"Lovely to meet you. I'm Norma and this is my husband, Norman. Your grandson's such a help. You must be very proud of him."

Kite colored with pleasure at the praise.

"I am," replied Venetia. "But he has his maverick moments, don't you, Kite?" she added with a wink.

The double doors swung open, and a man wearing a grubby overcoat, worn-out Wellingtons, and a red woolly hat shuffled in and

brought with him the musty smell of dirty laundry and stale urine.
His face was the livid red of a long-term drinker and ingrained with
grime and hardship. His hair and beard were so long and unkempt
that it was impossible to tell where one ended and the other began. Ignoring everyone else in the room, he headed toward one of the tables
and slumped into a seat that was next to a radiator. He pressed as
much of himself as he could against its hot metal.

"Shall I take Tommy his tea?" Kite offered.

"No, I'll do it," said Norma, filling a mug with a steaming dark
brown brew and spooning sugar into it. "You get on with the decorations."

The fir tree in a tin bucket that stood in a corner of the room had
been donated by a local market trader whose mother attended the
church. It was much larger than any tree they had had previously, and
Evangeline had augmented the church's rather meager selection of
baubles with a job lot that included a set of colored fairy lights bought
from the junk shop on Castle Road. They began by winding these
around the tree, Liberty passing the bunch of lights around its girth
to Venetia, unfurling them as they went, and Evangeline balancing
precariously on a chair to reach the highest branches.

"See if you can find a star or an angel in amongst that lot for the
top of the tree," Evangeline called to Kite as she carefully dismounted
with an inelegant wobble. Kite rustled through the newspaper in
which the decorations were wrapped and eventually found a doll
dressed in silver with white feather wings and rather more cleavage
on display than was seemly for a messenger of God.

"Here's an angel!" he said triumphantly, holding her aloft.

Liberty grinned. "She looks more like 'Barbie Does Naughty
Nativity'!"

"I think she's pretty," Kite replied doubtfully.

"So do I!" Evangeline agreed, seeing Kite's crestfallen face. She
took the doll and climbed onto the chair to fix her to the top of the

tree. Once she had safely dismounted, Evangeline stood back to admire their handiwork.

"Venetia, would you like to do the honors?" she said, nodding toward the socket into which the fairy lights were to be plugged. Venetia obliged, and by some small miracle, the tiny bulbs flickered into life, bathing the tree in soft bursts of color. The sound of frail but purposeful clapping came from somewhere in the room. They all looked to see where the sound was coming from and saw Tommy gazing at the tree. Colin sat close beside him with his head resting on the man's knee.

As a reward for all their efforts, Norma made them mugs of tea, and Norman brought a plate of the "best" biscuits to the table where they had sat down. Kite took his tea and went to join Tommy and Colin.

"If the building is on the market again, I should be able to arrange with the estate agent for you to see the ballroom," Liberty told Venetia.

"Why would you want to do that?" Evangeline asked. "Don't tell me you're thinking of buying it now?"

Venetia shook her head with a smile. "Of course not. I used to work there. I just wanted to take a look around for old times' sake."

"Well, why didn't you say so before?" Evangeline took a sip of her tea and helped herself to a biscuit. "You're welcome to go up now. They never lock it, and even if they did, I have a key."

VENETIA PAUSED FOR just a heartbeat before pushing open the door and stepping back in time. The ballroom was a ghost from her past, its former glory shrouded in dust and cobwebs. The draft as she entered caused the spiderwebs to flutter just as the sight of the room disturbed myriad memories. She had asked for a moment alone before the others joined her; Kite and Liberty were both eager to see the ballroom too. It was almost exactly as she had remembered it, but tragically depleted by time and neglect, like an aging showgirl who had fallen on hard times. Venetia stepped softly across the grimy floor, recalling how many times Brendan had spun her around in his arms beneath those same chandeliers and past those same mirrors in a whirl of lights and music. But now there was only silence and stillness. It was heartbreaking to see the birthplace of so many of her hopes and dreams end up like this. Much like the hopes and dreams themselves, she thought wryly. But were they truly lost beyond reach? The ballroom could be restored, but what about the rest? Surely she should concentrate on the future now, rather than reach back to a past that could never be changed? The sound of footsteps on the stairs broke her reverie before she could answer her own questions.

CHAPTER 23

"Only one more to go!" Kite announced as he prized open the penultimate door on his advent calendar, which was pinned to the wall in the kitchen.

Venetia was rolling out pastry for mince pies, and she smiled to herself at his excitement. She was so glad that he would be here for Christmas, if a little concerned about the reason for his unexpected company. He should have flown out to France at the end of term to spend the holidays with his parents, but Heron had telephoned Venetia suggesting, or rather requesting, a change of plan. She knew at once by the tone of his voice that something was wrong. Her son's marriage had apparently hit "a sticky wicket," and he was hoping that if he and Monica were able to spend some time alone together over Christmas, away from the pressure of work, they might be able to smooth things out. "A sort of marital team-building exercise" was how Heron had described it. Venetia had been tempted to suggest something a little more romantic might be better if their relationship was floundering, but she had no idea what the problem was, and she knew better than to pry if Heron didn't volunteer any details.

Kite hadn't been particularly surprised when he was offered the agreed-upon and deliberately vague explanation of "something important has come up." His parents seemed to have had little time for him since they had been in France. He had been disappointed at first, but then thought about Christmas confinement with his parents in a rented apartment in a foreign town and consoled himself with the reality that it held few attractions compared with what was on offer at home. He had asked Venetia if everything was all right with his parents, and having readily accepted her reassurances, he demonstrated his delight by dancing up and down the hallway with Colin Firth. Besides, Kite was convinced that the French ate frogs' legs for Christmas lunch, and he much preferred them in a pond to on his plate.

"Can I make the stars to go on top of the pies?" he asked Venetia as she stirred a little brandy into the mincemeat before spooning it into the cases. She handed him the pastry cutter, and he set to work, the tip of his tongue poking out as his face crinkled in rapt concentration.

"And don't give Colin any mince pies," Venetia warned Kite. "Mincemeat is bad for dogs, and even a tiny bit could make him very ill."

Kite nodded seriously and paused to screw the lid back onto the jar as though its very fumes could endanger his four-legged friend.

"Those look good!" Liberty came into the kitchen carrying the post that had just dropped through the letterbox.

"Don't give any to Colin Firth," Kite replied immediately. "They're dog poison!"

"Cross my heart and hope to die. All the more for us."

The doorbell rang.

"I'll go," said Liberty, nodding at Kite's and Venetia's flour-covered hands.

Venetia frowned as she wiped her hands on her apron. "We're not expecting anyone, and the postman's already been."

She, Kite, and Colin listened and were astonished to hear a familiar voice bellow out, "Good God! Who are you? Where's Venetia? Are you the maid?" Without allowing Liberty to answer, the voice continued: "Pay the cabdriver, will you? I don't have any cash on me, and I can never remember how to work those plastic card things. And you'd better give him a tip, I suppose."

Venetia and Kite, followed by Colin, hurried out into the hallway to find that Swan had barged through the door and past Liberty, carrying a hot-water bottle in one hand and dragging a suitcase on wheels in the other. She was wearing a black wool cape, enormous sunglasses, a gray faux-fur Cossack hat, and snow boots. On seeing Venetia and Kite, she abandoned both the hot-water bottle and the suitcase and flung open her arms as though expecting a round of applause.

"There you are!" she exclaimed. "Your"—she gestured toward Liberty—"let me in. I've come to stay for Christmas!"

Colin trotted up to inspect the new arrival, and Swan clapped her hands in delight.

"A pet wolf! How marvelous!"

Half an hour later, the cabdriver had been paid, Swan's suitcase had been taken upstairs, and the woman herself was drinking coffee in the sitting room, unwrapped from her coat but still wearing her hat and boots. Kite had been set the task of entertaining her while Venetia briefed Liberty in the kitchen.

"She's Hawk's sister Swan," Venetia explained. "She's as deaf as a post, and a somewhat erratic relationship with her hearing aids means that she shouts quite a lot. I'm afraid it looks as though we're stuck with her now; we'll just have to muddle through."

Liberty smiled, recalling Kite's description of his grandfather's funeral. So, this was his great-aunt. The one who got drunk and swore and was apparently completely bonkers.

"I'm sure we'll manage," she replied. She had a sneaking suspicion that Swan might prove to be a rather entertaining houseguest.

Venetia piled a few of the freshly cooked mince pies onto a plate, and she and Liberty joined the others in the sitting room, where Swan was making friends with Colin.

"What a handsome chap you are!" she told him. "Although I'm not sure you ought to be keeping a wolf in the house," she added doubtfully, raising her eyebrows at Venetia.

"He's not a wolf, he's a German shepherd," Venetia replied, offering Swan a mince pie. She took two and dismissed her sister-in-law's response with an impatient shake of the head. "Now, Swan," continued Venetia, "what made you decide to come and spend Christmas with us? It's a lovely surprise, but it is rather . . . sudden."

Swan helped herself to another mince pie and shoved it into her dress pocket. "I didn't like to think of you all by yourself at Christmas. I had no idea that young Kite would be here, or that you'd gone and got yourself a . . ." She nodded vaguely in the direction of Liberty.

"This is Liberty," Venetia explained patiently.

"She's the granny—" Kite began, but Venetia interrupted before he could finish.

"She's my assistant."

"It's lovely to meet you," Liberty offered.

"I'm sure it is," Swan replied graciously.

"But what about Nightingale?" Venetia wondered if the two sisters had had one of their fallings-out. "What's she doing for Christmas?"

Swan scowled. "My feeble-minded sister has completely taken leave of her senses. She has found herself a gigolo with whom she will be spending the festive season in a seafront hotel in Hastings."

"Why?" asked Kite. "What's a gigolo?"

"A boyfriend," Venetia translated.

"Isn't she a bit old for a boyfriend?" Kite replied.

"He's hardly a boy, but he's at least five years younger than her!"

"Goodness. Where did she find him?" Venetia inquired.

"In *The Lady* magazine's personal column. Papa will be spinning in his grave. The man was virtually touting his services as an escort. He's a retired plumber! I warned Nightingale that it will only end in ignominy for the Hamilton Hargreaves name, but my words fell on deaf ears."

Venetia smothered a smile at the irony of this remark as Swan continued.

"My sister insists that they bonded over their mutual love of sudoku and musical theater and refused to be swayed. She sashayed off to the station yesterday reeking of Estée Lauder Youth-Dew with a new silk nightdress in her suitcase. She'll get no sympathy from me if he bursts into her bedroom brandishing his ball cock!"

Venetia wondered if Swan's vitriol might be tinged with sour grapes, but registering the curiosity on her grandson's face and hoping to divert any awkward questions, she swiftly moved the conversation on. "Well, we're delighted to have you with us, but I should warn you that we shan't be having our Christmas lunch until Boxing Day."

"Whyever not?" exclaimed Swan, sounding scandalized at this departure from the traditional festive schedule.

"Because we will be spending most of Christmas Day itself helping out at a community drop-in center run by our friend at a local church," Venetia replied.

"How very virtuous. I'll come and watch."

CHAPTER 24

"Do you believe in Father Christmas?"

It was the afternoon of Christmas Eve, and Kite was hanging up his stocking on the fireplace next to the one that Venetia had helped him make for Colin. Liberty had no idea how to answer because she had no idea whether Kite himself believed that Father Christmas was really a man or merely a myth. What did most ten-year-old boys believe? Not that that would have helped much even if she had known, since Kite wasn't like most ten-year-old boys. But if he did still believe that his presents came down the chimney courtesy of Santa and a sled pulled by Rudolph and his crew, she didn't want to be the one to suggest that Royal Mail and other well-known couriers might be responsible instead. She wished that Venetia were here to steer her in the right direction as she so often did, but Venetia was taking a bath while Swan was having a nap.

"What do you think?"

Kite smiled mischievously. "What do I think about Father Christmas, or what do I think you think about Father Christmas?"

"Both."

Kite fiddled with a glass bauble on the Christmas tree while considering his answer. "I think you don't believe in him because you can be a bit too sensible sometimes."

Liberty smarted a little at this description. It hadn't been very sensible to have a long affair with a married man who had turned out to be a complete and utter bastard. But then she could hardly use that in her defense to Kite. In what way did he think she was too sensible? she wondered.

"What about you, Kite? What do you think?"

"I think that Father Christmas is that word that sounds like 'allergy.'"

Liberty hadn't been expecting that. She waited, hoping for clarification.

"It's like Aslan in *The Lion, the Witch and the Wardrobe*. Grandpa explained it to me once. It's just a different way of telling the same story. Aslan is a lion who is brave and wise and good, and he dies to save his friends. He fights evil like Jesus—or Superman."

"You mean an allegory?"

Kite nodded. "I think so."

"So where does Father Christmas fit into all this?"

"I think he's a bit like God."

Liberty was intrigued. "In what way?"

Kite wandered over to the window and stared out at the river while he sorted his thoughts into words. "Well, lots of people believe in God, don't they? Even though they've never seen him. And they believe all those crazy stories in the Bible about him making the whole world in six days and then drowning it and getting Noah to build an ark, and sending plagues of boils and frogs and cockroaches and stuff."

Definitely not like other ten-year-old boys, Liberty thought.

"So, if you believe in all of that, what's so different about Father Christmas? If God made everything in six days, why can't Father Christmas deliver presents to all the children in the world in one night? It's just another miracle."

Liberty had no answer to that, but Kite wasn't finished yet.

"And the whole point about God is to make us better—nicer. To teach us to care about people and animals and the planet, and not be mean to anyone. And Father Christmas does the same thing. Kids always get told to be good, or else he won't come and they won't get any presents. His job isn't just to bring us presents; it's to make us nicer too."

Liberty couldn't fault his logic and found his innocence and sincerity strangely moving, but she was still none the wiser as to whether he was expecting Father Christmas in person that evening or not. Perhaps it didn't matter.

"So, are we going to leave out carrots for the reindeer and mince pies and a glass of milk?"

Kite wrinkled his nose in disgust. "Father Christmas doesn't drink milk! We always leave him a glass of whisky."

"Fair enough. Let's go and find some carrots."

They went through to the kitchen, where Colin was asleep on his bed, his nose twitching and legs paddling, acting out his dream. Liberty found some carrots in the fridge and began washing them, while Kite took some mince pies from a tin and put them on a plate.

"Did you know that in Germany they have a monster called Krampus who visits the bad children instead of Father Christmas?" he told Liberty with a grin. "He beats them with sticks and branches and then eats them. Or sometimes he just sends them to hell."

EVANGELINE STOOD IN the church and closed her eyes. The scent of evergreen and vetiver hung in the cold air, and spirit whispers shimmered across the silence like moonlight on the surface of a lake. Evangeline was about to lock up, having sent everyone else home. Everything was prepared for tomorrow. The tables were set and the kitchen was in order—plates stacked, pots in place, and aprons at the ready. But Evangeline couldn't resist taking a quiet moment for herself alone in the church that she loved. Christmas Eve had always been her favorite day of the year. When the magic felt real. It still did. She stood before the altar and spoke prayers for her family and friends, and for those who had neither, for whom

Christmas might be just another day. And she prayed that this church in which she stood—*her* church—might be saved. Somehow. Anyhow. *But please, God, let it be saved.*

It was late afternoon and shafts of light from the streetlamps streamed through the windows, illuminating the treasures piled on their sills. So many souvenirs of gratitude, of hope, of faith. Evangeline had faith. She turned away from the altar and reached into her bag, taking out a small plate that was covered in tinfoil. She placed it on the seat of the front pew and removed the tinfoil to reveal three homemade mince pies.

"I know it's probably just my foolishness," she said out loud to no one in particular. "But these are just in case."

For some time now she had had the feeling that someone was coming into the church at night. She had no proof and no idea how they might be getting into the building. Nothing was ever moved or taken, but the feeling persisted. It was as though the presence of whoever it was left an imprint on the atmosphere after they had gone. And then there was the silver egg cup—the one shaped like an acorn. She had first noticed it one morning when she had gone into the church to polish the brass crucifix. She was pretty sure that it hadn't been there the day before. But perhaps it had, and she simply hadn't seen it. It was very small and easily hidden among all the other things on the windowsill. Perhaps someone had simply moved it and that was why it had caught her eye. But if someone was visiting the church at night, who could it be? Evangeline couldn't help but feel it must be someone who was lost in some way. Someone who needed more than mince pies. But for now, that was all she could offer. That, and her prayers. And maybe it was nothing after all. Maybe it was just her imagination. But it was Christmas, and so she left the mince pies anyway. Just in case.

FROM THE FIRE escape, Crow could see Christmas lights twinkling in the darkness along the Embankment and in the gardens and doorways of the big houses that faced the river, but their gaiety only served to distill his sadness. The moon's reflection rippled on the water, and a pair of swans sailed through it, dislocating the silver orb before it re-formed in their wake. It was late and the bells of Saint Paul's were summoning worshippers to midnight Mass. Crow shivered. It was bitterly cold, and he made his way to the place where he had learned that he could break into the building. Inside the attic, enough moonlight filtered through the grimy windowpanes for him to pick his way through the shadows without using his flashlight. Besides, he had spent enough time there that he could probably find his way blindfolded. In winter, when it was too cold to stay on the fire escape for long, he came inside and sat by the window, just gazing out at the view or playing solitaire with an old pack of cards that he always carried. They had been his mother's, and she had used them to read fortunes back in Poland when he was a little boy. Whenever he dealt them, it brought back memories of his mother and her friends sitting at the kitchen table drinking tea and eating *sernik*. His uneven footsteps echoed on the stairs, but there was no one other than a few startled mice to hear him.

The church welcomed him with silence and the smell of ivy and pine needles. He took a deep breath and exhaled a cloud of steam into the sacred air. Peace enveloped him, and he felt the tension seep out of his flesh and bones. He walked over to the windowsill where the silver egg cup stood. He picked it up and cradled it gently in his hands as though it were a baby bird. It had belonged to his sister—a christening gift from their grandmother. It was the only thing of hers that he possessed and the only thing he owned apart from the cards that was of any real value to him. Which was why he had brought it here for safekeeping. The house where he lived in a single room was little more than a den of thieves.

At the altar he lit a candle and prayed for his family—all dead now, save for his ex-wife. And he couldn't bring himself to pray for her. He prayed for the friends he had once had in another life, and he prayed for the strength to carry on in this one. He thought that he would sit for a while, but when he turned from the altar toward the front pew, he saw a plate of mince pies. The hairs on the back of his neck prickled. He glanced around even though he knew he was alone. He pushed the plate to one side and sat down next to it. His racing pulse gradually slowed as he stared at the flickering flame of the candle on the altar. Finally, he risked another glance at the mince pies. They were homemade and dusted with icing sugar. It had been so long since he had tasted anything home baked. Who had put them there? Whom were they for? He knew that children left various treats out for Santa Claus and his reindeer, but usually under the Christmas tree or by the chimney. His mouth was watering. What harm would it do if he ate just one? Before he could talk himself out of it, he whispered a thank-you, took one of the pies, and bit into the buttery pastry.

When the bells of Saint Paul's sounded the end of midnight Mass, Crow blew out the candle he had lit and left the church, closing the door softly behind him. As he ascended the stairs, he paused at the door to the ballroom. He never went inside, keeping only to the church and the attic whenever he was in the building. But tonight, he let his curiosity get the better of him. He didn't dare use his flashlight in case the beam was seen from outside, but even in the gloom he could see that beneath the dirt and dust it was still a beautiful room. As a young man he had loved to dance, but his injury had put an end to all that. It had robbed him of both the ability and the inclination to dance. Dancing was for happy people. But there was something about this Christmas Eve that made him want to try. Just for a moment. Perhaps it was something in the mince pie, he thought, smiling to himself. He stood up straight and raised his arms as though taking hold of an invisible partner. Quietly singing

"What a Wonderful World"—an old favorite—he began with faltering steps, clumsy at first but growing easier as he moved across the floor. But as he tried to turn, his crippled leg buckled beneath him, and he winced with pain. Cursing his own foolishness, he limped back to the stairs and climbed up into the attic. His dancing days were done.

CHAPTER 25

Christmas Day dawned dank and drizzling. But the customary English festive weather did nothing to dampen Kite's spirits. At six thirty he rang his parents on his mobile, waking them grumpy and hungover from a party the previous evening. Oblivious to their lack of seasonal cheer, he wished them a happy Christmas and then bounced out of bed, dislodging a still-sleepy Colin from his cocoon in the duvet, and the pair trotted downstairs to open their stockings. By the time Venetia joined them, Kite had eaten two satsumas and a bag of chocolate coins, and Colin was demolishing a squeaky dog toy. Kite was already dressed in a striped shirt and one of his grandfather's bow ties, and Colin was sporting his new holly-leaf-print bandanna and a pair of plush antlers. Swan appeared for breakfast wearing a purple satin frock. And snow boots. Liberty joined them for tea and toast, and soon after ten they were ready to leave. Kite and his faithful canine led the way out of the house and onto the Embankment. Colin was still wearing his bandanna but had ditched the antlers and was probably planning to bury them in the garden at the first opportunity. Swan was once again swathed in her black cape and crowned with her Cossack hat, and she carried a walking cane with a silver swan's head handle—though more for effect than efficacy.

At the drop-in center, Evangeline and her small band of helpers were already hard at work peeling potatoes and washing sprouts.

"Merry Christmas! Merry Christmas!" Evangeline greeted them.

"It's so good of you to come and help. And just look at you, Mr. Firth! More handsome than ever in your Christmas finery."

Venetia handed her a tin of mince pies and a large Christmas pudding. "It's already cooked—just as you asked. It only needs warming up."

Swan, who had been ignored for quite long enough in her opinion, coughed affectedly.

"And who is this glamorous lady you've brought with you?" Evangeline inquired. "She looks like Lara from *Doctor Zhivago*!"

"This is my sister-in-law Swan," Venetia replied. "She arrived yesterday. It was a wonderful *surprise*." The emphasis was barely perceptible, but Evangeline's wry smile signaled her understanding.

"Well, it's lovely to meet you," she told Swan. "And an extra pair of hands is always welcome."

Swan looked horrified but managed to muster a tight smile. "I'm only here to watch. I'm afraid I have no waitressing experience."

Evangeline took her hand and patted it kindly. "Oh, don't you worry. I'm sure we can find you something to do."

"Might I take a look inside your church?" Swan had swiftly withdrawn her hand and was looking for an escape.

"I'll show you," volunteered Kite. "Me and Nisha helped to decorate it."

"It's 'Venetia and I,'" Swan corrected, wondering what on earth they taught him at that expensive school of his. "Lead on, Macduff," she instructed, waving her cane imperiously.

"Who's he?"

Clearly not Shakespeare, thought Swan as she followed Kite across the room.

"Isn't it beautiful?" Kite whispered as he pushed open the door and ushered his great-aunt inside. He breathed in deeply. "It smells of Christmas—and magic!"

Swan sniffed the air tentatively. "It smells of damp coats and musty old books to me." She poked at some of the cushions with her stick. "I shouldn't be surprised if there are mice."

"But look at all these treasures," Kite replied, sweeping his arm toward the windowsills. "These are what people bring to say thank you to God—and to Evangeline."

Swan peered at the jumble of trinkets and knickknacks. "Good heavens! Why on earth can't they just use a collection plate?"

"But don't you think this is much nicer?" Kite picked up a peacock feather and wafted it through the air like a magician's wand. "Besides, Evangeline says some of the people who come for healing or to get messages from their loved ones don't have much money."

Swan narrowed her eyes suspiciously. "Exactly what sort of church is this?"

"It's a spirit church."

Swan tutted and shook her head as she made her way down the aisle and sat in the front pew to inspect the nativity scene on the altar in front of her. She debated whether to risk a prayer. Her faith was steadfast but firmly rooted in the stalwart conventions of the Church of England. It had been nurtured at Sunday school and confirmation classes and entrenched at countless eucharists. She was loath to risk her eternal salvation for the sake of an "Our Father" in a place of dubious divinity. But before she could decide, she spotted the mince pies. Two mince pies on a plate right beside her. She put one in her mouth. Whole.

"I saw that!" Kite admonished.

Swan chewed slowly and deliberately before answering. "It was only small," she replied. "A mere amuse-bouche."

But Kite was concerned with her morals, not her manners. "It wasn't yours!"

"Well, it was only going to waste," she reasoned. "The Almighty is hardly going to eat it."

She offered Kite the remaining pie. He was sorely tempted, but reluctantly shook his head. Swan ate it herself and handed Kite the empty plate.

"I suppose we should return to the philanthropists and their impecunious guests," she told him.

Kite had no idea what she was talking about. She sounded like a dictionary.

"Who are they?" he asked.

"The do-gooders and the down-and-outs!"

Evangeline met them as they came out. "I was just coming to find you. It's getting busy."

The tables in the reception room were filling up, and Venetia was welcoming more people at the door. Some were elderly or frail and happy to have someone cook for them, and some were simply in need of a hot meal. Others were lonely or troubled and in need of some Christmas cheer, and some were faithful members of the church's congregation who just wanted to be there. In the kitchen, Liberty was beating the lumps out of a huge pan of gravy, and Norma was pouring glasses of soft drinks while Norman sliced turkey.

"Perhaps you and Kite could hand out the crackers? I forgot to put them on the tables yesterday."

Kite swapped the empty plate in his hand for the box that Evangeline offered him.

She smiled. "The mince pies were gone?"

"They are now," Swan replied. "I ate them."

Evangeline's smile faded.

"I'm sorry. I couldn't stop her."

Evangeline caught Kite's worried expression and gave him a wink. "It doesn't matter. It's fine."

Swan was unrepentant. Never apologize, never explain. She surveyed the tables, assessing the assortment of people already seated. Most of them looked surprisingly normal. Steeling herself, she took Kite's arm.

"Come along, then," she instructed him. "Let's get cracking."

Kite grinned. "You made a joke!"

"Not intentionally."

At each table, Kite passed his great-aunt the crackers, and she handed them out one at a time with a gracious, if slightly haughty, "Merry Christmas," in the manner of the Queen greeting her subjects on a royal visit. At the last table, Tommy sat alone save for Colin Firth, huddled up against the radiator as usual. He appeared to have made a perfunctory effort to smarten himself up for the occasion. His face looked a little cleaner, and his hair was dragged back into a ponytail. Even his beard looked as though it might have been hacked at with a pair of scissors.

"This is Tommy. He sometimes sleeps in the park. I bring him his tea when I'm here, and Colin Firth really likes him."

Tommy looked up at them with his bloodshot pale gray eyes. Hopelessness hung over him as palpably as his grubby overcoat, and something in Swan inexplicably softened.

"I'm Swan, Kite's great-aunt."

Tommy replied with a shaky salute, and Swan recoiled inwardly at his filthy hands and fingernails.

"Were you a military man?" she asked him.

"Twenty years—army," he muttered.

Swan nodded thoughtfully. "My father served in the Chindits in Burma."

"Bosnia and Afghanistan," Tommy replied.

Kite offered Swan a cracker, but she shook her head. "Tommy and I have something to do first."

To Kite's astonishment, she approached Tommy and took him by the arm.

"On your feet, soldier."

Once Venetia had seated all the diners, she found Evangeline and asked if there was anything else she could do.

"You can sit down and wait for your dinner," Evangeline told her. "Everything's under control, and we're just about ready to serve up!"

As Liberty, Kite, Evangeline, and Norma handed around plates of turkey with all the trimmings, Norman lowered the needle of an old record player onto an LP of Christmas favorites sung by Dean Martin. Having accompanied Tommy to the washroom and supervised a thorough hand-scrubbing, Swan chose to sit with him while he ate. Venetia watched her sister-in-law pull a cracker and coax him into a little conversation. Swan even persuaded him to wear a paper hat. Colin lay beside them and was occasionally rewarded with scraps of turkey.

"Who'd have thought it?" Evangeline nudged Venetia and nodded toward the old soldier and Swan.

"It's what her brother would have done," Venetia replied with a sad smile.

When the Christmas pudding and mince pies were served, Kite marched over to Tommy and Swan and retrieved Colin. "It's for your own good!" he told the dog.

Outside, it was getting dark, but inside it was bright and warm and cheerful. People sat chatting in a comfortable, cozy fug of contentment. The lights on the Christmas tree were soft smudges of color against the dark green branches, and the Barbie angel looked down over all with her feather wings and her splendid cleavage. Norman, who was acting as DJ, found a Louis Armstrong album and placed it on the turntable. As the first song began to play, he took Norma's hand and pulled her up into the small space in the center of the floor.

"Dance with me."

As Louis crooned "When You're Smiling," others joined them. A few elderly couples shuffled to and fro, clinging to each other for support. Some of those who had come alone found impromptu partners. Kite showed Liberty his best dance moves, and Evangeline stood swaying to the music and delighting in the smiling faces all around her. Venetia watched and wondered as she stroked Colin's silky head. Could she really do it? Should she do it? She had forgotten how much happiness the simple pleasure of moving to music could bring. On the other side of the room, the sound of a chair scraping across the floor cut across the music. Tommy had stood up and offered his hand to Swan. To Venetia's amazement, Swan took it and accepted his invitation to dance—albeit keeping a safe distance between them. When the song ended, Tommy returned Swan to her seat and pulled on his overcoat. He took her hand in his once more and kissed it gently before turning and heading for the door. Before he left, he turned and took a final glance at what happiness might look like before stepping out into the cold, wet night.

CHAPTER 26

It was one of those days in that strange temporal no-man's-land between Christmas and New Year, and dawn was still several hours away. Venetia padded into the kitchen in her slippers and dressing gown and switched on the kettle at precisely 4:23, according to the digital clock on the stove. She had been lying awake in rumpled sheets for hours, attempting to marshal her thoughts and make a decision, but her efforts had proven as fruitless as trying to gather mist in a butterfly net. She found her own dithering infuriating, but her heart was pushing her forward while her head was pulling her back. She was caught in a riptide of sense and sensibility. She made some chamomile tea and sat at the table, watching curls of steam rise from her cup.

Hawk's death had left her a rich woman, but her wealth made her uneasy and, at times, embarrassed. Perhaps it was because she hadn't worked for it and so felt that somehow she didn't deserve it. She had had no illustrious career or entrepreneurial acumen to account for her bank balance—only a marriage certificate. Although some might argue that for all her years spent as a loyal wife and mother, she had earned it.

Venetia sipped her tea. It was still too hot, and it burned her tongue. She had grown up in a model middle-class family, her mother and father a teacher and engineer, respectively. Her mother had been a strong, determined woman and had, somewhat unusually for the time, returned to teaching not long after her children were born, leaving them in the care of her own mother. Venetia's father had disapproved, but not strongly enough for it to come between him and his wife, and her desire for a little independence and more intellectual stimulation than motherhood alone could provide had prevailed. They had lived on a quiet suburban street in their own detached 1930s villa with a Border collie called Flash. There had been dancing lessons for Venetia and tennis lessons for her brother; RV holidays on the coast once a year and then, later, camping trips or package holidays abroad. It had been a comfortable but modest life.

All that had changed when she married Hawk. Hawk "came from money" and was making money—a good deal of it at that. He was a topflight barrister with a lifestyle to match. Over the years, Venetia became accustomed to the beautiful houses, the luxury holidays, the expensive gifts, and the champagne social life, but never wholly comfortable. Often guilt would gate-crash her enjoyment. Guilt that through no merit of her own, she was one of the haves instead of the have-nots. She had tried, over the years, to placate her nagging conscience: she had donated to various good causes, volunteered at an animal rescue center, sat on the boards of several charitable trusts, and sponsored the education of two orphans in India, but it all felt so piecemeal somehow. Her attempts at patronage felt awkwardly patronizing and, for the most part, squeamishly remote, like a well-to-do Victorian lady throwing coins through the window of her fine carriage to paupers on the street. But now she had the chance to use her money to do something practical to help people she actually knew. But would she really be doing it for them or for herself?

She heard footsteps in the hallway, and Swan appeared wearing an enormous cardigan over striped silk pajamas, a satin turban, and tartan slippers.

"What's that stench?" she demanded. "It smells like cat wee!" She wrinkled her nose in disgust.

"It might be my tea," Venetia replied. "It's chamomile."

Swan pulled a face. "Do you mind if I make myself some *normal* tea?"

"Be my guest."

"I already am," replied Swan archly. She made herself a mug of dark brown Assam and sat down at the table opposite Venetia.

"Somniphobia!" she announced grandly. "The older I get, the less inclined I am to sleep. It's too much like death, and that will catch me soon enough. The more I sleep, the more I miss out on what life I have left." She blew gently across the surface of her tea. "What about you? Nightmares?"

Venetia shook her head. "I'm trying to decide what to do with Hawk's money."

"Well, it's yours now, so you can do as you please with it."

Venetia frowned. "Yes, I know. But I want to do something worthwhile."

"Aha! You mean good works. God preserve us! Why not buy a villa in Tuscany or an apartment in Venice? I should love to go to Venice. And if I'm not mistaken, your name means 'from Venice,' so it would be very fitting."

"I'd like to do something that Hawk would be proud of—a fitting memorial to him, if you like."

"Well, Hawk loved Venice too! He was in a production of *The Gondoliers* once at his university. You know how fond he was of Gilbert and Sullivan."

Venetia smiled. "I was thinking about something a little closer to home."

Swan sighed, her dream of vacations in Venice sinking fast. "Well, come along, then. Out with it!"

Swan listened attentively and at times incredulously as Venetia explained what she was considering. When Venetia had finished, Swan sat silently for a moment or two before declaring, "It's madness. Complete and utter madness!"

But then she reached over and patted Venetia's hand.

"It's also bloody marvelous! Of course you're absolutely stark raving bonkers, my dear, and the chances are it will be an unmitigated disaster. But I take my hat off to you!" She removed her turban and waved it in the air before ramming it back onto her head.

"So . . . you think I should do it?" Venetia inquired tentatively.

"It is of no consequence what I think. It's what you think that counts. But I'm pleasantly surprised that you've come up with such a crackpot idea, and if it's what you want, then what's to stop you?"

"But am I really doing a charitable thing, or am I doing it for myself?"

"Quite possibly both, but does it really matter? If you succeed, you will have done something good for a good number of people—yourself included. There's no shame in that."

And that was it. That was the moment when Venetia made her decision.

"Then I think we should drink a toast to my new venture," she told Swan.

"So long as you're not going to make any more of that appalling tea."

"Oh, I think we can do better than that," Venetia replied, going to the fridge and taking out a bottle of champagne.

Swan clapped her hands. "How splendid! And could I have some toast and Marmite with that?"

WHEN KITE APPEARED in the kitchen with Colin Firth an hour later, he found his grandmother and his great-aunt pink-cheeked and giggling.

"What are we going to do today?" he asked.

Venetia smiled at him and raised her empty glass. "Today, we're going to buy a ballroom!"

CHAPTER 27

New Year's Eve 1971

C ome on, sis—we'll be late!"

Venetia's brother, Paul, stood checking his hair in the hall-stand mirror. He wolf-whistled as she appeared at the top of the stairs in a sequined minidress with long, wide sleeves.

"You don't scrub up too badly for a squirt of a little sister," he joked.

They were going to the New Year's Eve dance and disco at the ballroom. Paul, who was two years older than Venetia, no longer lived at home and shared a flat in town with two friends. But he had agreed to collect Venetia and see her safely home, even though she had insisted that he didn't need to.

"It's not safe for a young woman to be wandering the streets at night—especially on New Year's Eve," her father had cautioned.

"I'll hardly be wandering the streets! I could get a bus there and a taxi back."

"Your father's right," her mother had agreed. "I know you're sensible enough, but once some people have had a few too many—well, you never know. Besides, you'll never get a taxi on New Year's Eve."

"We're off, then!" Paul called to his mother, who was in the kitchen making sausage rolls and vol-au-vents. Venetia's parents were seeing in the New Year at home and had invited their neighbors Tom and Barbara Bowler to join them for drinks and a light buffet.

Their mother came out of the kitchen wearing an apron over her new Laura Ashley maxi dress. Her large gold hoop earrings glinted under the hall light.

"Have a good time, you two, and be—"

"Careful!" her son and daughter chorused good-naturedly.

Venetia leaned forward and brushed a smudge of flour from her mother's temple before kissing her on the cheek.

"You look lovely, Mum," she told her, but in truth her mother looked like a watercolor wash of herself. Her skin was strangely pearlescent and so pale that it was almost colorless. Her blue eyes were still bright, but they seemed sunken in their shadowy sockets. She'd probably been overdoing it, Venetia told herself. She'd organized the school concert and the nativity play, and then with all the hustle and bustle of Christmas she was probably tired and now it had caught up with her. That was all it must be. Venetia gave her mother a quick hug. "Have a nice time with Tom and Barbara."

"We will. If your father ever emerges from that shower!" She called the last sentence up the stairs, grinning at her son and daughter.

"And don't go letting that Tom take any liberties with you at midnight, Mum. I reckon he's got the hots for you!" Paul winked at his mother before dodging her playful clip around the ear on his way out the front door.

It was a cold, clear night, and the stars were brilliant pinpricks of light in an ink-black sky. There was already a sparkling of frost on car windscreens and privet hedges as they walked to the bus stop. The 7:22 was on time, and twenty minutes later it delivered them to their destination. Venetia stepped gingerly down from the bus, mindful that her silver high heels weren't the most suitable footwear for negotiating slippery pavement.

"Don't do anything I wouldn't!" the bus conductor called after them as he rang the bell, and the bus pulled away. They could hear snatches of music and laughter coming from down the street and see people eagerly making their way toward the ballroom.

"Come on," said Paul, offering her his arm with a grin. "Try not to fall over and break your neck in those ridiculous shoes!"

Inside, they left their coats in the cloakroom on the ground floor and climbed the carpeted stairs toward the sound of "Let's Face the Music and Dance" and the smell of beer and cigarette smoke. The floor was almost full of couples dancing the quickstep. Brendan was partnered with one of his most ardent admirers, and when he spotted Venetia an expression of relief lit up his face. Paul began edging his way around the tables to get to the bar, where one of his flatmates was already waiting for him.

"What do you want to drink, sis?"

"Bacardi and Coke, please."

As the cold bubbles from her first sip prickled on her tongue, Brendan arrived, a little agitated, by her side.

"Thank God you're here!" he exclaimed. "You have to rescue me!"

Venetia smiled. "But Pauline *really* likes you."

Brendan rolled his eyes. "I've only escaped her clutches because she's gone to the ladies'. You've got to promise me that you won't leave me alone. Not for a second."

Venetia looped her arm around his waist and gave him a squeeze. "I promise! Unless someone else comes along who takes your fancy. I can't believe you're still single—you always have women falling at your feet."

"And most of them are my pupils. They fall for the idea of who they think I am: the dreamy dance teacher straight out of a romance novel. They only ever see me here, dressed in my best and showing them how to strut their stuff. They only know this version of me, the one I get paid to be. They have no idea who I really am."

"So, who's your perfect woman, then?" Venetia nudged him as

she saw Pauline return from the ladies' and glance over at them. She didn't look very happy.

"You, of course! And Cher. Not that she's likely to be popping in for tango lessons any time soon. But speaking of admirers, I see your bashful beau is here with his flat-footed friend."

Venetia followed Brendan's gaze and saw Hawk Hamilton Hargreaves standing on the other side of the room with a drink in his hand, chatting with Andrew. His shirt and tie were a little too formal for the occasion and he looked ill at ease, but Andrew, as usual, was laughing and joking and seemed to be having a good time.

"He doesn't look as though he's enjoying himself very much."

Brendan grinned. "That's because he hasn't seen you yet!"

"Don't be daft! As you're so fond of saying yourself—he's just a pupil and I'm his teacher."

At that moment, Hawk saw her. He smiled and began to raise his hand to wave, but then obviously thought better of it, resulting in an awkwardly aborted gesture that made him blush and turn away.

Venetia danced with Brendan. They both enjoyed the opportunity to showcase their talents without the constraints that teaching necessarily imposed. They were perfect partners, and when they were together on the floor, Venetia felt as though they almost became two halves of the same dancer, such was their synchronicity. Their tango in particular brought gasps of admiration from the other dancers, who moved back to give them more space in which to perform their extravagant moves. At the finish, they were greeted with a round of applause. Breathless, they made their way to the bar.

"You're such a show-off!" Paul greeted her with a laugh. "And you just encourage her," he joked with Brendan. "I suppose you're both after a drink now?"

Venetia shook her head. "It's my round. What do you want?"

"I'll have a pint of lager. And seeing as you're buying, I'll have a packet of cheese and onion crisps too."

Brendan raised his eyebrows. "Are you sure? I don't fancy your chances of getting a kiss at midnight with cheese and onion breath!"

As Venetia paid for the drinks, she felt someone lightly touch her arm. She turned to find Hawk standing next to her.

"Congratulations! Your tango was wonderful."

"Thank you. Perhaps you might like to give it a go at your next lesson?"

Hawk shook his head. "I'm sensible enough to know my own limitations and quit while I'm ahead. I consider myself fortunate to have mastered a basic quickstep, waltz, and foxtrot. Speaking of which . . ." The music had begun to play again, and the drama and daring of the tango was followed by a decorous waltz. "I wonder if you'd do me the honor?"

He held out his hand and Venetia took it. As she accompanied him onto the dance floor, Brendan caught her eye and mouthed, "I told you so!"

Hawk had been a conscientious pupil and was now a confident partner as he led Venetia around the floor. Venetia leaned into his embrace and breathed in the scent of his clean skin, freshly laundered shirt, and Acqua di Parma cologne. His footwork, like his person, was clean and crisp, but still lacked a little fluidity. Hawk and his beautifully tailored shirt were buttoned up just a bit too tightly. It was a shame, Venetia thought. He would make someone a lovely husband. Someone sensible and refined called Elizabeth or Margaret, who knew how to arrange flowers, set the table for a six-course meal, and make appropriate small talk with members of the peerage. But he wasn't likely to find the future Mrs. Hamilton Hargreaves here, Venetia mused. He would surely have more luck at one of those balls he had spoken of at his first lesson. When the dance ended, Venetia excused herself and went to the ladies'. By the time she returned, the lights had dimmed, and the disco had begun.

For the next hour, she and Brendan danced to T. Rex, David

Bowie, Elvis Presley, Marvin Gaye, and anything else the DJ played. They even persuaded Paul to join them when Tony Christie began asking the way to Amarillo. At five minutes before midnight, the DJ announced the final dance of the year, and the opening chords of Frank Sinatra's "My Way" invited couples to take to the floor. Brendan was about to take Venetia's hand when his arm was grabbed from behind by Pauline. Emboldened by five brandy and pear ciders, she was clearly determined to be in his arms at the stroke of midnight. Venetia registered the irritation that flashed across Brendan's face before he recovered his professional smile, and she couldn't help but be glad. She too had wanted this dance to be with Brendan, but she knew that there would be many other chances for her but maybe not for Pauline. She could see Hawk making his way toward her, but before he could reach her, a young man who was clearly very drunk slipped and grabbed Hawk's arm to prevent himself from falling, spilling most of his drink over his reluctant savior. As Venetia grimaced in sympathy at Hawk, she felt someone touch the small of her back.

"Would you like to dance?"

Clifford Sykes was a regular at the ballroom and almost as popular with the ladies as Brendan. He was dark and attractive in a textbook way, but without any distinguishing features to elevate him beyond homogenously handsome. His good looks encouraged a self-confidence that came perilously close to cockiness at times. He wasn't the kind of man that made Venetia's heart beat faster, but she was nonetheless flattered that he had chosen her for the last dance. He led her to the dance floor and pulled her tightly into his arms. Hawk stood, beer-soaked and bitterly disappointed, and watched for a moment before turning and walking out the door.

CHAPTER 28

New Year's Eve 2022

From the top step of the fire escape, Crow could see for miles. At least, he could see miles of darkness and lights. Here in town, the lights were more densely distributed, shining from streetlamps, windows, and traffic. But in the distance, where buildings gave way to open countryside, the lights dwindled into a sparse scattering across an expanse of almost total blackness. Above him, the stars were lost behind swollen storm clouds that scuttled across the sky, granting only fleeting glimpses of a bright crescent moon. Crow climbed up onto the roof. The wind that battered him came from the east, and it was raw and brutal. It stung his cheeks and whipped tears from his eyes. Tonight was New Year's Eve, and it had been another year wasted, wallowing in shame and guilt. Another year skulking in the shadows, hiding from all the specters in his past. He thought about his sister and about the child's grave in Poland where she was buried that he hadn't seen for so long. He thought about his parents and how many lies he had told them—how much he missed them. He hoped that now, they were reunited and a family again.

He wondered where his ex-wife was and if she ever thought of him, and how different things might have been if he'd never met her. She had walked into his office one rainy Friday afternoon to collect some program designs he had prepared for the auction company that she worked for, and they had ended up in the pizza place around the corner, sharing a bottle of Montepulciano with their Margheritas. Their wedding day had been the happiest of his life. He could still picture her smile as she walked down the aisle toward him and her slender hand in his as he slipped a gold band onto her finger. She had left him after fifteen years of marriage for another man, and since that day his life had spiraled inexorably out of control. He had sought solace in the bottoms of countless bottles of booze until he was barely ever sober. He had lost his home, his job, and every last shred of self-respect. He had almost lost his leg too, when he stumbled out of the pub and into the road in front of a car. His pain had been equaled only by his shame at what he had become. It had been terrifying how fast the descent had been from a man with a profession, a wife, and a home to an unemployed, vagrant drunk with nothing. Not even hope. And without hope he *was* nothing.

It began to rain. It didn't fall but was flung across the roof in icy spears by the relentless wind. Crow stood and let the elements thrash him. As the final seconds of the eleventh hour ticked away, he made his way to the very edge of the roof. When the first chime of midnight rang out from the steeple of Saint Paul's, he threw his arms wide open and turned his face heavenward.

"Happy New Year!"

Evangeline was at home, surrounded by her friends and family, celebrating. The party was in full swing, but all evening Evangeline had been unable to shake a feeling of dread that clung to her like smoke from a bonfire. Something was wrong, and she was connected to it by some ethereal thread. As the twelfth chime rang out from Big Ben on the television, she closed her eyes and offered up a silent prayer. It was a spark of light tossed into a terrible unknown darkness, for she had no idea what she was praying for. She could only hope that her God, who knew everything, did.

CHAPTER 29

Kite stood at the window watching the rain trickle down the pane in rivulets. Across the road, council workers in hi-vis jackets were working in the ornamental gardens beside the river, tidying the flower beds in preparation for the impressive display of tulips and daffodils that would bloom there in spring. It was almost the end of the school holidays, and Swan still hadn't returned home, nor had she given the slightest indication that she was planning to leave any time soon. She was currently reclining on the sofa, reading the newspaper. Venetia came in carrying a cup of tea, which she set down on a small side table next to her sister-in-law.

"I wish it would stop raining!" moaned Kite. "I wanted to take Colin Firth to the park this afternoon, but he hates it when it's wet."

Venetia smiled sympathetically at her grandson. It was true. The dog detested rain. He could barely be persuaded to take a few steps beyond the back door to relieve himself in wet weather. Having been forced outside for a few minutes that morning to do the necessary, he was now upstairs sulking on Kite's bed.

"Perhaps if we got him a coat of some sort, it might help," she suggested.

Kite's face immediately brightened. "That's a brilliant idea, Nisha!"

There was a rustling noise, and Swan emerged from behind *The Telegraph*. "I don't know why they keep calling it 'Dry January'! It's been chucking it down for the last two days! Bloody awful weather," she bellowed. She clearly hadn't turned her hearing aids on.

"It's not that kind of dry," Kite explained patiently—and loudly. "It means giving up alcohol for the month."

Swan looked at him aghast. "Why on earth would anyone do that?"

"It's good for your health."

Swan shook her head in disbelief. "Horse manure!" she exclaimed. "It certainly wouldn't be good for my health. What kind of imbecile believes that?"

"Well, Dad did it last year."

"And was his abstinence rewarded with renewed vim and vigor?"

Kite shrugged. "I don't know, but I don't think he's doing it again this year. He didn't say he was."

The previous day, Kite had FaceTimed his dad, who had seemed a bit sad. They had talked for longer than they usually did. Usually, Heron had only a few minutes to chat because he was so busy with work. But yesterday he had sounded as though he was interested in what Kite had to say and had the time to listen for once. Kite had wanted to tell him about Nisha buying a ballroom, but Nisha had asked him to keep it a secret for the time being, just in case it didn't come to anything. He had wanted to speak to his mum as well, but she was out. His dad had promised to ask her to call Kite later, but he must have forgotten because she hadn't rung him yet.

Kite returned to the window and traced the path of a raindrop down the glass with his fingertip. "Would you like to play chess, Swan?" he shouted.

He only ever called her by her first name at her own request. She said that anything else made her sound like an ancient crone. He had been delighted when he had discovered that she knew how to play his favorite game, but not so happy when she had beaten him twice. He was eager for a rematch.

"Not today, thank you. I'll teach you how to play poker if you like? But I give you fair warning—I'm a bit of a card shark!"

"Why don't we find a game that we can all play together this afternoon?" Venetia suggested. "And, Swan, could you please sort out your hearing aids? We shall all be as deaf as you at this rate!"

Swan rolled her eyes and adopted an exaggeratedly pained expression but did as she was asked.

Venetia was worried that Kite was bored and that he didn't have anyone of his own age to do things with. She felt sure that it wasn't healthy for him to spend all his time with adults, but it was what he seemed to prefer. He had been to the drop-in center with Liberty several times since Christmas to help Evangeline, and other than that he spent his time walking or playing with Colin or at home with her and Swan. She had made up her mind that when the new school term began, she would encourage him to bring a friend home and she would take them to the cinema or out for pizza, or whatever it was that boys of his age liked to do.

"We could play Clue," Kite proposed. "And I could go and ask Liberty if she wants to play."

"It's Liberty's day off," Venetia reminded him.

"I know. But it's not work, is it? Playing Clue is fun. Anyway, she might be lonely."

"We don't even know if she's in."

"Her car's still in the drive," Kite replied eagerly.

"She might have gone for a walk."

"Well, if she's gone walking in this god-awful weather, she must be a complete ninny!" Swan declared, folding up her newspaper.

Kite was already on his way out of the room when Venetia called after him: "Don't try to persuade her. Just ask her, and if she says no, come straight back and leave her in peace."

LIBERTY HAD BEEN looking forward to her day off. She had planned to go for a walk along the river and then into town, and maybe visit the antiquarian bookshop. It was the kind of shop where you could browse for as long as you liked without being pestered by the staff, and it had lots of little alcoves and a bargain room where all the books were less than five pounds. There were even a couple of sofas where you could sit and read—try before buying, so to speak. She had also considered popping into a nail bar and having a manicure. But the weather was so awful that she couldn't face it, and then she'd seen the email from Mr. Court reminding her that they were due to meet for lunch in a few days' time. He had suggested a pub on the Embankment, so at least she wouldn't have to drive, which meant that she could have a glass of wine. She had a feeling she was going to need it. The thought of being questioned by that oh-so-superior solicitor to gratify some whim of her mother's made her want to beat her fists on the table in frustration. But instead, someone beat a tattoo on the door.

"It's me!" yelled Kite.

She got up and opened the door.

"What are you doing?" he asked, peering around her into the flat with unabashed inquisitiveness. He hadn't been inside it since she had moved in and was desperate to see what it was like.

"Do you want to come in?"

Kite was through the door before she had finished her sentence. He wandered around the room, inspecting the books on the shelves, the film posters she had fixed to the walls, and the records that were neatly stacked in a row against one wall.

"Who's that?" he asked, pointing at a framed photograph of Liberty's mother that stood on one of the bookshelves. Bernadette was standing beside her VW camper van, wearing a bright pink cotton caftan. Her fair hair was loose and windswept, and her face was deeply tanned, but the first thing anyone looking at the photograph would have noticed was her smile.

"It's my mum."

"She looks lovely! Is that her van?"

"It was, yes."

"What happened to it? Didn't you get it when she died like I got Grandpa's chess set?"

No, I didn't, thought Liberty crossly. *I got bugger all.*

"No, she sold it a few years ago."

Kite looked at her quizzically. "You don't look much like your mum."

Thanks! Liberty thought. *Nice to know that I don't look in the least bit lovely.* And she was disappointed too, because she realized, with some surprise—and irritation—that it truly mattered. It mattered what Kite thought about her.

"She looks really cheerful and happy," Kite clarified. "But you're quite serious, aren't you?"

Liberty didn't know how to answer him, but fortunately she didn't have to. He was ready to reveal the purpose of his visit.

"We wondered if you'd like to play Clue with us? Swan was going to teach me how to play poker, but Nisha wants to play Clue instead. I'm not supposed to persuade you, only ask. And if you say no, I'm supposed to leave you in peace. But I thought you might be lonely—or bored." He waited.

His honesty was disarming and, for Liberty, rather painful. She *was* bored, and she *was* lonely. But it was somewhat humiliating to have a ten-year-old boy call you out. She might have said no and manufactured some scintillating activity that she was about to engage in, or pretended that she was about to go and meet a friend for afternoon tea, had it not been for what Kite said next.

"And I want you to come and play with us." He grinned. "But only if you want to. Because I'm definitely not going to persuade you."

CHAPTER 30

Miss Scarlett had stabbed Mrs. White with the dagger in the kitchen, Professor Plum had dispatched Reverend Green with the revolver in the conservatory, and Mrs. Peacock had bludgeoned Colonel Mustard to death with the lead pipe in the billiard room.

"Serves him bloody well right!" Swan pronounced. "I never could stand Colonel Mustard!"

"But he's not real, so how do you know?" Kite asked.

"I know the type!" Swan replied. "Your great-grandpapa was in the military, and he was a bloody hero! An officer and a true gentleman. But I remember one of his army compatriots—a bombastic, red-faced bully with preposterous facial hair. He was a colonel something-or-other, and I couldn't bear the sight of him. He gave me the creeps." She shuddered. "He was always asking me to sit on his knee."

The way she clasped her hands together until the knuckles showed white betrayed her discomfort at the memory, even after all these years, but she swiftly dismissed it.

"Venetia, if we're to play another game, might we have some drinks and nibbles to keep us going?"

"Good idea!" Venetia had noticed Swan's reaction, and it had struck an uncomfortably familiar chord. "That's exactly what we need," she replied, just a little too brightly.

"Would you like me to do it?" Liberty asked, getting up.

"Certainly not! It's your day off. Kite, would you like to get some crisps and peanuts out of the pantry and put them in bowls?"

When the gin and tonics—fizzy orange for Kite—and nibbles were on the table, they began again. Colin rested his head on Kite's foot, nudging him every now and again for a crisp. This time around, Professor Plum strangled poor Miss Scarlett with the rope in the ballroom.

"I hope no one dies in our ballroom," Kite said, helping himself to some peanuts. He had assumed joint ownership with Venetia ever since she had announced her intention to buy it.

"It isn't ours yet," she reminded him gently.

"One mustn't count one's chiffchaffs before they've hatched," pronounced Swan, draining her glass.

"I thought it was chickens." Kite was using his finger to scoop up the last crumbs of crisps from a bowl.

"The specific bird is irrelevant—the general principle remains the same. I prefer chiffchaffs. But that aside, what *is* the latest news on the ballroom, Venetia?"

"As you know, I've made an offer, which the agent is fairly confident will be accepted. There appear to be no other buyers in the frame, and the owners are supposedly keen to be rid of it after the last sale fell through. My solicitor has told me that there's nothing more we can do now other than wait for the owners' response."

"Can't we tell them to hurry up?" Kite asked.

Swan tutted and rolled her eyes. "This is exactly why I need to teach you to play poker! You must be inscrutable. You must never let them know how keen you are!"

"Why not?"

"Because they'll take advantage and manufacture a reason to put the price up."

"But that's cheating!"

"Well, it's not going to happen," Venetia intervened, "because I've made my final offer and I'm sticking to it. Now, who fancies Chinese takeaway for supper?"

Venetia was keen to move away from the subject of the ballroom. Whenever she considered her prospective purchase, her emotions swung between fear and elation, calling in disbelief, doubt, and determination along the way.

"Liberty, please stay if you'd like to," Venetia continued. "You're more than welcome to join us. Kite, can you put the game away? And I'll see if I can find the menu for the Purple Elephant."

She got up and began searching through one of the drawers beneath the kitchen counter. She couldn't remember the last time she had shared a takeaway supper with anyone other than Hawk. It was wonderful to have her kitchen so full of chatter and laughter—so full of life.

"I think I'd make an excellent private detective," Kite announced as he gathered up the Clue cards and replaced them in the box. "I won two games! I could be like Sherlock Holmes. You could be my Watson, if you like," he said to Swan with a mischievous grin.

"Nonsense!" Swan replied. "You could be *my* Watson. I'm more qualified to be Sherlock Holmes. *I* can play the violin."

Kite was suitably impressed. "I didn't know that!"

"Young man, I have a great many talents that you know nothing about. I can drive a tractor, speak a little Arabic, and I once won an arm-wrestling contest with a lance corporal called Orlando from the Queen's Household Cavalry. But sadly, I doubt that any of this would prove useful to a modern-day detective. Crimes appear to be so much less imaginative these days."

Venetia found the menu and handed it to Kite and Liberty to look at. "Well, you can't expect real life to be much like Poirot or Miss Marple, or even Sherlock Holmes—especially now."

"Which is precisely why I don't watch these modern detective mysteries anymore," Swan replied. "It's all far too depressing and predictable. And the clothes are awful. Everyone in *Poirot* dressed so beautifully!"

Venetia laughed. "I agree there doesn't seem to be much mystery about it now. The perpetrator is nearly always a dodgy neighbor, a friend, or one of the family."

"It certainly was in my case," Liberty muttered under her breath, but not quite quietly enough.

"What was your case?" Kite asked, sounding excited. "Was it a murder or a robbery? Did you have to call the police?"

Liberty hadn't meant to say the words out loud. But her upcoming lunch date with Mr. Court was still playing on her mind and had inevitably resurrected her anger about the whole fiasco of her mother's will. Perhaps a couple of drinks on a fairly empty stomach and a few games of Clue had paved the way for her to share her very own real-life mystery. The one where Mrs. Bell disinherits Miss Liberty in the solicitor's office with a photograph album and a copy of *The Lady*.

While they waited for their supper to be delivered, Liberty told them everything. Well, almost everything. She didn't tell them about her affair with Graham. It would hardly have been appropriate in front of Kite, and besides, she felt humiliated enough already by admitting that her own mother had treated her so badly. She was also concerned about how Venetia would react, now that she knew that Liberty hadn't been completely honest at her job interview. But her worries were unfounded.

"How awful for you—to lose your mother and then your home too!" Venetia sympathized.

"But lucky for us," Kite added, "because you came to live here. But you must have done something really bad to make her so cross with you. Even if you didn't mean to," he added, seeing Venetia's warning frown.

"It isn't always that simple," Venetia told him. "Families can be very complicated."

"And a damn nuisance as well!" Swan banged her empty glass down on the table and Venetia got up to refill it—with tonic water. "Present company excepted, of course," Swan continued. "Look at that floozy of a sister of mine, gallivanting around the country with her tradesman boy toy! No sooner had they returned from their seedy sojourn in Hastings than they were off again, having packed their bonnets and breeches, to some Jane Austen reenactment weekend in Bath. Nightingale gives no thought for me whatsoever, left behind and all alone."

Venetia handed Swan her drink. "Well, you're not *exactly* alone, are you, now you're here? And we're very pleased to have you."

Kite was far more interested in Liberty's mystery than his great-aunt's unsuccessful play for sympathy. "I can't believe your mum didn't leave you her camper van. We could have all gone to the seaside in it. I bet Colin Firth's never been to the seaside."

"I can't believe any of the things that the solicitor told me after Mum died," Liberty replied with a rueful smile. "But I have to because they're true. And if I don't find out what it is that I'm supposed to do to pass his ridiculous test, then I won't get whatever it is she *did* leave me."

"Well, my dear, I shouldn't worry about that anymore," said Swan, reaching across and patting her hand. "You now have two of the greatest bird brains in the detecting business at your service—Swan and Kite Hamilton Hargreaves."

"And Nisha," Kite added. "She can be our Mrs. Hudson!"

Venetia raised her eyebrows. "As it's my house, I think I already am!"

"Well, if you really want to help, I'll bring the photo album over for you to look at tomorrow. You can see if you can detect any clues."

What harm could it do? Liberty thought.

The doorbell rang, and Colin was on his feet at once, barking and racing toward the front door. Venetia went to answer it while Liberty and Kite began to set the table.

Swan sipped her drink and grimaced.

"There's no bloody gin in this!"

CHAPTER 31

The photograph album had been a disappointment. The amateur sleuths had pored over it the following morning but had been unable to deduce anything useful at all. The photos were a seemingly random collection taken at various times throughout Liberty's life. They were arranged in chronological order, except for the last two, but there appeared to be no common theme to connect them. The first was of Liberty as a toddler sitting at a table holding a spoon, with a bowl of something in front of her. The next was of a slightly older Liberty wearing a frilly dress and dance shoes, standing in the garden. There was a teenage Liberty with a gaggle of girlfriends all dressed up and waving tickets to a Take That concert. There were ten photographs in all, and the final one was taken outside a beach hut. Liberty looked to be about the same age as Kite and was sitting on a sand dune with her parents. All three were suntanned and windswept and smiling for the camera, their eyes squinting in the bright summer sunshine.

Swan had insisted that Liberty tell them again exactly what the solicitor had said. On hearing that her next meeting with Mr. Court was imminent, Swan quickly lost interest in the photographs, saying that they probably had nothing to do with the mysterious terms of Bernadette Bell's will and had most likely been left to Liberty as a keepsake. She declared that she should accompany Liberty to the lunch on what could be regarded as a reconnaissance mission. Liberty had readily agreed. Swan would be a welcome reinforcement.

Kite had wanted to go too, but the lunch was scheduled for the first day of term.

Liberty was now waiting for Swan with Venetia in the hall. It was a fine day, and the pub was just a short walk from the house. Swan descended the staircase wearing a heavily embroidered coat with a faux-fur collar over a black velvet dress and a great many strings of pearls. On her head, a black beret with a large silken tassel was perched at a rakish angle. Liberty felt distinctly underdressed in her Next skirt and cardigan.

"I'll just pretend to be your slightly batty but charming friend," she told Liberty as they headed for the front door. "Your Mr. Court will have no idea that I'll be watching his every move and analyzing his every word. I've even put new batteries in my hearing aids."

Venetia thought that Swan might prove more convincing with the batty rather than the charming aspect of her assumed persona. Heaven help Mr. Court.

Liberty and Swan arrived at the Bubble and Squeak slightly early at Swan's insistence. She said that it would give them a tactical advantage. They chose a table with a clear view of the entrance, ordered drinks, and sat in silent suspense awaiting the arrival of their advocate adversary. If Mr. Court was surprised to see that Liberty had brought along a companion—and such an eye-catching one at that—he hid it well. He greeted Liberty with an outstretched hand and a formal smile, and when introduced, he declared himself to be delighted to meet Miss Hamilton Hargreaves.

We'll see about that, thought Swan.

A waiter brought menus, and once food had been ordered, the interrogation began.

"So, Miss Bell, how have you been getting on since we last met?"

He sounds more like a therapist than a solicitor, Liberty thought wryly.

"Professionally or personally?" Swan interjected with her version of a charming smile.

"Well, both, I suppose," replied Mr. Court.

"Only it's so much easier to give an accurate answer if the question posed is specific rather than generic, don't you agree, Mr. Court?" Swan continued coquettishly, winding her ropes of pearls around her fingers.

Liberty hoped that her dirty vegan burger and double-cooked chips were good. It was clearly going to be a long lunch. As they ate, Liberty told Mr. Court about her new job and her new home. Her tone was polite and her narrative dispassionate and strictly factual. She felt as though she were reading aloud one of those school essays, "What I Did on My Holiday," only this one was entitled "What I'm Doing with My Life." As Mr. Court listened attentively and nodded every now and then, Liberty struggled to keep her resentment in check. The ridiculous process felt both intrusive and demeaning.

"And are you enjoying your new situation?" the solicitor asked in a friendlier voice.

"It's fine," Liberty replied flatly. "Everything's fine." *Except for the fact that I'm here, reporting to you, because of some sodding stupid game that my dead mother insisted that we play,* she thought. Swan appeared to have lost interest in her undercover operation once her lunch had been served and was mopping up every last morsel of her beef and ale pie with relish.

"Would anyone like dessert?" Mr. Court's somewhat deflated tone implied that he hoped no one did. Liberty shook her head, eager to bring the torturous proceedings to a close. But Swan had other ideas.

"I should love dessert!" she piped up. "The steamed apple pudding with custard sounds divine!"

Mr. Court and Liberty settled for coffees while Swan enjoyed her pudding. After a few mouthfuls she narrowed her eyes and waggled her spoon accusingly at Mr. Court. "It must be very difficult playing God."

The solicitor looked a little startled. "I'm not sure I know what you mean," he replied.

"Well, as I understand it, you're here to judge this woman against some mysterious set of criteria in order to decide whether or not she has *earned* her inheritance."

Liberty shifted uneasily in her seat. It seemed that the two glasses of Malbec Swan had enjoyed with her lunch were kicking in. Mr. Court sighed.

"I'm simply doing my job," he replied evenly. "I am obliged to carry out Mrs. Bell's instructions as they were specified in her will."

Swan arched a single eyebrow high in disapproval and attacked a piece of apple viciously with her spoon. "What sort of mother abandons the fate of her only child—a loving daughter who gave up everything to nurse her mother faithfully in her final days, I might add—to the mercy of a solicitor who knows nothing about her? And what sort of solicitor is prepared to participate in such shameful she-nanigans? I hope your fee is worth it, Mr. Court, because frankly I don't know how you can sleep at night!"

The tassel on her beret swung back and forth and her pearls rattled as Swan delivered her speech with all the passion and projection of a wronged protagonist in an episode of *Poirot*. Several of their fellow diners were now openly eavesdropping, fascinated by the plotline that was unfolding before them. Swan had evidently dropped the promised charm from her offensive, but Liberty was grateful for her support. And Swan had more to say.

"Miss Bell is an efficient, hardworking, clean-living woman of impeccable morals. She has proved to be an invaluable assistant to my sister-in-law and a responsible carer for my great-nephew. What more do you need to know?"

There was just a moment of expectant hush from the diners at the tables around them before the spell was broken by the clatter of a dropped mobile phone falling onto the tiled floor, and the hum of conversations began again. Liberty's cheeks flushed with pleasure at Swan's praise, but also with guilt at her rose-tinted representation of Liberty's morals. She had made her sound like Mary Poppins. Mr. Court sipped his coffee before replying.

"I can't pretend that I enjoy all aspects of my job, but in the words of Dolly Parton, if you want the rainbow, you gotta put up with the rain. Your mother told me that, Miss Bell—I understand she was a fan—and I've never forgotten it. Believe me, I have no desire to withhold from you what is rightfully yours, but I am legally bound to comply with your mother's wishes."

"Yes, yes!" Swan replied impatiently. "You've already said. There's nothing wrong with our hearing—or our memories. What happens now?"

Before Mr. Court could answer, the waiter arrived with the bill, which Mr. Court duly paid. Having tapped his card, he returned to Swan's question. "I shall email Miss Bell in a few months' time to arrange another lunch appointment," he said.

Liberty looked exasperated. "So that's it? I've failed whatever test it was she set?"

Mr. Court shook his head slowly. "It really isn't like that. But I must be satisfied that her conditions are met. Believe me, your mother only wanted the best for you."

"Well, she had a bloody funny way of showing it!" Swan was struggling to get her arm into the sleeve of her coat, and Mr. Court gallantly went to assist her. She managed to thank him through gritted teeth before making one final remonstration on Liberty's behalf. "So, you mean to tell us that despite everything I've told you about Miss Bell being an exemplary employee and model citizen, you are still not satisfied?"

"I'm afraid not." He picked up his own coat and shrugged himself into it. "Perhaps, in some ways, because of what you said," he muttered, almost to himself.

"And there's nothing more you can tell me? No clues as to how I might 'improve my rating'?" Liberty asked, as she and Swan followed Mr. Court outside.

He turned to face her and tipped his head thoughtfully to one side. "Perhaps, Liberty, you're overthinking this. I'll be in touch."

They watched him walk off in the direction of the town before crossing the road to walk the opposite way beside the river back to Venetia's house.

"Well, that was a complete waste of time!" Liberty rammed her hands deep into the pockets of her coat.

"I'm not so sure."

Swan took her arm, and they began their way home, negotiating a careful path through the patches of goose poo.

"I think we need to write down everything that happened when we get back and everything he said. Well, everything that we can remember. He may have given something away without realizing it. Even his choice of food might have some hidden significance."

Liberty laughed out loud. "I hardly think that toad-in-the-hole is going to tell us anything!"

WHEN KITE GOT home from school that afternoon, he wanted a blow-by-blow account. He sat at the kitchen table drinking tea and eating biscuits while Swan consulted her notebook. She had written her report of the lunch appointment as soon as they had returned, but as she read it aloud, it all sounded rather inconsequential—and Kite said so.

"I can't believe you didn't find any clues! I told you I should have been Sherlock Holmes."

"And Mr. Court didn't ask you anything else?" Venetia peered over Swan's shoulder, trying to read her untidy scrawl. "Didn't give you even a hint of what he's looking for?"

Liberty shook her head. "Not a sausage, save for the ones in his toad-in-the-hole."

"I hate toad-in-the-hole when we have it for school lunch!" Kite pretended to stick his finger down his throat to demonstrate his disgust. "The sausages are always gristly like witches' fingers."

"*Which*, no doubt, you have eaten on numerous occasions, thus qualifying you to make the comparison?" Venetia teased him.

"Mr. Court did, in fact, say one thing worthy of note."

They all looked at Swan, and having captured their attention, she paused for a moment for what Hawk had always called *actio effectus* when it was used in the courtroom.

"Just before he left, he said, 'Perhaps, Liberty, you're overthinking this.'"

"He never calls me Liberty."

"Precisely."

CHAPTER 32

Venetia hung up the phone and took a deep breath, which she exhaled forcefully, as though blowing out the candles on a birthday cake. For better or worse, it was done. She was the legal owner of a church and a ballroom. All she had to do now was figure out what to do with them. Evangeline would, no doubt, take care of the church. But the ballroom? *Be careful what you wish for*, she thought.

It was the first day of half term, and Kite was spending it with his friend Ravi, whose parents had taken the boys to the Natural History Museum. Once Kite had become a day boy again, their friendship had been tentatively reestablished, much to Venetia's relief, and since Christmas, Kite had brought Ravi home several times, and they had even had a sleepover at Ravi's. But she knew that Kite would be disappointed not to have been there at the precise moment when *their* ownership was confirmed.

Liberty had taken Swan to the hairdresser. It was now clear that the duration of Swan's stay with Venetia had become indefinite—quite possibly permanent. Nightingale was rarely at home, and when she was, she invariably had her "boy toy" with her. Swan had met him only twice but had taken an instant and apparently irrevocable dislike to him, which was unfortunate because he had recently become Nightingale's fiancé. Venetia felt sure that it must have been lonely for Swan on her own in the family home once Nightingale had begun dating. The sisters had lived there alone since their parents had died and their brothers had left to have families of their own. Swan and Nightingale had cared for their parents in their dotage and then stayed put after their deaths. Venetia had sometimes wondered why neither of them had married, and now it appeared that Nightingale was making up for lost time in the however many years she had left. And good for her, thought Venetia. But she also felt sympathy for Swan, who had suddenly found herself supplanted in her sister's affection by a playboy plumber. Besides, Venetia's was a big house—built for a family. And that's what they were. *Who* they were. Liberty seemed to spend less and less time in her flat these days, and she had readily extended her role as assistant to include Swan without being asked. Venetia had spoken to her privately about it, not wanting to impose on her goodwill by assuming that she was happy to help Swan too. But Liberty had assured her that it wasn't a problem. It seemed that she and Swan had bonded over their lunch date with Mr. Court and their subsequent efforts to decipher the clues that Swan still insisted he had let slip.

And so, when her solicitor had telephoned that morning, Venetia was alone in the house with Colin, and she was glad. She needed some time to allow this new reality to sink in and for her emotions to settle. She reached down and allowed her fingertips to ruffle the soft fur on the dog's neck.

"We'll have a cup of tea," she told him, smiling again to herself at the age-old cliché that was nonetheless a reliable source of succor in times of disquiet.

Colin drank his tea lukewarm from his bowl, his untidy tongue splashing milky droplets onto the kitchen floor. Venetia made hers in a porcelain cup and saucer, piping hot with a shot of brandy to mark the import of what had just happened. And to calm her nerves. She carried it through to Hawk's study, which she had taken to using more and more these days to deal with the paperwork that had been associated with the purchase of the ballroom. Despite all her best intentions after Hawk had died, she still hadn't finished clearing the contents of his desk. Liberty had dealt with the files in the cabinet, but his appointment diaries still sat in a tidy tower on the floor and the desk drawers had yet to be emptied. Venetia had begun to look through the diaries when they were still searching for a way to contact Francis Taylor and Torin McGuire, the mystery guests at Hawk's funeral. But many of the entries meant nothing to Venetia. Hawk had often just written times and initials with only an occasional more detailed note, and nothing seemed to relate to Messrs. Taylor and McGuire. After a while, Venetia had run out of steam, and as the weeks and months went on, the activities of the living took over from the enigmas of the dead. But now, Venetia realized, these unanswered questions had begun to unsettle her.

She had promised herself that when Hawk died, she would start afresh. That she would discover who she was and who she wanted to be, independent of any role she might fulfill. And she had made a promising beginning with her new clothes and new hair. She had welcomed her grandson and sister-in-law to share her home, and even the granny nanny—although Liberty was turning out to be so much more than that. And now she had a project—her very own ballroom! And not just *any* ballroom, but the one where she had spent some of the happiest days of her life. Where she had worked, danced, laughed, made friends, and met her future husband. Where she had also met the man who had left an ugly stain on her life, like the ink from Hawk's pen on the carpet beneath her foot now. An indelible mark that she had learned to live with. But that man had had nothing to do with her decision to buy the ballroom. He was no longer a specter requiring exorcism. She had made her peace with the legacy that he had left her many years ago. No, the ballroom was destined to be a place of joy. Not just for her, but for as many people as she could share it with. So why was it that she could not allow herself to feel joy, now that her new life had truly begun? Why did she feel as though she were trying to drive away in an Aston Martin with the hand brake on? It was understandable that she should be a little daunted by what she had taken on, but it was exciting too. She knew that, but she couldn't feel it. Something was holding her back, and she needed to work out what it was.

Venetia picked up the copy of *The Lion, the Witch and the Wardrobe* that lay on Hawk's desk—the one she had found at the back of the drawer. She flicked open the cover to the page where the inscription was written above the initials A. F. Perhaps it was the ghosts that Hawk had left behind that were troubling her? The elusive funeral guests and the unfamiliar A. F., whose C. S. Lewis quotation was so apposite for Hawk. Was it a warning or a dare—or both?

When I became a man, I put away childish things, including the fear of childishness and the desire to be very grown up.

Whatever their intention, the words implied an intimacy between A. F. and Hawk that had afforded an insight into her husband's nature and an affection that had permitted the proffering of gentle advice. An intimacy and affection that Venetia had known nothing about, from a person she had never met and Hawk had never mentioned. Of course, the book could have been bought secondhand and the inscription intended for someone else entirely—a memorandum of previous ownership. But if that were the case, why wasn't it on one of the bookshelves in the study rather than hidden at the back of a drawer?

When Liberty had been unable to track down Francis Taylor and Torin McGuire, Venetia had thought it of little importance. But now she remembered their striking sincerity, the pale green eyes of the one who had said, "We thought of him often," and the way he had taken her hand in both of his instead of shaking it. She recalled how they had stood apart from Hawk's other friends and acquaintances and disappeared without saying goodbye. These two men and the enigmatic A. F. were a triptych of strangers to her. But were they known to each other? she wondered.

"Oh, Hawk!" She sighed out loud, and Colin was immediately by her side. He echoed her sigh and dropped his head into her lap. He stared up at her with his soulful brown eyes.

"What would you do in my shoes?" Venetia asked him. "Would you want to know, or would you be happy to let sleeping dogs lie?"

The dog burped. He had drunk his tea too quickly.

"Good point," Venetia replied with a smile. But she knew now that she couldn't move forward without looking back. Her marriage to Hawk had been one that was largely founded on compromises, tacit agreements, and mutual respect and affection. But perhaps not complete honesty—not full disclosure. She had always trusted him to be a decent man, a good husband and father, and as far as she knew he had been. But there was a part of Hawk that had always been indistinct, like a distant horizon. And no matter how far Venetia had walked, she had never come close enough to comprehend its landscape. It was a foreign country to her, but could it be home to A. F., Francis Taylor, and Torin McGuire? Venetia needed to know. She needed to understand, finally and fully, the man she had agreed to marry "till death do us part."

At the sound of the front door opening, Colin jumped to his feet. Venetia followed him into the hallway at a more decorous pace. Swan was standing in front of the mirror, her hair a crown of rigid curls and her face a gargoyle of fury.

"That bloody hairdresser has made me look like a cauliflower!"

CHAPTER 33

Any doubts that Venetia might have had about buying the ballroom were swept away in the tsunami of relief and joy that burst from Evangeline when she heard the news. Venetia had taken a stroll down to the drop-in center with Colin to tell her in person while Liberty was preparing lunch for Swan. Evangeline and Norma were busy serving sandwiches and cups of tea to a few of the regulars, including Tommy, who was in his usual spot by the radiator. But today he had a companion: a scruffy little dog with wiry fur that stuck out in all directions, giving him the look of a long-legged hedgehog. While Colin wandered over to introduce himself to the newcomer, Venetia took Evangeline through to the church so that she could speak to her in private. She didn't want to make a big announcement just yet, and she anticipated that Evangeline's reaction might not exactly be discreet. She was right. Evangeline flung her arms around Venetia and sobbed. It was as though a dam had burst and all the months of stress and uncertainty were being washed away in a torrent of messy, hiccuping tears. When she had recovered herself a little, she managed a few words of thanks.

"God bless you, Venetia! I swear that even if I live to be a hundred, I'll never be able to thank you enough! I've been so scared about what would happen if we had to leave. I couldn't bear to let everyone down like that."

Venetia was a little taken aback. Until then, she had always judged Evangeline to be indomitable. But in that moment, she understood that Evangeline's steadfast portrayal of strength and optimism was for the protection of those under her care, and hid the true burden of her fears, which she had borne in secret and alone. Venetia also realized that it meant she had more in common with Evangeline than she had ever thought.

The following morning, Venetia returned with her full cohort. Liberty was armed with a clipboard, and, not to be outdone, Kite had brought along his own notebook and pencil. Swan had brought a hip flask containing apricot brandy. Both she and Kite were disappointed that Tommy and his new dog were nowhere to be seen, but according to Evangeline he might put in an appearance around lunchtime. Swan elected to stay downstairs with Evangeline and do her daily crossword while the others headed upstairs to the ballroom. Venetia was keen to make a proper assessment of what needed doing before it could be used again. A building survey had shown it to be structurally sound, but the decor and furnishings were in need of urgent attention.

"What's up there?" Kite pointed to a door at the top of the steps that led up to the floor above the ballroom.

"From what I can remember, it's just the attic," Venetia replied.

Kite's eyes lit up. "Can I go and explore? There might be things up there that we can use. There might be treasures!"

Venetia smiled. "It's probably just full of dust and cobwebs."

"But can't I just go and check?"

"All right. But be careful."

Kite galloped up the stairs before his grandmother could change her mind. Colin went to follow, but Venetia grabbed his collar.

"Not you, lovely boy. We don't know what the floor's like up there. You might tread on something sharp."

In the attic, Kite was already wondering if he could persuade Nisha to let him turn it into his den. It was a huge space. Light poured in through the windows despite the layers of grime encrusted on the glass, and Kite could see for miles over the treetops. It *was* very dusty, and the beams across the ceiling were festooned with cobwebs that trembled every now and again, disturbed by a draft that crept in through some crack or crevice. There were numerous boxes, a few bits of furniture—several small tables, a couple of metal music stands, and dozens of chairs—a record player, a box full of records, and a large trunk. Kite heaved the lid of the trunk open to reveal piles of sheet music and old posters. The posters advertised dance lessons, dances, discos, and special events that had been held in the ballroom. Kite pulled a few of them out. Although the trunk itself was thick with dust, its contents had been protected from both dirt and sunlight, and the colors on the posters were still bright. Excited by his discovery, Kite selected a few samples to take downstairs to show the others. But as he headed toward the stairs, something caught his eye.

At the far end of the room beside an upturned packing crate, a single chair was positioned by a window as though someone had been sitting there, admiring the view. Kite moved closer to take a better look. Strangely, the chair looked clean, as though someone had wiped the dust from its seat, and on the floor poking out from under the packing crate was a single playing card. Kite picked it up and turned it over. The five of diamonds. He sat down in the chair and looked out over the river. Who else had been sitting here, he wondered, and what were they doing in the attic? He would ask Evangeline. Leaving the card on the packing case, he gathered up the posters and trotted off downstairs to the ballroom, where Liberty was making notes as she worked her way around the room with Venetia.

"Look what I found! I knew that there'd be treasure!" Kite unrolled some of the posters to show them. "And there's tons more up there. And a record player and records."

Venetia was almost as excited as Kite. "These would look wonderful in frames on the wall," she said. As she leafed through them, one in particular caught her eye. "New Year's Eve Dance and Disco, December 31, 1971," the bright red and blue letters proclaimed above an illustration of a man and woman dancing beneath a disco ball, surrounded by balloons and colored streamers. She held it up for Liberty and Kite to see.

"I was there," she told them. "And so was your grandpa," she added, smiling at Kite.

"Well, that one definitely has to go up," said Liberty, making a note on her clipboard.

Venetia had already explained to Liberty that she was keen to restore the ballroom to its former glory and wanted to keep as much of the original furniture as possible, so the posters were a fortuitous find.

"These mirrors just need a good clean," Venetia said as she traced a pattern across the mottled glass with her fingertip. "And the chairs will look as good as new once they've been reupholstered. Dark blue velvet, I think."

Liberty made another note.

"But I don't think the curtains can be saved," Venetia continued. She held up the tattered fabric of one of them to survey the damage wreaked by moths and sunlight. "We'll need to measure the windows and get new ones made."

"What about the chandeliers?" asked Liberty, pointing up at them with her pen. "Do they still work?"

Venetia tried the light switches on the wall, and the chandeliers flickered reluctantly before settling into a feeble glow that was barely visible through the dust and cobwebs. Venetia turned them off.

"Well, they work. But they need a professional clean—and it looks as though the wiring needs checking too."

By the time they had finished, Liberty had filled six pages of notes, and they were in desperate need of a cup of tea. Downstairs, Norma and Norman were serving sandwich lunches, and Evangeline was in the church preparing for an afternoon service. Kite went to show her what he had found in the attic.

"Nisha was actually there," he told her, unfurling the New Year's Eve poster. "And so was Grandpa."

"Well, well." Evangeline nodded and planted her hands firmly on her hips. "I think it must be a sign. A sign that your grandmother was meant to buy this place."

"And there's other stuff up there too. There's a record player and records, and boxes that I haven't even looked in yet! I'm going to ask Nisha if she'll let me have it as my den."

"Maybe you'll find more treasure," Evangeline told him with a wink.

Kite remembered the chair by the window. "Does anyone else ever go up there?"

Evangeline frowned. "I'm pretty sure the estate agent had a look around, but that was ages ago, and the surveyor of course. But other than that . . ." She shook her head. "I certainly don't. I'm too afraid of the mice! Now, how about a sandwich?"

As Evangeline had predicted, Tommy had arrived and was seated at his usual table, where he had been joined by Swan. His little dog was having a fine time playing with Colin.

"What's his name?" asked Kite, scratching the dog's ears.

Tommy shrugged. "I dunno. He's a stray."

"But haven't you given him one now you've adopted him?"

"He's not mine. He just follows me, and I give him a bit of food," Tommy replied gruffly as he stirred more sugar into his tea.

"But you must call him something?" Kite persisted.

Tommy didn't answer.

"Can I give him a name, then?"

Tommy looked up in exasperation. "Suit yourself."

Swan took the hip flask from her handbag and unscrewed the lid.

She sloshed some of its contents into Tommy's tea and then a little into her own cup.

"He looks as though he's stuck his paw into an electric socket, the way his fur sticks out. And he could do with a bath," she said, wafting her hand back and forth in front of her nose. "So I'd call him Spiky or Smelly."

"Don't be mean!" Kite admonished her. "Although he does look quite spiky," he conceded. "I know—let's call him Hedgehog!"

Venetia, who had been discussing her plans for the ballroom with Evangeline, was ready to go home. "Come along, Kite. Time to go," she said. "Put your coat on, and don't forget the posters."

Kite had left the posters in the church where he had shown them to Evangeline. On the way to fetch them, he had an idea. He galloped back up the stairs to the attic. He took his notebook and pencil from his pocket and wrote a few words before carefully tearing out the page, then hurried over to the single chair by the window and left his message on the seat.

Who are you?

CHAPTER 34

L iberty leaned back in her chair and gazed out the window into the garden, where the watery dawn light was just beginning to dilute the darkness. It was only seven, but she had been sitting at her laptop for over an hour already. She stretched her arms above her head and felt her stiff shoulders crack with relief. The half-drunk mug of coffee by her side had grown cold, and she got up to make herself another. As she waited for the kettle to boil, she picked up the photograph album for the umpteenth time and traced her forefinger over the gold embossed initials with which her mother had had the front cover personalized.

L. S. B.

Liberty never told anyone her middle name. She hadn't even told Graham. It was too embarrassing. "Liberty" was bad enough, but her full name was "Liberty Starlight Bell." It had been her mother's doing, of course. Her dad would have been perfectly happy with Claire or Karen—something comfortable and unremarkable. Nothing that would invite raised eyebrows or wry smiles. When she was a little girl, her mum used to tell her that she was her twinkling star. But Liberty had never felt like a star—twinkling or otherwise. She had been a timid child, and her name had always felt ill-fitting, as though she had been given someone else's coat from the cloakroom by mistake. Someone bolder and brighter—someone with swagger.

She couldn't help but fear that she had been a disappointment to her mother. Liberty remembered her mother's excitement when she had been offered a place at university. Perhaps she thought that it would be the making of her daughter, that it would prize Liberty out of her shell or maybe even encourage her to discover her wild side. But it turned out that Liberty didn't have one. After three years, she had returned home having gained a degree and lost her virginity (the result of a brief fling in her final year with an anthropology student), but otherwise much the same. No tattoo, no belly button piercing, no burning desire to change the world.

Liberty had been happy to be inconspicuous and allow life to happen to her rather than steer her own course. She had taken a string of safe but boring jobs and drifted into a series of unmemorable relationships with men who had been so nondescript that they were almost interchangeable. Most of these relationships had not so much broken up as ground to a halt, like a clockwork toy that neither party could be bothered to wind up again. There had been only one that was special. Or at least it had been to Liberty. She had met Jake at a friend's wedding. They had been seated next to each other—the victims of her friend's matchmaking. Jake had been handsome in an untidy way, with floppy hair, long, loose limbs, and a lazy smile, and he had radiated an easy confidence that was both reassuring and irresistible to Liberty. He had just returned from a season working as a chef on a luxury yacht and was full of tales about the pampered guests who had chartered *The Diamond Empress*. Much to her surprise, he had asked her out. He had gotten a job in a local hotel restaurant that came with accommodation, and they had dated for around eighteen months. Afterward, Liberty always wondered if their relationship was only ever an interlude between adventures for Jake, or whether he had genuinely intended to make a go of it. Whatever the answer, in the end his wanderlust had won. He had packed his bags one day and returned to the yachting life, leaving Liberty a bouquet of red roses and a note of apology and farewell. She had kept the roses until the petals withered and the leaves dried up and crumbled into pieces at the slightest touch. *Like me*, she had thought, after he had gone. And then there had been Graham.

At least the fact that she had never married meant that she had been spared the mother of all mother-of-the-bride outfits that she was sure Bernadette would have worn. But she worried that her mother would have liked grandchildren—and she knew that her dad would have loved them. She had never intended to let them down, and her dad would have been so happy simply to see her make a home with a family of her own. But somehow, these modest milestones in life that seemed to come so effortlessly to others had inexplicably eluded Liberty. She hadn't even managed the ordinary, and she was pretty sure that her mum would have been hoping for the extraordinary.

But now, for the first time in a long time, Liberty was excited for the future. And perhaps for the first time ever she had a sense of purpose and direction, and a growing conviction that she was capable of far more than she had ever attempted up until now. Venetia was trusting her to manage the restoration of the ballroom and to come up with ideas that might enable it at least to break even as a business, if not turn a profit. Liberty's degree had been in business studies, but she had never really used it. University might have been years ago, but surely the principles couldn't have changed that much? It was the morning after their visit to assess the ballroom, and Liberty had been tapping away on her laptop, checking out upholsterers, professional cleaners, and painters and decorators. She was also researching insurance options for the building and what would be required for them to obtain a license to sell alcohol on the premises.

She put down the album and made her coffee. It was ironic that one of the photographs in the album had a connection to the ballroom, but one so unhappy and humiliating that Liberty had no intention of revealing it to Venetia. Liberty's mother had taken her to a music and movement class there when she was about four or five years old, and she had taken a photograph of Liberty wearing a frilly dress and dancing shoes in the garden just before they had left for the ballroom. Liberty hadn't wanted to go, and when the class began, she had stood in the corner trying hard not to be noticed. It was the exposure that terrified her: trying new things and potentially failing in front of people she didn't know. But she had been so nervous that she had wet herself and become the focus of everyone's unwelcome attention anyway. She could still remember the sting of hot urine running down her leg and soiling her new white socks and her mother's look of embarrassment. Or perhaps it was disappointment. Well, whatever it was that her mother wanted her to do now—and Mr. Court to approve—would have to wait. She had something more important to occupy her time. She had a ballroom to get up and running.

She had been working for another thirty minutes or so when there was a knock at the door. She checked her watch. She had been so busy that she had forgotten to go over to the house and help Kite make his breakfast. She opened the door to find Kite holding a plate piled high with toast and strawberry jam. The toast was a bit burnt and the slices cut rather raggedly, but Kite was smiling proudly.

"I thought you must be really busy because you forgot about me," he said without a trace of judgment or self-pity in his voice. "So I made enough toast for both of us."

Liberty wished she had the nerve to hug him.

CHAPTER 35

Colin led their procession up the Embankment at a brisk trot, and Swan brought up the rear at a more regal pace. In the middle, Kite was torn between keeping up with one and waiting for the other. The dog paused outside the Bubble and Squeak as a tantalizing waft of cooked breakfast tickled his nostrils, allowing their party to regroup. But Kite was so excited at the prospect of returning to the ballroom attic that he would have been quite happy to gallop all the way there. Nisha had agreed that he could make part of the attic his den, but that he would also need to clear a space and go through the other boxes first to see if he could find anything else that might be useful. It was an important job, and Kite was so proud to be helping his grandmother with their ballroom. But he was also keen to see if anyone had left an answer to his note. Liberty had been too busy to take him, and Nisha already had plans for that morning, but fortunately Swan had volunteered to go with him and "help out." She had no intention whatsoever of clambering up into a dirty attic, nor did she ever provide Evangeline with any practical assistance, but she quite enjoyed watching the comings and goings at the drop-in center and would always sit with Tommy and exchange a few words with him whenever she saw him.

It was midmorning, and the drop-in center was still quiet when they arrived. Evangeline was helping Norma wipe the tables and sweep the floor before their first visitors arrived.

"Good morning! Good morning!" she greeted them. "I thought

you might be back today," she said, winking at Kite. "I expect you're going back up in that attic to look for more treasure, aren't you?" She shuddered. "Just don't bring any creepy-crawlies with you when you come back down!"

Kite grinned and headed off upstairs, eagerly followed by Colin.

"And what about you?" Evangeline turned her attention to Swan. "Aren't you going with him?"

Swan arched one eyebrow and tilted her head slightly. "Do I look as if I'm about to go rooting around in the roof in the company of incontinent rodents?"

Evangeline laughed and held out the broom she was carrying. "Then perhaps you'd like to give us a hand getting this place ship-shape before our friends arrive?" she teased.

"I'm afraid I'm not dressed for domestic chores. But I suppose I could switch on the tea urn and set out some cups and saucers," Swan replied magnanimously.

Upstairs, Kite pushed open the door to the attic and Colin followed him inside, his nose immediately twitching at the smorgasbord of smells that greeted him. Kite went straight over to the chair by the window. His note was gone, but there was something in its place.

VENETIA SETTLED HERSELF at Hawk's desk and slapped her palms down with a purposeful thud on a surface richly patinated by years of paperwork and penmanship. Liberty was working at her laptop in the kitchen, and Kite had gone to the ballroom with Swan. Venetia hoped that giving him the independence and responsibility of sorting through the boxes in the attic might bolster his confidence. She had loved seeing him so excited to be given the opportunity to contribute something to his grandmother's madcap project. Meanwhile Venetia, having delegated the initial tasks concerning the ballroom to Liberty, had decided to make good her resolution to clear out Hawk's desk and try to uncover the people and places in his life that he had withheld from her. She knew that she was taking a serious risk by visiting a past that had lain undisturbed and inaccessible to her until now. Perhaps inaccessible for good reason—but good for whom? Hawk, or herself? Perhaps both. But the book with its inscription was an oddity among the remnants of Hawk's ordered life, like an imperfection on an otherwise smooth facade. If Venetia prodded at a patch of loose plaster, would the whole wall come tumbling down? There was only one way to find out.

She began emptying the desk one drawer at a time. Her husband had been tidy and methodical. The top drawer contained pens, pencils, erasers, sharpeners, paper clips, rulers, a spare blotting pad, and a bottle of ink. In the next were blank sheets of paper—plain, lined, A4, and A5—with an assortment of envelopes. There were empty folders, both paper and plastic; sticky labels; and unused notepads. Hawk's desk was a stationery store in miniature—practical, professional, and entirely predictable. Except for the bottom drawer on the left-hand side. When Venetia pulled it open, it stuck a little. It was very full and unexpectedly untidy, crammed with a miscellany of mementos. There was a battered cricket ball with its stitching coming undone—Venetia remembered Hawk teaching Heron how to bowl with it in the garden, and how their son's first attempt at a googly had scored a smashed pane of glass in the greenhouse roof. There were several hand-drawn birthday cards from Kite, a key ring with a plastic hawk attached (a Father's Day gift from Heron years ago), and a small tin box containing a few old photographs. Among them was a snapshot of Hawk and Venetia on a windswept beach in Norfolk. They were both smiling, and Hawk had a protective arm around her shoulders.

Venetia stared at the photograph. She had been around twelve weeks pregnant with Heron, and her hands had been constantly drawn to the slight swell of her stomach, in wonder that a new life was ripening inside her. Hawk had taken her away for the weekend to make up for the fact that he had been unable to attend her first ultra-sound. He had been in court, and she had gone alone. The weekend had been spent taking long walks on the beach, having lazy lunches in the pub, and Venetia snoozing in the afternoon while Hawk read P. G. Wodehouse novels. The photo had been taken by a woman walking a springer spaniel called Zebedee. It was strange, Venetia thought, that she could still remember the dog's name. Hawk had asked the woman if she would mind taking the picture.

"My wife's pregnant," he had said out of the blue. The woman had smiled and congratulated them. Hawk had been so pleased—and proud—when Venetia had told him. And that weekend he had been carefully solicitous, insisting that she rest after their walks and eat plenty of fresh, healthy food. Venetia had been touched at first, but mildly irritated after a while. Later, she had put it down to unruly hormones.

In the very bottom of the drawer was a large brown leather wallet, tatty with use and age. It contained one of each denomination of old English paper currency: ten shillings, one pound, five pounds, twenty pounds, and fifty pounds. Tucked away in its folds were a couple of train tickets, a few receipts, and a scrap of paper on which was written a string of numbers. A phone number, perhaps? It didn't look like Hawk's writing. At that moment Venetia's mobile rang, and she scrabbled to retrieve it from underneath the contents of Hawk's desk drawers that she had piled onto the desk. She glanced at the screen. It was Heron's number.

"Hello, Mum? It's me, Heron." He sounded exhausted, as though the enunciation of each word was a Herculean effort. "I think I'm in trouble."

Venetia pressed the phone to her ear, and as her son began pouring out his woes, there was a commotion in the hallway.

Kite had arrived home for lunch with Colin and Swan. Liberty came out from the kitchen, and while she was helping Swan out of her coat, Kite galloped up the stairs, taking them two at a time. Once in the privacy of his room with the door closed behind him, he shrugged off his rucksack, unzipped one of the side pockets, and took out the object that had been left on the chair in the attic. He had folded it flat to bring it home, but now he gently pulled the folds apart to reveal an origami model of a bird made from old newspaper. Kite stood it on his windowsill. It looked like a crow.

CHAPTER 36

Crow would need to be more careful in the future. No more daytime visits now that the building had been sold. The boy had almost caught him. He had been about to sneak into the attic when he heard a noise. He risked a quick glance through the window and saw the boy rummaging through the contents of a trunk, watched by a large dog. For a moment he had been tempted to go in anyway and speak to him. But he didn't. Crow had no right to be there. He was trespassing on private property—breaking and entering. And besides, he didn't know how the dog might react to an intruder. But he couldn't help watching for just a few moments—shooting glances that captured snapshots of the boy's curiosity and excitement.

Crow had always assumed that he would be a father, maybe a grandfather, by now. He had assumed that his life would follow the template laid down by his parents—if not in detail, then at least in principle. He knew, of course, that things weren't always straightforward, that there were obstacles to overcome and heartaches to endure. This was real life and not a fairy tale. His parents had been almost broken by the death of their youngest child, but together they had survived and found the strength to leave their beloved Poland and build a new life in a strange country with their eleven-year-old son. Together, as a family, they were home—no matter where they were. Home was never a place, but rather the bond between them. And since that bond had been broken, Crow had never made another home, never managed to re-create for himself the example that his parents had given him. He could only imagine their disappointment, but it couldn't have been any worse than his own.

After a final glimpse through the window, he turned away. He would come back tonight when the place was empty. He retraced his steps down the fire escape, and his left leg thrummed with pain as he struggled to control its defective movement. Tears of frustration pricked his eyes; it was bad enough that his lame leg was a constant reminder of a past he would prefer to forget, but the fact that one of his own limbs was always working against him felt like the ultimate betrayal. Back on the ground, he steadied himself for a moment. It was cold and he really wanted a coffee. He knew that he could simply walk around the corner and into the drop-in center, where he could sit in the warmth and drink free coffee. They would probably give him lunch too. And they would be kind. It was the kindness that he couldn't bear. He had been to one of their church services once, more out of curiosity than anything else. He had heard that it was a spiritualist church, and yes, perhaps he had hoped for something—a message or a feeling, some kind of connection to his sister or his parents. But what he had received was kindness. The woman called Evangeline had introduced a visiting medium who had given messages to others but not to him. After the service, Evangeline came and spoke to him. Thanked him for coming and apologized that no one had come through for him.

"Perhaps next time," she told him with a smile.

When she leveled her steady gaze at him, he felt as though she were looking inside him to see what he was hiding. Her smile faded just a little, and she reached out and placed her hand on his arm. He could feel the warmth even through his shirtsleeve. He couldn't remember the last time anyone had deliberately touched him like that.

"Come back. You're always welcome here."

And so he had. But he kept to the attic unless the building was empty—so that no one could be kind to him. Because kindness, he feared, could be his undoing. Kindness might tempt him to lower the guard that had been his protection for so long. It might seduce him with possibilities of friendship and belonging—of happiness. If he were to accept kindness, he would be vulnerable again. After everything he had sacrificed to make himself strong and reliant only on himself, it was a risk that he couldn't take. So instead of warmth and free coffee, he chose to walk in the cold over the suspension bridge to the café by the boating lake. He bought a flat white he could ill afford and sat down on a seat close to the bandstand. He turned up the collar on his coat and cupped his hands around his coffee. The bandstand was a Victorian construction of curlicued wrought iron. Its stone steps were littered with leaves and old conker shells, and a squirrel sat among them, watching him warily with its blackcurrant eyes, tail twitching.

Crow sipped his coffee and tried to convince himself that this was the best way. For years now he had kept himself apart. Marek, the friend who had found him work and a place to stay after his marriage had ended, had moved to London a few months later in pursuit of a better job. He had asked Crow to go with him and his family, but Crow had declined. He would have felt like a cuckoo in the nest.

When Crow had first arrived in Bedford, Marek had shown him around and taken him to the town's Dom Polski club to introduce him to the local Polish community. Crow had tried to fit in and make new friends, but there were always too many questions about his past and his family that he had to dodge or answer with lies. He had stopped visiting his parents, unable to bear the anguish in their eyes each time they saw what their son had become. He hadn't even felt able to tell Marek the whole truth. How could he have allowed a woman to reduce him to this? Crow and Marek had known each other since they had been small boys back in Poland, and their friendship had survived the years since then despite sporadic contact and physical distance. When Crow had turned to Marek for help, he had agreed without asking for an explanation. Crow had told him that his marriage had broken down, but his pride would not allow him to confess that his wife had been unfaithful with a bastard who had once been Crow's friend. When he had offered no further details, Marek hadn't pressed him. Perhaps the damaged version of Crow who had arrived at the train station late one Sunday evening with a single bag stuffed full of his belongings and eyes emptied of all emotion had been explanation enough.

The squirrel cackled a warning at a passing dog and scampered down the steps of the bandstand and up a nearby tree. Crow drained the last of his coffee and threw the cup in a litter bin. An elderly couple, arm in arm and wrapped up against the cold, stopped beside the bandstand to admire it. The old man turned to look at his wife.

"If there was a band playing," he said, "I'd ask you to dance."

His wife shook her head. "You don't need a band, you could sing. Go on—I dare you!"

The old man winked at Crow. "We've been married for sixty-one years today, and she can still wrap me around her little finger. Mind you, I wouldn't have it any other way!"

He took his wife's hand and led her up the steps into the bandstand.

"Happy anniversary!" Crow called after them, and without turning around, the man raised his hand in acknowledgment. Crow watched them dance for a moment before walking away. But something inside his head—or maybe his heart—had shifted.

CHAPTER 37

Kite lay down on his tummy and stretched out his arm to reach for the box that his new sneakers had come in and that he now kept hidden under his bed. The box was home to his recently acquired menagerie. The crow had been joined by a frog, a mouse, and a rabbit. Kite was amazed that such realistic figures could be made simply by folding old newspaper. He had returned to the ballroom's attic every day for the rest of his half-term holiday, and every day a new creature had been waiting for him. But today was Sunday, and Nisha had insisted on taking him and Ravi to the cinema and then for pizzas afterward.

"You can't spend all your time in that attic," Nisha had told him. "And anyway, you can tell Ravi all about your new den."

Ravi may have been appalled when Kite asked for artichoke and pineapple on his pizza, but he had been suitably impressed when Kite had told him about the attic full of treasures that was going to be his new den.

"It's brilliant!" Kite had told him. "And full of old stuff from the ballroom that we're going to use again. But the attic's going to be mine, isn't it, Nisha?"

His grandmother had smiled and nodded, and Ravi had dropped a piece of his pepperoni pizza down his front, staining his white T-shirt.

It had been a fun afternoon, but Kite wouldn't be able to go back to the attic until next weekend now. He lifted the lid of the box and

picked up the frog. He held it carefully in the palm of his hand, trying to read the newsprint that adorned its body. Yesterday, he had
taken a bar of chocolate that he had bought with his own money and
left it on the chair. He hoped that whoever was leaving the animals
for him would realize that the chocolate was a present. To say thank
you. Kite hadn't told Ravi about the mysterious visitor in the attic.
He hadn't told anyone. He sometimes felt a bit guilty about keeping it
from Nisha, but he liked the idea of having a secret friend whom no
one else knew about.

"Kite! Are you ready?"

It was Nisha's voice coming from the bottom of the stairs. They
were going to take Colin for a walk while Liberty cooked their supper and Swan interfered. Kite returned the frog to the box and shoved
it back under the bed, then quickly changed his shoes.

Venetia was waiting in the hallway, where Colin was wagging his
tail with excitement and pawing at the door. Kite pulled on his coat
and grabbed his beanie, which he dragged down over his ears.

"We're off now!" Venetia called, and Liberty appeared in the hallway, wiping her hands on her apron.

"It'll be ready in about forty-five minutes," she said, "so don't be
too long. Although I shouldn't think you're very hungry after all that
pizza," she added, grinning at Kite.

Kite rolled his eyes in protest. "I'm starving!"

"Come along, then. The sooner we go, the sooner we'll be back."

Rather than crossing the road and walking beside the river, they
headed toward the park and the bowling pavilion where Kite had hidden out when he had run away from school. The park was bisected
by a well-lit footpath, and the route they took retraced some of Kite's
wanderings on that day that had, thanks to the kindness of a stranger,
ended happily for all of them. Kite still thought about Lukasz. He
had asked Evangeline if she knew him, but she hadn't recognized the
name, and Kite's description of him had been too vague to help much.

"But he knew you," Kite had insisted. "He knew your name."

"Lots of people know my name, sweetheart—but it doesn't mean that I know them. Your friend has probably been here at some time or another or spoken to someone who has. But who knows," she had added, seeing Kite's downcast expression, "maybe he'll be back one day."

As they crossed the park, Colin kept his eyes peeled for late-to-bed squirrels, and his nostrils flared for the scent of Sunday suppers cooking in the houses that faced them. Venetia and Kite chatted about the film they had seen and the merits of pineapple on pizza.

"Are you all ready for school tomorrow?" Venetia asked. "Homework done and uniform ready?"

"Yes and yes!" Kite replied.

"And did you ring your mum and dad?"

He nodded thoughtfully. "I FaceTimed them." There was a brief silence. "Are Mum and Dad getting a divorce?"

Venetia was grateful that Colin chose that very moment to pause and relieve himself, giving her a chance to compose an appropriate answer while doing what was necessary with a poo bag. She batted the question back to her grandson. "Whatever gives you that idea?"

"Because they're always arguing, and Mum calls Dad 'your father' instead of 'Dad,' and sometimes when I ring and she's supposed to be there, she's out. And when I ask Dad where she is, he says she's had to go and see a man called Maurice about work and Dad seems really sad. And once when I FaceTimed them, Dad wasn't there, but Mum was. And so was Maurice."

Venetia wasn't entirely surprised by this news. She knew from her last conversation with Heron that things weren't going well and that he suspected Monica of having a dalliance with one of their French competitors in the property business. Heron was hoping that it was simply a fleeting fling. "Women of Monica's age are often held hostage by their hormones and behave completely out of character," he had proclaimed to Venetia with more hope than conviction in his voice, evidently forgetting that his mother was also a woman and had once been Monica's age herself. But he had never mentioned divorce. Venetia would have to ring Heron tomorrow and try to find out what was going on. But in the meantime, she did her best to reassure Kite, while taking care not to make any promises that might turn out to be false.

"Your mum and dad have both been working very hard, and it's probably been quite stressful starting up a new business. Married people sometimes have fallings-out and arguments, and times when they don't get on very well. It happens to everyone. But more often than not they just sort it out, or soldier on until things get back to normal."

Venetia remembered the "soldiering on" in her own marriage. But they had never really argued. And she and Hawk had made it through "till death do us part."

They had reached the other side of the park now and turned left to cut through to a tree-lined street of large Victorian houses that ran back down toward the river.

"But what if things don't get back to normal? What if Mum and Dad do get divorced and Mum marries Maurice and stays in France? Will *I* have to go and live in France?"

"That's a lot of what-ifs," Venetia replied gently. "But I promise you that whatever happens between your mum and dad—"

"And Maurice," Kite interjected.

"—they will love you every bit as much as they do now."

"Yes, but will I have to go and live in France?"

Venetia hesitated, recalling her intention not to make any doubtful promises. But then she saw the anxiety in her grandson's face. Kite had been so much happier, and his confidence had burgeoned, since he had been living with her. She was damned if she was going to allow the conjugal complications of his parents to undermine his progress. She had kept her concerns to herself when Kite was sent off unwillingly to boarding school, and look how well that had gone.

"No," she replied with absolute certainty. "You won't have to go and live in France."

Kite grinned. "I'm really starving now!"

"We'd best get a move on, then. We'll be in trouble with Liberty if we're late."

"And if Swan's drinking gin she'll be hammered!" Kite giggled uncontrollably at the hilarity of his own joke.

Venetia couldn't help but smile. "Who on earth taught you to say that?" she asked.

"Tommy."

CHAPTER 38

The day after Venetia's discussion with Kite about divorce, news came of a wedding. Venetia, Swan, and Liberty had just finished lunch when the phone in the hall rang. Swan, who was on the way to the sitting room to retrieve her newspaper, answered it and began a conversation with someone she clearly knew. Venetia wasn't intentionally eavesdropping, but Swan's horrified "Good God! How could you?!" was loud enough to be comfortably heard in the kitchen. Venetia and Liberty exchanged interrogative glances. Venetia got up, uncertain whether to go and see if Swan was all right. But before she could decide, Swan hung up, crashing the phone down into its cradle, and disappeared upstairs to her room. When she was still there more than an hour and a half later, Venetia began to feel uneasy. She went upstairs and knocked softly on Swan's door.

"I'm making some tea. Would you like a cup?"

There was silence. She knocked again, more purposefully this time, and tried the door, which opened to reveal Swan sitting on the end of her bed, staring out the window. Her face was as gray as the late-afternoon light. Her eyes were bloodshot and swollen, and her bony fist clutched a tissue that was soaked with tears. In that moment she looked both desperately old and pitifully childlike. Venetia sat down beside her and took her hand.

"Whatever's the matter, Swan?"

Swan took a deep, shuddering breath. "Nightingale has married her boy toy. They eloped to Brighton yesterday."

Venetia squeezed her sister-in-law's hand and tried to fathom why this news had precipitated such distress. Swan had known for some time that her sister was engaged. Why then had the marriage come as such a shock? Her question was answered without her having to ask.

"She didn't invite any of us. Her family. Me—her only sister!"

"Perhaps she didn't think you'd want to go," Venetia replied gently. "She knew you didn't like him. Perhaps they just wanted to keep it small—private."

"Private!" Swan expostulated with a strangled sob. "For all these years, we've lived together. Done everything together. We were so close—always there for each other—and now she's just abandoned me. Discarded me like an old shoe!"

"Oh, Swan! I'm sure it's not like that. She rang you to tell you. She wanted to share her news with you."

"After the fact! How could she exclude me like that?" Silent tears streamed down Swan's face, and she didn't bother to wipe them away.

Venetia wrapped her arm around Swan's shoulders and clasped her in a comforting hug while trying to recalibrate her understanding of this woman whom she had evidently misjudged for all these years. She had always taken Swan's tough, waspish demeanor at face value, assuming her to be as self-reliant and phlegmatic as the persona she presented. But it was clear now that beneath her prickly exterior there was an underbelly as soft and vulnerable as any hedgehog's. It was also clear that Venetia's perception of Swan's relationship with Nightingale was merely that of an outsider looking in and seeing only what was revealed at family get-togethers. She had sorely underestimated the strength of their sisterly bond and the sense of betrayal that Swan had felt over the past few months. Hawk had been very fond of his brother and sisters, but they were not a family given to public displays of affection or any meaningful discussion of emotions. He had also been a considerate and caring husband, but not exactly romantic, and never passionate or spontaneous. It had always seemed to Venetia that the Hamilton Hargreaveses' collective view was that emotions were something to be governed like a high-spirited horse—held on tight reins for fear that they might bolt. But Venetia knew only too well that to deny the expression of feelings didn't prevent or subdue their existence, and sometimes when they became too powerful or painful to command, they would burst out like air from an overfilled balloon. And here was Swan, the steely mistress of composure and caustic wit, weeping as though her heart was broken. Venetia was glad. Glad that Swan was able to rant and cry and berate her beloved sister and her hapless husband, because it might bring her some relief. Glad, because Swan's anguish was testimony to her love, and now that she had shared it, Venetia knew what was broken and would do everything in her power to mend it.

"I'm sure that Nightingale didn't mean to hurt you. Why on earth would she? As you say, you've always been so close. Isn't it more likely that she just didn't think? That she's so excited by her late-flowering love that it's made her a bit giddy?"

Swan sniffed and, looking up at Venetia, arched an eyebrow. "You've stolen that from Betjeman," she said, a little of her customary spirit returning.

"I believe his poem was called 'Late-Flowering Lust,'" Venetia replied.

"Well, I expect it's that too. Although the conjugal consummation of two geriatrics is not something that I particularly want to think about," Swan added with a theatrical shudder.

Colin appeared in the doorway and padded across the carpet to Swan. He looked up at her and sighed heavily before placing his head in her lap. As Swan trailed her fingers across his silky fur, Venetia saw her shoulders relax and a little of the sadness lift from her face.

"How about that tea now?"

Swan managed a half smile. "With a gin chaser?"

Venetia shook her head and grinned, relieved to see that Swan was rallying at last. "For medicinal purposes only," she agreed.

They had their drinks in the sitting room with the curtains still open as daylight dwindled and streetlights came on, casting pools of light onto the pavement below.

"Perhaps you could ring Nightingale later," Venetia suggested gently as Swan sipped her drink. Swan set down her glass with a clatter, and Venetia wondered if she had pushed her too far too soon. Swan took a deep breath and placed her slender hands down into her lap, pushing hard before exhaling as though preparing for something arduous or painful. But when she spoke, her voice was soft and wistful.

"I want her to be happy—I do. I want her to love and be loved. I want her to have what I once had. What I gave up for her."

Swan paused, and as the silence continued, Venetia wondered if that was all she was going to say. Venetia was desperate to ask her what she meant but worried that any interruption might distract Swan and stall her confessions. Then the silence was broken by Kite bursting through the front door, wearing two bags like panniers containing his games kit and schoolbooks, and brandishing a hockey stick in both hands like a sword.

"Guess what?" he called out to no one in particular but everyone in general. He began disentangling himself from his school paraphernalia, and Liberty appeared in the hallway to help him.

Damn! thought Venetia, silently cursing the interruption while out loud declaring, "I couldn't possibly—you'll have to tell us!"

"I scored a goal in hockey!" Kite replied triumphantly, charging into the room miming a shot with his stick.

Venetia raised her eyebrows in surprise. "I thought you hated hockey?"

"I do! It's rubbish. But everyone cheered and they all liked me for once."

His final comment pinged on Venetia's protective radar. She made a mental note to have a chat with Kite about how he was getting on at school. He seemed happy enough, but after his great escape she was taking no chances.

"That's brilliant!" Liberty appeared behind him. "Well done, you!"

Kite grinned sheepishly. "It was a complete accident," he confessed. "I think I had my eyes shut when I hit the ball."

Liberty shrugged. "It makes no difference—it was still a goal. Now go and get changed, and I'll make you a snack to fuel your brain for your homework."

Kite took himself and his hockey stick upstairs, and Liberty closed the door to the sitting room on her way out, leaving Venetia alone with Swan once more.

"Now, what were you saying before Kite came home?" Venetia verbally nudged Swan, trying not to sound unduly inquisitive.

Swan stared down at her hands, which were still in her lap, and spread her fingers wide. "It was so long ago," she replied eventually. "A lifetime ago."

She sighed, and Venetia waited.

"I met him at a friend's twenty-first birthday party. He was someone's older brother, sent along to chaperone his sister and bored out of his skull. I found him skulking in the garden when I went outside to get away from the blaring music and have a sneaky cigarette. He was leaning against an apple tree, smoking a St. Moritz. He offered me one and then coolly flicked open his Zippo." Swan looked up at Venetia. "I suppose you could say it was love at first light," she added with a wry smile.

"His name was Tommaso—his father was Italian—and he taught classics at Cambridge. For our first date he took me punting on the Cam. It was such a cliché, but I thought it was terribly romantic. He told me that one day we would ride together in a gondola in Venice."

Swan's eyes filled with tears again, and she dabbed at them with a fresh tissue.

"We were together for about a year, and it was all going swimmingly until he was offered a position at Ca' Foscari University in Venice. Tommaso was over the moon, and he asked me to go with him. His father was from Venice but had moved to England when he met and fell in love with Tommaso's English mother. But by all accounts, the greater part of his heart remained in Venice, and after ten years his homesickness got the better of him and he returned to Italy. Tommaso's parents never divorced, and the family spent holidays together in Venice, but until I met him, Tommaso and his sister lived with their mother in England."

Venetia was astounded. All this must have taken place just a couple of years before she had met Hawk, and yet she had never heard anything about it before. "What happened?" she asked. "Didn't you want to go to Venice?"

Swan sighed. "I was desperate to go to Venice. It was the one place in the world that I had always longed to go to, and suddenly I had the chance to live there with a man I loved more than anyone in the world."

She looked up at Venetia almost defiantly.

"Does that shock you?" she asked. "That I loved a man whom I had known for only a year more than my own family?"

Venetia shook her head. "Of course not. Besides, it's a different kind of love. But if you loved him and were desperate to go to Venice, why didn't you go?"

"Because of Nightingale."

Venetia waited. And waited. The silence was taut with anticipation. Eventually Swan spoke.

"I promised my sister all those years ago that I would never speak about this to anyone, but I think now that what she asked of me was too much. Both the secret and the sacrifice. So, I will spare the details but tell you enough so that you can draw your own conclusions."

Swan drained the last of the gin from her glass before she began.

"Nightingale was always much more *sociable* than I was. She was young and free-spirited—a little too free-spirited, as it turned out. Just two weeks before I was due to leave for Venice with Tommaso, she confessed that she was in trouble and begged me to stay and help her to sort it out. I told Tommaso that I would follow him as soon as I could—he couldn't wait with me because the new term was about to start at the university. I covered for Nightingale with everyone while she decided what she wanted to do. We pretended that she was ill. Fortunately, there was nothing like the mention of 'women's troubles' in our family to send the men running for the hills, and Mother was too busy caring for her own elderly parents at the time to notice much. Sorting out that particular kind of 'trouble' back then wasn't so easy, and afterwards, to make matters worse, Nightingale really was ill with an infection, and I couldn't leave her. I wanted to, with all my heart, but I couldn't. I let duty come before love. Weeks turned into months, and Tommaso wrote to me time and again, telling me how much he missed me and pleading with me to join him. I kept telling him that I would be there as soon as I could, but eventually, I could feel him slipping away from me, swept along by his new life and new friends. By the time Nightingale had fully recovered, Tommaso had found a nice Italian girl to replace me."

Venetia sat in stunned silence. That ruddy family! Damn their stiff upper lips, "duty firsts," and "keep calm and carry ons." But Swan wasn't finished.

"He wrote to me just once more—a year later, and one month before he was due to marry his Italian fiancée. He said that although he loved her, he could never love anyone as much as he loved me, and I only had to say the word—and get on a plane—and he would break off his engagement. He said that he bitterly regretted not waiting for me to join him and that he would never be able to forgive himself if he didn't try one last time to be with me."

"But you didn't go?"

Swan shook her head slowly. "And I've spent the rest of my life regretting it—regretting that I didn't at least give it a chance."

"What stopped you?"

"Hawk," she replied flatly. "I really wanted to go, but I was afraid. I wish I could say that I was concerned for the other girl's feelings, but it wasn't that. What if I got there and it didn't work out? What if, when he saw me again, Tommaso realized that he didn't love me anymore after all? I looked up to Hawk. He was my big brother, and he always knew what to say and what to do. He seemed so self-assured. I went to him hoping that he would dismiss my fears and tell me to go. But I should have known that his sense of propriety would come first. It always did. He was appalled. He told me that I couldn't possibly go. That if I did, I would be little better than a marriage-wrecker. He said that if 'that bloody Italian lothario' had really loved me, he would have waited for me. Hawk convinced me not to go—no, he frightened me into staying at home. I still have Tommaso's letter, but I never replied to it."

By now, Venetia was close to tears herself. Swan's doomed love affair was heartbreaking enough in itself, but her story held up a mirror to Venetia's own disappointments—the missed opportunities, the roads not traveled, the tedious compromises, and the numerous sacrifices. Well, not anymore! They had wasted enough time.

"Do you realize, Swan, that we are both younger than Cher?"

Swan narrowed her eyes and fiddled with her hearing aid, wondering if she'd heard correctly.

"We're not that old!" Venetia continued. "Seventy is the new sixty, and it's time we started having some fun and living for ourselves! Damn Hawk and his sense of propriety—let's misbehave for a change!"

A slow smile spread across Swan's face. "Well, in that case, I'm going to need some more gin."

Venetia stood up to fetch the bottle and poured more drinks.

"And if you still want to go to Venice," she said, raising her glass in a toast, "I'll gladly go with you!"

CHAPTER 39

Liberty fought the urge to giggle as Bob and Derek stood at the top of their stepladders, holding out a large canvas sling beneath the chandelier while they waited for their colleague, Mick, to unscrew the locking nut that was holding it in place up in the attic. Derek glanced across at Liberty and grinned.

"I know exactly what you're thinking," he said, and he was right. Liberty couldn't help but picture the classic scene in *Only Fools and Horses* where Grandad unscrews the wrong chandelier and Del and Rodney watch in horror as it falls to the floor and smashes into smithereens. But Swell and Noble, Restoration and Refurbishment Specialists—the company that Liberty had engaged to clean the chandeliers and mirrors, and reupholster as many of the chairs as were still usable—had come highly recommended, and Mick, Bob, and Derek managed to load everything into their dark green van without any mishaps.

"We should have the chandeliers and mirrors back to you in a couple of weeks," Derek told Liberty, handing her a receipt for the items they were taking away. "The chairs will take a bit longer, but we'll give you a ring once we know what's what."

Liberty's footsteps had a hollow echo now that the ballroom was almost empty. Only the piano remained, hidden under a dust sheet in the corner, and a few chairs that were too far gone to save. The decorators were arriving tomorrow to begin cleaning the ceiling and repainting the walls and window frames. She couldn't wait to see the stars above her restored to their brightest gold and the floor beneath her feet cleaned and polished until it gleamed. She had ordered frames for the posters that Kite had found and a vintage storage unit to house the record player and records from the attic. She would arrange for a piano tuner to sort out the piano once the refurbishment was complete. She pulled a metal tape measure from her bag, along with a notepad and pen, and began to measure the dimensions of the windows. The old curtains were still hanging, but when she gave a gentle tug on the hem of one of them, its fragile hold on the brass rings that held it up failed, and the fabric collapsed onto the floor with an exhausted sigh. The remaining curtains surrendered at the slightest touch, and Liberty piled them together in a huge, dusty heap on top of the chairs. She would ask the decorators if they could dispose of them the following morning.

That was as much as she could do here today, so she went downstairs where Evangeline was making soup in the kitchen. Seeing her, Evangeline came out to speak to her.

"My, you're looking a lot perkier these days!" she said. "Have you changed your makeup or something?"

"Don't be daft!" Liberty replied, her cheeks reddening.

"Perhaps you've got a new man, then?"

Liberty laughed. "Chance would be a fine thing! Besides, I'm off men these days. I always seem to choose the wrong ones."

"Maybe that's because you've been looking in the wrong places."

"I'm not looking at all now."

"And that's a shame! A fine woman like you. Any man worth his rice and peas would be proud to have you by his side! Maybe you should try one of those dating app things."

"You must be kidding, Evangeline! Nobody tells the truth on those. Everyone lies about their ages and posts photos that are filtered and airbrushed until they look nothing like the real person. Imagine turning up for a date expecting Hugh Grant and getting Piers Morgan!"

Evangeline hooted with laughter. "I'd be more than a match for that Piers Morgan! But never mind. I think there's a man coming for you. I just have a feeling . . ."

"Well, he can turn right round and go back to where he came from. I'm not interested."

Evangeline gave her a hug and returned to the kitchen. As she stirred the soup, she thought about her old friend's daughter and how much Bernadette had worried about her.

"Liberty's doing just fine now, Bernadette," Evangeline said out loud. "Her new job suits her, and Venetia's a good woman. And mark my words, the right man for her is out there somewhere, and I've a feeling he's not too far away."

LIBERTY WALKED HOME at a leisurely pace. It was cold but sunny, and the public gardens beside the river were carpeted with gently nodding snowdrops. She thought about what Evangeline had said and wondered if she had answered truthfully. Was she really not open to another relationship, or was she simply afraid of getting hurt again? Was it worth the effort and the risk? Her parents had been happily married, and her mum had had several successful relationships after her dad had died. But then it seemed to Liberty that her mum had led a charmed life in every way. Even her death had been completely on her own terms. Venetia had been married to Hawk for longer than Liberty had been alive, but was longevity a gauge of success or merely tenacity? Since Hawk's death it seemed as though Venetia was intent on rebirth. She had revamped not just her wardrobe but her whole life, and Liberty was very much enjoying being a part of that. And now, from what she could gather, Heron's marriage was on the rocks. But despite all of this, Liberty couldn't help but feel it would be nice to have someone to share things with—someone to love who loved her back. She thought of Nightingale and her whirlwind romance and smiled. Perhaps there was hope for her yet.

Back at the house, the sound of Michael Bublé singing "Sway" was coming from the sitting room. Liberty peered through the open doorway to see Venetia dancing with Swan.

"I'm teaching Swan to cha-cha," she explained.

"And I have to say, I think I'm a natural!" Swan added with an elegant swirl.

Venetia smiled. "You're an excellent pupil! And I need to get some practice in before the ballroom reopens."

Liberty's face betrayed her surprise. "I hadn't realized that you were going to be teaching classes yourself."

"Why on earth wouldn't I? Dancing used to be the thing I loved most in the world. I shall only teach a few classes a week, but there's no point in me having my own ballroom if I'm not going to dance."

Venetia's face was flushed with excitement, and she looked years younger than her age. Liberty suddenly felt proud of her and proud to be working for this wonderful woman. But Venetia's next words filled her with dread.

"I thought that perhaps I could use you and Swan and Kite as my practice pupils—and maybe Evangeline, if she's up for it. I'll have you all doing the quickstep before you know it!"

Liberty immediately thought of the photograph album. The picture of her in the frilly dress and the humiliation of her first and only dance class. Cold sweat prickled her skin, but she managed a thin smile. "Well, I expect you're ready for lunch now. Can I get you anything?"

CHAPTER 40

Tonight, Crow had brought an origami phoenix for the boy. It was one of the most complex models he had attempted, and he was pleased with how it had turned out. In his previous life he had been a graphic designer, but these days his paper models were the only outlet for his artistic abilities. Most of the other men in the house he shared spent their time drinking, fighting, and doing or dealing drugs. Many of them were career petty criminals, and to them Crow was an oddity like an exhibit in a freak show. He had given up closing the door to his room because, when he did, it was always kicked open. Seeing him making his models and concentrating so hard to fold sharp, precise creases in sheets of old newspaper, they had mocked him. They had called him "soft" and "daft in the head," but he took no notice.

It was the same if they ever found him reading. He spent as much time as he could in the town library, where it was warm and quiet and no one bothered him, but he hadn't joined so that he could actually borrow books, because he knew that if he left them in his room they would be stolen or destroyed. He would occasionally wander into the local branch of Waterstones just to inhale the distinctive scent of new books, to inspect their covers, and to perhaps hold one or two briefly, flicking through their pages. But he never had the money to buy new books. One of the charity shops in town had a box outside filled with free books that were too tatty to sell, and Crow always picked a couple out when he was passing. There was one great lump of a man whose room was next to Crow's who never missed an opportunity to abuse him for whatever spurious reason took his fancy. His face was usually twisted into a snarl, and his nose looked as though it had hit the pavement more than once. He always stank of booze and cigarettes, and his belly hung over his belt like a sack of raw pizza dough. He had once caught Crow reading *Three Men in a Boat*.

"Three men in a boat! I always thought you were a fucking weirdo, and now I know it's true. Three men in a fucking boat! Sounds like a fucking kiddies' book to me!"

He snatched the book from Crow and flicked through the pages.

"Or maybe it's dirty?" he sneered, licking his fat lips. "Because that would explain why you're always hiding away in your room *reading*. Are the three men fucking poofters?"

Crow ignored him. He ignored all of them whenever they tried to start something. Despite his lame leg, Crow was a powerfully built man, and on the rare occasion he made eye contact with any of them, there was something in his stare that made them back down.

The attic was looking very different now. Boxes had been sorted through and rubbish cleared. Most of the chairs had disappeared, and there was an area that had been organized into a sort of room. A small table was surrounded by four chairs, and a large beanbag cushion had appeared on the floor along with a rug and a pile of children's books. A packing crate had been turned on its side and was being used to store several small bottles of Coke, bags of crisps, and a packet of Garibaldi biscuits. Crow wondered how long it would be before the mice found them. He had been touched to see that throughout the progress of these rearrangements, his chair and makeshift table remained by the window. One night he had arrived to discover a bar of chocolate left on his chair. There had been no note, but he had assumed—hoped—that it was for him.

He sat down in his chair and retreated into his heavy coat, pulling up the collar around his ears. It was cold, and his breath blew white plumes into the darkness as he watched the lights of the traffic taking people home to their families, to their dinners, to their television sets. Home to love and food and comfort. Home to all the things that he had had—and lost. He thought about the couple he had seen dancing on the bandstand and the promise that he had made to himself that day. He was going to get a life. Not the same life that he had once had and thrown away. He knew that wasn't possible. His wife was long gone, and his parents were dead. But what he also knew was that he could have something better than the paltry existence that he had now. Hadn't he already made a start by leaving the animals for the boy? He had reached out to another human being without any agenda other than to be kind. His kindness had been reciprocated with the chocolate and an atom of faith restored. Perhaps, next, he might visit the drop-in center. When it was actually open. The thought of it was both exciting and frightening, but then weren't those emotions simply two sides of the same coin? The trick was to flip the coin onto the right side. Besides, it was unlikely that he would be able to continue with his clandestine visits to the ballroom attic for very much longer, now that the place was being renovated. No doubt the security of the building would be updated, locks would be mended, and alarms fitted so that he wouldn't be able to break in at night without being detected.

He stood up and cursed. His bad leg had stiffened in the cold, and he staggered a few paces before regaining his normal lopsided gait. He would go down to the church and say a prayer. He would ask for strength to stick to his new resolutions. He took the origami phoenix from his pocket and set it down carefully on the chair that he had just vacated. As he reached the door of the attic that led to the stairs, the hairs on the back of his neck prickled and his muscles tensed—his body's response to danger kicking in just seconds before his brain processed the information that had precipitated it. He could smell smoke. He opened the door. The stairwell was filling with a dense gray fug. He closed the attic door behind him and reached for the phone in his pocket to dial 999. He had no signal. He clambered down to the first floor and saw that the smoke was coming from behind the door to the ballroom. He grabbed the fire extinguisher that was mounted on the wall and approached the door, placing the back of his hand on the wood to test for heat. It was barely warm. He took a deep breath and pushed the door open. Through thick smoke he could see what looked like a large bonfire blazing halfway down the room against one wall. Fierce orange flames licked the skeletons of chairs that appeared to have been covered with something that was now almost completely burnt away and floated up toward the ceiling in black scraps fringed with glowing heat. The fire roared and spat and crackled, fed by the fresh oxygen supply coming through the open door. Crow grabbed the pin on the extinguisher and pulled. Nothing happened. He tried again. Still nothing. It was stuck. He struck it on the floor, but the pin wouldn't budge. There was nothing he could do. His lungs were filling with smoke and the heat was unbearable. He lurched toward the door. He needed to get somewhere where he could use his phone and raise the alarm. Back in the stairwell he closed the door to the ballroom behind him and clambered down the steps. He could barely see through the smoke. His eyes stung and watered, and every breath was agony. And then he was falling, tumbling, flailing helplessly, and when he stopped, he was at the bottom of the stairs and his leg was broken. In the moment's respite where shock kept pain at bay, he somehow managed to pull his phone from his pocket and dial 999. Moments later, searing agony flooded his body and everything went black.

CHAPTER 41

Venetia and Liberty were at the ballroom only minutes after Evangeline. As the official key holder, Evangeline had been notified first, and she had immediately rung Venetia. Kite had been desperate to come too, but Venetia had insisted that he remain at home with Swan. The blaze had already been extinguished, and the firefighters were standing outside the building pulling off their masks and helmets. One of them was talking to a police officer, and an ambulance with blue lights flashing drove off at speed just as Venetia and Liberty arrived.

"Who was in the ambulance?" Venetia asked Evangeline. "Please God, it wasn't one of the firefighters?"

Evangeline shook her head. "I have no idea. I haven't been able to find anything out yet."

The firefighter approached them, along with the police officer.

"Is one of you ladies the owner of the building?" the police officer asked.

"I am," Venetia replied. "Venetia Hamilton Hargreaves."

"I'm Sergeant Wilson, and this is Lead Firefighter Stokes."

"It could have been a lot worse," Stokes reported. "The real damage is confined to the large room on the first floor, although the rest of the building will need a good airing because of the smoke. There's no structural damage—it's all cosmetic—although part of the floor in that big room looks pretty bad."

"Who was in the ambulance?" Venetia couldn't worry about the ballroom until she knew if anyone had been hurt.

Sergeant Wilson consulted his electronic notebook.

"It's a Mr. Kowalski. He was found unconscious at the bottom of the stairs, but the ambulance crew managed to bring him round before taking him to hospital. It seems he was the one who reported the fire."

"Is he going to be all right?"

"I'm afraid we can't say," replied Stokes. "His leg was pretty badly broken, and he'd inhaled a lot of smoke by the time we found him."

"But who is he, and what was he doing inside the building?" Venetia looked at Evangeline, who shrugged.

"We were rather hoping that you would be able to tell us that," Sergeant Wilson replied. "But if you don't know him, it would appear that he could be guilty of breaking and entering—and trespass. We'll need to speak to him once he's well enough. It's always possible that he started the fire himself."

Evangeline shook her head in disbelief. "Why on earth would he do that? Set the place on fire and then call the fire brigade?"

"You'd be surprised how many arsonists do exactly that. They enjoy the drama and the spectacle—and the feeling of power that they created it."

"Well, I think that's unlikely in this case," Stokes interjected. "It looks as though the source of the fire was a socket just above the skirting board, so in all probability it was caused by an electrical fault. It's quite common in older buildings for mice to chew through the wires, resulting in a short circuit, and if there's enough flammable material nearby it won't be long before a fire takes hold. Also, we found a fire extinguisher in the room. It looks like your man tried to put out the fire himself, but the extinguisher was an old one and the pin was stuck. Someone will be back tomorrow to carry out a proper investigation for your insurance. You'll need to get an electrician in and have all the wiring checked and quite possibly upgraded. Oh, and another thing—if that part of the building hasn't been used for a while, you should check the batteries in the smoke detectors."

Evangeline's thoughts were still with the mystery good Samaritan. Who was he? She remembered all the times when she had felt that someone had visited the church at night, when no one else was there. The reason she had left the mince pies at Christmas. It had always been nothing more than a feeling—there had never been any physical evidence of an intruder. But Evangeline was inclined to trust those feelings when she had them, because they were usually right.

"Does the man have any family?" she asked Sergeant Wilson. "Did he want you to call anyone to let them know where he was or to get them to go to the hospital?"

"I did ask, but he just shook his head. I didn't get a chance to see if he had any ID on him, but I'm sure they'll sort that out at the hospital."

Once the emergency services had left, Venetia, Liberty, and Evangeline went inside to inspect the damage. Liberty immediately took out her mobile and began searching for a twenty-four-hour locksmith to repair the lock on the front door where the fire brigade had been forced to break in. In the drop-in center, the smell of smoke was only faintly discernible, and in the church, which was farthest away from the stairs and behind another closed door, there was barely a trace of it.

"Well, it's not too bad so far," said Evangeline, squeezing Venetia's arm and doing her best to sound positive.

"The locksmith will be here within an hour," Liberty reported as she caught up with them.

It was only in the stairwell that the acrid stench really hit them.

"That poor man!" Venetia stood staring at the foot of the stairs. She covered her nose and mouth with her hand and coughed.

"We don't have to do this now," Liberty said gently. "I can wait here until the locksmith comes and Evangeline can take you home. We can come back tomorrow."

Venetia pulled back her shoulders and pursed her lips in determination. "No, we'll take a look now. I shan't get any sleep wondering and worrying about what state my ballroom is in if I don't see it for myself. At least then I'll know what we're dealing with. And, Liberty, first thing tomorrow I want you to order new fire extinguishers for every room in the building and to check the batteries in all the smoke detectors. That man could have died, and I would have been partly to blame."

They climbed the stairs, taking care not to touch anything. Every surface was coated in a strangely greasy gray residue. The door to the ballroom had been closed, and Venetia braced herself before opening it. The ballroom was a blackened, stinking, sticky mess. Liberty looked up at the filthy ceiling and her eyes filled with tears. After all her work to get the renovation started, it was ruined before it had begun. It was clear that the fire itself had been confined to a relatively small area, but the combination of smoke and whatever had been used to extinguish the flames had desecrated the entire room.

"Well, there's no question that it's an absolute bloody mess!" Venetia declared. "But on the positive side, at least the chandeliers, the mirrors, and the decent chairs are safe. So well done, Liberty. Excellent timing. And another thing—none of the windows are broken."

"But the decorators are supposed to be starting tomorrow. They were going to clean the walls and ceiling ready for painting." Liberty's voice cracked, and Evangeline gave her a quick hug.

"They might get more than they bargained for when it comes to cleaning now," Venetia replied with a wry smile. "But this can all be fixed. It's a setback rather than a disaster."

She pointed up at the ceiling.

"Those stars are still there under all that muck. And they will shine again. That I can promise you!"

CHAPTER 42

Evangeline had barely slept and was swallowing her second cup of black coffee in gulps while she brought Norma and Norman up to speed with the previous evening's events, and issued instructions concerning what they could do to help while she was away from the center that morning. She had telephoned the hospital and managed to persuade them to tell her which ward Mr. Kowalski was on and that he was "as comfortable as he could be." Venetia had been as anxious as Evangeline to find out how he was doing, and Evangeline had promised to keep her updated.

"It's so good of you to come in this early," she said gratefully to Norma and Norman. "If you can deal with the teas and coffees and maybe start getting the lunches ready. Liberty and Venetia will be in later because the decorators are arriving—but dear Lord, the mess upstairs! There's a lot of cleaning to be done first. Don't let anyone use the stairs, and keep the door to the stairwell shut. I've opened a couple of windows in there—I know it's cold, but you'll just have to keep your coats on."

She paused for a moment, breathless. Her thoughts were racing ahead of her words, and she took a moment to gather herself. Norma and Norman stood patiently in front of her, waiting to see if she had finished.

"Please tell Venetia that I'll be back as soon as I can—I should only be an hour or so."

Norma nodded. "Don't worry—Norman and I can hold the fort.

And I do hope that poor man is feeling better. It doesn't bear thinking about, what might have happened if he hadn't raised the alarm."

Just then, the door opened and Tommy and Hedgehog wandered in. They both raised their noses in the air and sniffed.

"Fucking hell!" said Tommy. "It stinks in here!"

EVANGELINE WAS IMMOVABLE. She was not going to take no for an answer. She stood face-to-face with the ward manager, wearing a fixed smile and an adamant gleam in her eyes.

"I know it's not visiting hours until two P.M., but Mr. Kowalski doesn't have any family and I'm his friend. He didn't have anything with him when he was brought in last night, and he needs some toiletries, pajamas, and a phone charger. If you'll just let me have a few words with him and drop these off"—Evangeline held up a shopping bag—"I'll only stay a couple of minutes."

The ward manager held out her hand. "I can take those and give them to him for you."

Evangeline lowered the bag. "Yes, you could. But I'd prefer to do it myself. And I'm sure you're very busy." She amplified her smile.

"And if I say no?" The ward manager was almost smiling now herself—in the face of inevitable defeat.

"I'll just wait until your back is turned and sneak in anyway!"

"I thought as much. But please, just a few minutes. Mr. Kowalski is still quite unwell and needs to rest. He's in bay six, next to the window."

Evangeline walked down the corridor that bisected the ward with bays on either side. It was warm and brightly lit, and the air was heavy with the slightly sweet, peculiar scent of sickness. Machines beeped, and somewhere a patient's alarm buzzed like a frenzied bee. From one of the bays a frail but persistent voice wailed, "Nurse! Nurse!" Evangeline wondered how anyone could get any rest in a place like this. Bay six was the last bay on the left, and it was mercifully quiet.

Several of the patients were asleep, one was wearing headphones, and another was staring at the screen on his phone. The bed nearest the window was hidden by curtains. The occupant was a well-built man of around fifty years old with a shock of charcoal-gray hair. His eyes were closed, and an oxygen mask covered his handsome features. His left leg was elevated and cocooned in plaster. Evangeline moved closer and was struck by an instant shock of recognition. She stared at his face, trying to place him in the context where she had seen him before. Because she had definitely seen him before. The man stirred and groaned a little, and Evangeline instinctively reached out and touched his arm.

"It's okay, sweetheart, you're fine. You're in hospital, but everything's going to be okay."

The man forced his eyes open and looked up at her, clearly puzzled.

"You had an accident, remember? There was a fire and you fell down the stairs? If it wasn't for you, the whole building would have gone up in flames! Anyway, I brought you some things—toiletries, pajamas, a bottle of squash, and a phone charger. I'll leave them here and I'll be back later."

The man tried to sit up, and as he did the hospital gown slipped from his shoulder, revealing part of a large tattoo that appeared to cover most of his upper back. It looked like a crow.

"No, no! You rest now. Lie back down," Evangeline told him. "That ward manager will be after me if she thinks I've disturbed you! And speaking of the devil—I'd better go before she kicks me out on my backside. I'll be back at visiting time to check that you're okay and see if you need anything else."

The man stared at her with wet, red-rimmed eyes. He reached out his hand and she took it in hers.

"Thank you," he rasped, his voice barely audible beneath the mask. "Evangeline?"

She smiled. "That's right. Evangeline."

When Evangeline returned that afternoon, the man was sitting up in bed wearing the pajamas that she had brought him. They were a little short in the sleeves but better than the hospital gown. He was still wearing the oxygen mask, but his face had lost its deathly pallor, and there was a smudge of color on each of his cheeks. He even managed a smile when he saw her approaching. She sat down in the chair next to his bed and slipped off her coat.

"Aren't you looking better! How do you feel?"

The man pulled down his oxygen mask and took a sip of water from the plastic cup on the tray in front of him.

"I'm sorry," he said. "I'm so sorry for being so much trouble. I know I shouldn't have been there. I only go at night for a bit of peace and quiet, and sometimes down to the church to say a prayer."

The penny dropped. That was where Evangeline had seen him before. In the church.

"And you came to a service once, didn't you? But you didn't get a message. Why didn't you come back?"

"I did," he croaked. "But I could only face it when no one else was there."

"Well, you just listen to me—you have nothing to be sorry for. In fact, we have so much to thank you for. If you hadn't been there and called the fire brigade, things would be a whole lot worse. As it is, the fire was only in the ballroom and the damage can be repaired. And as luck would have it, the chairs, the mirrors, and the chandeliers had already been taken away, so the room was almost empty."

The man nodded and held the oxygen mask up to his face for a moment before saying, "I'll pay you back for the things you brought in for me. I don't have much cash in my wallet, but as soon as I get out of here—"

Evangeline didn't let him finish. "You can pay me back by getting well again! I don't want your money, I want to see you dancing around on that leg—well, maybe both legs might be better."

The man shook his head slowly. "But why do you care? Why would you do all this for me? You don't know me. You don't know anything about me."

It was almost true. Evangeline knew only that he had saved the ballroom and, in so doing, had almost certainly saved her drop-in center and church too. It was true that he had been trespassing at the time—one of many times by his own admission—but what harm had he ever done? And what good was a church if it couldn't provide sanctuary, even if it was outside opening hours? Maybe that was when it was needed most. And then, of course, there was that feeling, the feeling she had always had about the nighttime visitor. That it was some lost soul looking for solace.

"Did you visit the church on Christmas Eve?" she asked.

The man smiled. "Yes. I'm afraid I stole one of the mince pies left out for Father Christmas."

"I didn't leave them out for Santa Claus—I left them out for you!"

The man's eyes filled with tears. "But I don't understand. Why were you—are you—being so kind to me? I don't deserve it."

Evangeline patted his hand and passed him a tissue. "Kindness isn't a reward—it's a gift. And it's mine to give wherever I choose. And I choose to give it to you."

They sat in silence for a moment, and it suddenly occurred to Evangeline that she still didn't know the man's first name.

"I could keep calling you Mr. Kowalski," she said with a mischievous grin, "but now that I've seen you in pajamas, perhaps we could be a bit less formal?"

"My friends call me Crow," he began. "I have a tattoo—"

"I know. I've seen it!" Evangeline replied with a wink. "Then *I* shall call you Crow."

CHAPTER 43

"You make the best macaroni and cheese in the world!" Kite shoveled another forkful into his mouth. "When we have it at school it's too stodgy. And it smells like vomit."

"Well, it sounds as though I don't have too much competition from your school's kitchen," Liberty replied with a smile.

Kite considered for a moment. "They do a brilliant chocolate sponge and custard, but you haven't made me that yet so I don't know if yours would be better."

Liberty made a mental note to add it to the following week's menus. She and Kite were having supper in the kitchen with Colin. Venetia had taken Swan along to a meeting of her book club. The dog sat very close to Kite and looked up at him with pleading eyes.

"I think Colin Firth thinks your macaroni and cheese is the best in the world too."

"Flattery will get him everywhere!" Liberty got up and spooned a dollop into the dog's bowl.

"Nisha says we shouldn't feed him while we're eating because it will encourage him to beg," Kite told her. "But I think it's mean to make him watch us eat before he can have something." He reached over and stroked the dog's head.

"I'm no expert when it comes to dogs," Liberty replied, "but I don't think it will do any harm just this once."

Kite looked up at her and grinned. "You like him now, don't you? When you first came you were frightened of him, and you never stroked him. But now sometimes you do—*and* you've given him some macaroni and cheese."

Liberty chewed her food thoughtfully. Kite was right. She had been frightened when she'd first arrived—and not just of the dog, but of everything. Frightened of not getting things right. Frightened that Venetia wouldn't take to her. Even, in a way, frightened of Kite. But most of all frightened that she wouldn't be good enough—not for the job, and not for life in general. After what had happened with Graham, and then her mother's will, she had felt inconsequential. Both unloved and unlovable. But somehow, since she had been at Venetia's house, her fears had gradually subsided—or perhaps just been superseded by a sense that she was finally succeeding at something. Venetia seemed to enjoy her company and trusted her to help with the house, the ballroom, and even her grandson. Swan had come to rely on her for so many little things, and now Kite had called her macaroni and cheese the best in the world. And it was true that she wasn't frightened of the dog anymore and that she did occasionally stroke him when no one was looking.

Kite interrupted her thoughts. "Look! He's licked his bowl clean, so he agrees with me about your macaroni and cheese. Is there any more?"

"For you or the dog?"

"Both?"

Liberty served another spoonful onto Kite's plate. "I think Colin has had enough. We don't want him to be sick on the carpet."

The dog lay down with a contented sigh.

"I won't tell Nisha that we gave him any," Kite said as he scraped the last of his supper onto his fork. "It can be our secret."

Something in the way Kite intoned the word "secret" drew Liberty's attention like a beckoning finger. Liberty was no more an expert on children than she was on dogs, but she had a feeling that Kite wanted to share something with her.

"Okay," she replied. "I can keep a secret."

Kite trailed the tines of his fork in a circle around his empty plate.

"I've got another secret," he said, without looking up at her. "Do you want to know what it is?"

"I do if you want to tell me."

Kite sighed and then turned to face her. "I think I know who the man who reported the fire is."

"Mr. Kowalski?"

"I don't know his name, but he's sort of my friend."

"But how do you know him?"

Kite explained about the chair in the attic and the note he had left. "And the next time I went back, there was a paper bird on the chair. And every time after that there was a different paper animal. I've got a frog, a mouse, and a rabbit. They're amazing. Only a really kind person would do something like that."

"And have you ever seen anyone in the attic?"

"No. But I left a bar of chocolate to say thank you for the animals and someone took it."

"So, what makes you think that it was Mr. Kowalski?"

"Nisha said that he told Evangeline at the hospital that he used to go to the attic at night sometimes. That's why he was there on the night of the fire."

Liberty tried to think how Venetia might respond to her grandson's revelations. A small boy making friends—albeit remotely—with a strange man in an attic seemed to her to raise an entire bunting of red flags, but then why should she assume that Mr. Kowalski's intentions were anything but kind? Why be so keen to suspect rather than trust? Is that what life had taught her?

"Do you think I'll be in trouble for not telling Nisha?" Kite studied her anxiously, waiting for an answer.

"Well, I can't speak for her, but Nisha knows that you're a sensible boy, and we all know now that Mr. Kowalski risked his life to save the ballroom. Evangeline is the only one of us who has met him, but she says he's a good person."

Liberty knew full well that she had given him a politician's nonanswer to his question, but she didn't want to give him any false reassurances.

"I think you should talk to Nisha when she gets home from book club and let her know what's been going on."

Kite brightened. "Yes—and I can ask her if I can go and visit Mr. Attic Man in hospital to see how he's getting on."

"Good idea!" Liberty replied, hoping to bring the conversation to a close before she said anything that Venetia might not agree with. "Off you go and get started on your homework. What is it tonight?"

Kite pulled a face. "Fractions and spelling." He trudged up the stairs, followed by Colin.

Liberty had just finished loading the dishwasher when the doorbell rang. On the other side of the glass at the front door she could just make out the shape of a stout male figure. She opened the door and was astonished to see Heron looking sweaty and flustered. He barged his way past her, dragging a suitcase behind him. Before she could say anything, Colin came bounding downstairs into the hallway. He took one look at Heron and, with a deep-throated growl, slunk toward him, his hackles rising.

"What in God's name . . . ?"

As Heron retreated, he fell backward over his suitcase, and Kite joined them just in time to see his father flailing on the floor like an upturned tortoise.

"Dad! What are you doing here? And why are you rolling around like that?"

Kite began giggling as his father tried to disentangle himself from his suitcase and get to his feet. Seeing Kite's response to the stranger, Colin relaxed and began sniffing Heron's trousers.

"Get that sodding dog away from me! Where the hell's your grand-mother?"

Kite took hold of the dog's collar and pulled him away. "Don't call him a sodding dog. His name's Colin Firth, and Nisha rescued him from a drug den. And you're not supposed to say swear words in front of me."

Liberty had managed—but only just—to keep a straight face throughout the undignified slapstick of Heron's unexpected arrival and now sought to restore order. "Venetia's at her book club with Swan, but she should be home soon. We weren't expecting you. Can I get you a cup of tea or coffee?"

Heron was standing now and brushing himself down, but he was clearly still agitated. Kite thought of something that might cheer him up and delay his own return to fractions homework. "Would you like to see the paper animals that the man in the attic made for me?"

Liberty had turned toward the kitchen to put the kettle on, but now turned back, anticipating that further explanations might be required.

"Who on earth is the man in the attic?" Heron looked up toward the ceiling in bewilderment.

Kite sighed and then spoke slowly with exaggerated patience: "The man in the attic of Nisha's ballroom, who's my friend and leaves me presents and nearly died when the ballroom caught fire but saved the whole building from burning down."

It seemed that now that Kite's secret was out, he was happy to share it with everyone. For a moment Heron was speechless while he tried to process what his son had said, and Liberty took the chance to intervene.

"Kite, why don't you go back upstairs and finish your homework, and then you can talk to your father once he's had a chance to take off his coat and sort himself out."

She gave him a look that she hoped conveyed that he should make himself scarce while she tried to placate his father. Kite trotted off upstairs with Colin but stopped on the landing and hung over the banister, eavesdropping.

"Why don't you take off your coat and I'll make you a cup of tea." Liberty was surprised at how calm she felt.

"Never mind the damn tea! I should like to know what sort of madhouse I've come home to! What the hell was my mother thinking, taking in a dangerous dog from a drug dealer? And what's all this about a sodding ballroom? Dear God, please tell me she hasn't actually bought one?"

Unable to hear the dog maligned without defending him, Kite stomped back down the stairs and stood defiantly facing his father, his hands on his hips.

"Colin Firth is not dangerous, and Nisha rescued him from a horrible place and horrible people. And yes, she *has* bought a ballroom, *and* a place where poor and lonely people go for sandwiches and cups of tea, *and* a church. And it all caught fire, but the man in the attic called the fire brigade, who put it out."

Heron turned to Liberty. "Is this true?" he demanded coldly.

"I think that's a pretty good summary of exactly what's been happening," Liberty replied. "We've had an exciting few weeks, haven't we, Kite?"

Heron's face had turned so red with fury that he appeared to be in imminent danger of spontaneous combustion. "You!" he expostulated, pointing at Liberty. "This is all your fault! I employed you to keep an eye on a vulnerable old lady, and instead you've been letting her run riot, wasting her money and getting involved with criminals and all manner of undesirables! You, Miss Whatever-Your-Name-Is, are fired!"

Liberty very much wanted to slap him, but Kite was still in the hall with them, standing open-mouthed in amazement.

"Kite, please go upstairs and finish your homework while I talk to your father."

Kite shook his head. "Please don't make me—I want to watch."

Fair enough, thought Liberty. *Watch and learn.*

"Firstly, Mr. Hamilton Hargreaves, you are not my employer, your mother is, and therefore you can't fire me. Secondly, your mother is neither vulnerable nor old. She's a vibrant, intelligent, independent woman and perfectly entitled to do whatever she pleases and spend her money on whatever she likes. Lastly, she's bought a ballroom, and frankly, she's having a ball! Get over it!"

Heron made to reply, but Liberty held up her hand to silence him.

"And since you can't even be bothered to remember, let me remind you. My name is Liberty Bell, and don't you ever speak to me like that again!"

CHAPTER 44

By the time Venetia and Swan returned home from their book club meeting, Heron was in his father's study nursing a large glass of whisky, Kite was in his room doing his homework, and Liberty was in the kitchen eager for their return so that she could escape to her flat. She waited for them to hang up their coats and come through to the kitchen so that she could warn Venetia about their surprise visitor.

"Well, I still say that the book was dreadful!" Swan clearly hadn't enjoyed the chosen novel. "It was unmitigated misery from start to finish. Each character spent the entire novel trying to outdo everyone else in the misery stakes."

"I completely agree. It was thoroughly depressing. But I think Rowena chose it because it had been shortlisted for some literary prize or other. Although why misery should equate with merit is beyond me," Venetia replied, leading the way through to the kitchen. As they entered the room, Liberty stood up.

"Heron's here," she announced without preamble. "He arrived about half an hour ago. He's in the study."

"What the devil's he doing here?" Swan sounded a little put out. "He's supposed to be in France. You said he was in France, Venetia."

"He was. Do you know what's going on, Liberty?"

Liberty pushed her hair back from her face and sighed. "I don't know why he's here—he hasn't told me. But I'm afraid we've had words."

Swan perked up immediately. "Good for you! What about?"

"He threatened to fire me. He doesn't think I'm doing my job in a satisfactory manner."

"What the hell would he know about it? Damn fool! He hasn't even been here. You're doing a splendid job—isn't she, Venetia?"

But before Venetia could reply, another voice piped up.

"He called Colin Firth 'dangerous' and a 'sodding dog.' He said 'sodding' quite a few times actually, and he's not supposed to swear in front of me."

Kite had appeared in the doorway, accompanied by the dangerous dog.

"We should have stayed at home instead of going to book club," Swan answered him with a wry smile. "It sounds like you had all the fun."

"Well, it's certainly not funny that Heron threatened to sack Liberty. He had no right—and no authority," Venetia said, frowning.

And that's exactly what I told him, thought Liberty, feeling quietly proud of herself.

Meanwhile, Venetia was concerned for her son—clearly something was wrong—but she was not prepared to tolerate him throwing his weight around as soon as he set foot through the door. It was her house and her rules. Things had changed since he had left for France, and now that he was back, he would have to get used to the new order of things.

"Right, then. Kite—it's bedtime for you. Upstairs and into your pajamas."

"But I need to talk to you about something. Liberty said that I should talk to you about it when you got home."

Venetia looked at Liberty, who raised her eyebrows apologetically. "I'll come and talk to you once you're in bed—after I've spoken to your father. And if you're asleep by then, we can talk about it in the morning."

Kite climbed the stairs reluctantly, and Venetia went into the study and closed the door behind her.

"Would you like me to make you a cup of tea or hot chocolate before I go?" Liberty asked Swan, although she was desperate to get back to the peace and privacy of her own space.

"Hot chocolate be damned!" Swan replied. "I'm going to have a large G and T and take it upstairs to watch *Father Ted* in my room. Night night!"

VENETIA WOKE EARLY the next morning and lay in bed, staring at the ceiling. It was quiet save for the sound of the garbage truck outside stopping to empty the litter bins along the Embankment. She had spent two hours the previous evening talking to Heron, and her heart ached for him in the way that only a mother's can for her beloved son. Because although he could be a pompous, foolish prig, as he had demonstrated last night with Liberty, she knew that he was a decent man with a good heart who loved his family very much. She also knew that his infuriatingly bombastic persona hid a vulnerability that he rarely showed—that he was tethered to insecurities that kept him doggedly adhering to the life he thought he should lead, rather than the one he might choose for himself. He was so like his father that there were times when Venetia wanted to shake him. But this wasn't one of them.

Monica had left him. Of course his pride was hurt that she had gone off with another man, but his heart was hurting too. He had truly loved her, and the rejection was devastating. Venetia had wanted to gather him up in her arms and comfort him like she had when he'd fallen off his bike as a little boy and skinned his knees. But this could not be fixed with hugs and kisses and a dab of antiseptic. And then there was Kite. Heron was terrified that Monica would want to take their son to live with her in France. He had raged and wept as he had spoken about it, and Venetia had struggled to quell her own panic at the thought of losing her grandson. In the end, she had let him talk everything out until he ran out of words, and then she had sent him to bed. Today they would begin to unravel the mess and try to find a path through to the other side.

LIBERTY HAD WONDERED whether she should come over to the house to have breakfast with Kite after her altercation with Heron, but had eventually decided that she would carry on doing what she normally did unless Venetia told her otherwise. She found Kite already up and dressed and shoving slices of bread into the toaster.

"Is your father still here?" she asked him, trying to sound unconcerned.

Kite nodded. "But he's still asleep."

"Unlike some of us!" Swan strode into the kitchen wearing a velvet dressing gown and her hair hidden under a silken turban. She slumped down at the table and swept the back of her hand over her brow. "I hardly slept a wink! Your father snores so loudly that the wall between our rooms was trembling. I swear there's a crack by my headboard that wasn't there yesterday!"

Kite giggled as he spread a slice of toast liberally with peanut butter. But then his face became serious. "Why do you think he's come home? And why isn't Mum with him? He was very cross, wasn't he, Liberty?"

"He *was* very cross, and he was very tired. But it's nothing for you to worry about."

Venetia joined them in the kitchen and went straight to the teapot to pour herself a mug of tea. She looked tired, but she smiled brightly at Kite. "Now what was it that you wanted to talk to me about? Do you want to tell me now, or is it a secret, and do we need to go to Grandpa's study?"

"Well, it was a secret, but I've told Liberty now—and Dad—so it isn't really anymore."

"Well, come on, young man. You haven't told *me*, and I'm quite agog!" said Swan. "Spill the beans!"

Kite repeated everything that he had told Liberty about the chair in the attic and the paper animals and then waited anxiously for Venetia's response. Venetia sipped her tea and wondered if she should lace it with a slug of brandy. It seemed that all her exciting plans for the future were being sabotaged by fire and infidelity, and now her grandson had been forging a potentially dubious friendship with a complete stranger while he was in her care. Perhaps she had been foolish to think that she was capable of reinventing her life at her age. But if not now, when? She had allowed her dreams to be crushed by cruel circumstances once before, and now she had been given—no, she had made for herself—a second chance. Was she really going to waste it? Would Cher give up at the first sign of trouble? Hell no! And neither would she.

"I think that I should talk to Evangeline and find out how Mr. Kowalski is doing. If she thinks he's well enough, I'll take you to visit him, and we'll ask him about the paper animals. I very much want to speak to him anyway to thank him for saving the ballroom."

Kite grinned. "Can we go today—after school?"

"I think it might have to wait until the weekend. But if you want to make Mr. Kowalski a get-well-soon card, I could get Evangeline to give it to him."

"It should be a thank-you card too. Thank you for calling the fire brigade and nearly dying."

"Hmm, I think the wording might need a little finessing," Swan suggested. "But perhaps I could help you with that when you get home from school."

There was the sound of footsteps in the hall, and Heron shuffled into the kitchen. Liberty instinctively bristled, but then she saw his face and how broken he looked. She poured a cup of tea and handed it to him without a word.

CHAPTER 45

Evangeline was already sitting at the patient's bedside when Venetia and Kite arrived at the hospital. She had been to see Crow every day since he had been admitted and was delighted to see how much he was improving. When she saw them approaching, she waved them over.

"Here come your visitors," she told Crow.

Crow had been anxious about meeting the woman who owned the ballroom ever since Evangeline had told him she was coming. The boy, whom he now knew was her grandson, had made him a colorful card, which Evangeline had delivered. It had a painting of the ballroom on fire and the fire brigade on the front, complete with himself being loaded into the ambulance on a stretcher, and inside were little drawings of each of the paper animals that Crow had made for him. He hoped that the card was a good sign. As the woman and the boy approached his bed, the boy's face lit up.

"It's you!" he exclaimed. "You're the man who rescued me from that creep who punched me in the alley. You took me to Evangeline!" Kite stared at him in amazement. "I can't believe it's you! We brought you some biscuits and some apples."

Evangeline smiled. "Well, it appears that you two are already acquainted. But, Venetia, let me introduce you to Mr. Kowalski—or Crow, as he's known to his friends."

Venetia looked stunned but offered him her hand. "I'm so pleased to meet you, Mr. Kowalski. And it seems that I'm more in your debt than I realized. Is it true that you are responsible for the safety of my grandson on the day that he ran away from school, as well as the survival of the ballroom?"

"Of course it's true!" Kite could barely contain his excitement. "I was there—I should know! But you told me your name was Luka."

"Lukasz," the man corrected him quietly. "It is. But my friends call me Crow."

"Why?"

"Because when I was a little boy in Poland, I rescued an injured crow, and he stayed with me until he died almost five years later. He was my friend and I loved him. He was clever and funny, and he used to bring me little presents—pebbles and bits of string, all sorts of things. I had a tattoo made on my back to remember him."

"Can I see it?" Kite's eyes were wide with wonder.

Evangeline laughed her rich, throaty laugh. "You can't be asking Crow to take off his clothes in front of everyone to show you his tattoo."

"I can draw the curtains round." Kite was up and ready to act, but Venetia intervened.

"Come and sit down, Kite. Poor Mr. Kowalski needs to rest." Turning to the patient, she added, "I have no idea how to thank you. If there's anything I can do, anything at all, then please let me know."

Crow smiled uncertainly. "You mean I'm not in trouble?"

"Why on earth would you be?" Venetia was genuinely puzzled.

"For trespassing. For breaking into your building. I know it was wrong and I'm really sorry, but I didn't damage anything."

"Mr. Kowalski, you rescued my grandson from a violent mugger and delivered him to a safe place, and then you prevented my ballroom and Evangeline's drop-in center and church from being burned to the ground. I think I can safely say you're one of the good guys."

"He's a hero!" Kite exclaimed a little too loudly, causing the nurse who was taking the blood pressure of another patient to look over and frown. Venetia raised her hand in silent apology.

"And it was you who left me the animals, wasn't it?" Kite continued in a stage whisper.

"Yes, it was. And thank you for the chocolate."

Kite grinned. "And the first one you left me was a crow. Was it a clue?"

Crow winked at him. "Maybe. You're a smart boy."

"Will you teach me how to make paper animals?"

"It will be my pleasure."

"Perhaps you can give classes at the drop-in center," Evangeline suggested. "We're always looking for ways to keep our visitors entertained. But that will mean that you'll have to keep more conventional hours from now on and come in when we're actually open!" She squeezed his arm to show that she was teasing.

"How long will you need to keep the cast on for?" asked Venetia, gesturing toward his leg.

"The orthopedic surgeon said around eight weeks, and then I might have to wear a walking boot for a couple of weeks after that."

"Goodness! How will you manage? Do you have anyone at home to help you?"

Crow reddened slightly. "My family are all gone. I have a room in a shared house, but I'll be fine."

"Can't Crow come and stay with us, Nisha? We've got a spare room—and then we can look after him."

Venetia knew it would be the right thing to do. After all, she owed him at least that much. But now that Heron had come back, things weren't so simple. She was pretty sure that he would have a fit if she invited Crow to stay, regardless of Crow's record as a good Samaritan. And in truth, there was only so much she could cope with at one time. She had to get the ballroom back on track as well as support her son through his divorce, and she already had Swan as a permanent houseguest. She felt terrible—ungrateful—for even hesitating, but before she could reply, Evangeline stepped in.

"I'm afraid he can't come and stay with you, because he's already taken! He's coming to live with me until he's back on his feet."

It was clear from the expression on Crow's face that it was the first he'd heard of this, but his protests were instantly dismissed by Evangeline.

"Answer me this," she demanded. "Would you like to sleep in a clean and comfortable bed, eat delicious home-cooked food, and enjoy the company of a fabulous, witty—and very modest—woman, or would you prefer to go back to that house of yours?"

Crow blushed. "Well, obviously—" he began.

"That's settled, then! We'll say no more about it. And don't worry—I'll find you plenty to do. You can still do the dishes on one leg!"

Crow smiled, but he was flagging. He looked exhausted.

"I think it's time we went and let Mr. Kowalski get some sleep." Venetia stood up and started putting on her coat.

"Please, call me Crow. And thank you for coming to see me. You're very kind."

Venetia took his hand. "And you are a remarkable man, Crow. I'm very grateful for everything you've done."

"We'll be back!" Kite promised. "Do you play chess? I could bring my chess set in and we could have a game."

"I do. I'll look forward to it."

As they made their way through the parking lot back to Venetia's car, Kite walked ahead of them, eager to get home and tell Swan all about their visit.

"Are you sure about having Crow to stay?" Venetia asked Evangeline. "I hate to be so suspicious, but we know very little about him, and you live alone. Do you think it's safe? God, I know how awful that sounds, but still . . ."

"It doesn't sound awful—it sounds very sensible. But I know a little more about him than you do. We've had some long chats these past few days, and I firmly believe that he's a good man who has had some very hard times. Yes, he's made some bad choices—but which one of us hasn't? He used to visit my church at night, not just the attic. *And* I have one of my feelings about him."

Venetia smiled. "You're a wonderful woman, Evangeline!"

"We both are! Don't forget that without you I probably wouldn't have a drop-in center or a church anymore. And don't worry," she said with a wink, "if there's any trouble from Mr. Crow, I'll whack him with my Dutch oven!"

CHAPTER 46

Just seven days later, Venetia was back in Hawk's study, sitting in his chair and reflecting on how much things had moved on in the past week. Monica had appointed a solicitor to handle her side of the divorce, and so Heron had been obliged to do likewise. He had apparently exchanged several frosty emails with Monica, who had reassured him that she had no intention of taking Kite to live in France. She was happy for his current schooling arrangements to continue and had suggested that it might be best for her to visit him in England during the school holidays and occasional weekends.

"I expect her fancy man doesn't want any children cramping his style," Swan had said to Venetia, when she had shared the news.

"I wouldn't have gone to France anyway," Kite had announced in a determined voice. "Venetia promised me that I wouldn't have to. And I don't like Maurice."

"Why not?" Swan was curious as ever.

"He's got mouth cheese when he talks."

It had been agreed that, for now, Kite would continue living with Venetia while Heron stayed in their family home, which was only a few streets away, until a decision was taken as to whether it would be sold.

Mr. Kowalski—or Crow, as she must remember to call him—was making good progress and would soon be out of the hospital. She had taken Kite to visit him yesterday, and they had played chess while she and Evangeline had gone for a cup of tea in the hospital canteen. Today, Kite was with his father, and Venetia had insisted that Liberty take a day off. Since the fire, she had been working tirelessly to make up the ground that had been lost. She had organized an electrician to carry out the rewiring, ordered new fire extinguishers, and helped Venetia to choose curtain fabric and then arranged for the curtains to be made. She had been at the ballroom most days, supervising the cleaning and reparation of the smoke damage, and had even managed to find a carpenter to restore the damaged section of the floor. Today she was going to visit an old friend in Cambridge.

Venetia leaned back in the chair and the leather creaked. In her hands she held the old wallet that she had found in the bottom drawer of Hawk's desk. Recent events had diverted her attention away from Francis Taylor, Torin McGuire, and A. F., but she hadn't forgotten them, and today, while the house was quiet, she had resolved to resume her investigations. She took the scrap of paper with the telephone number written on it from the wallet and began to tap the digits into her mobile phone, but there was no signal. In the hall, using the landline, she tried again. If it had ever been a phone number, it was no longer in use.

"Who are you calling?"

Swan had finished her crossword and was looking for some company.

"I've no idea."

Swan frowned.

"It's a long story."

"Good. I've got nothing else to do."

"Well, we'd better go and sit down."

Venetia led the way through to the sitting room. It hadn't occurred to her to ask Swan about the funeral guests because she had assumed that they'd become part of Hawk's life during their marriage, but she realized now that she had no real evidence to support this.

"I've been going through Hawk's things in his study," Venetia began, "and I found this."

She handed the wallet to Swan, who immediately inspected its contents and was clearly disappointed. "The money's no good now, although I suppose a bank might change it for you."

"I also found this," Venetia added, showing Swan the piece of paper. "I thought it might be a phone number, but when I dialed it just now, I didn't get through to anyone."

Swan glanced at the numbers. "Well, that's not much of a story. I was expecting something more exciting than that."

Venetia smiled. "Have you ever heard of Francis Taylor or Torin McGuire?"

"No. Why? Should I have done?"

"They came to Hawk's funeral, but I have no idea who they are."

"It's no good asking me about Hawk's funeral—Nightingale got me completely wasted on champagne! But surely there must have been lots of people that you didn't know? Hawk's former law cronies and his rugby friends? Why are these two so important to you?"

Venetia sighed. "I'm not sure. I met them briefly, and there was just something about them. They weren't like any of Hawk's other colleagues or friends."

Swan remained silent for a moment as though she was weighing something up in her mind before asking, "Is there anything else?"

"It may not be relevant, or connected in any way to Messrs. Taylor and McGuire, but I also found a ragged old copy of *The Lion, the Witch and the Wardrobe* in the bottom drawer of Hawk's desk. It was . . ." Venetia hesitated. "It was pushed to the back of the drawer—almost hidden, but not quite."

"But why on earth would Hawk want to hide it? And if he did, he surely wouldn't have hidden it there. He would have known that you would find it after he died."

"But perhaps that was the point. Perhaps he didn't want anyone to find it until after he'd died."

Swan shook her head dismissively. "It's only an old book. He probably just shoved it in there one day and forgot all about it."

Venetia recalled the other drawers in Hawk's desk, their contents arranged with military precision. Hawk wasn't a man to shove anything anywhere at random.

"There was an inscription in the book."

Swan rolled her eyes. "Why didn't you say so? Is this the juicy bit?"

"I don't know—maybe. Or maybe the inscription wasn't meant for Hawk at all, and it was already there when he bought it."

"And are you ever going to tell me what this blasted inscription says?"

Venetia had read it so many times now that she knew it by heart. "*When I became a man, I put away childish things, including the fear of childishness and the desire to be very grown up.* And underneath, it's signed A. F."

"C. S. Lewis's plagiarism of Corinthians—how intriguing. It doesn't sound like Hawk at all."

"That's exactly what I thought. The very opposite, in fact. But what if it was a message *telling* him to—I don't know—loosen up? Have a bit more fun?"

"If that was the case, then A. F. had a lot of nerve. Hawk didn't take kindly to being told how to behave."

Venetia nodded. "Precisely. Which means that whoever A. F. was, they knew Hawk well enough to tease him—or maybe offer him some heartfelt advice. Can you think of anyone whom Hawk knew who had the initials A. F.?"

Swan shook her head. "No one springs to mind. What about the funeral? Was there anyone there with those initials?"

"I got Liberty to check the book of condolences—although I didn't tell her why—and the only A. F. was Andrew Frobisher, who was a junior clerk in Hawk's chambers. I always got the impression that he was rather scared of Hawk, so I don't think it's likely to be him."

"And is this why you rang the number on the piece of paper? Were you hoping that it might be A. F. or one of the other two?"

Venetia shrugged. "I know it probably sounds daft, but there was always a part of Hawk that felt unavailable to me. I didn't resent it and I still don't. But now I just need to know. And I can't help but feel that if I could only find out who these people are, they might have some of the answers that I'm looking for."

Swan was still holding the wallet. She ran her fingers over the leather thoughtfully and then stopped as though something had suddenly occurred to her. She pulled out the money and then closed the wallet and squeezed it between her hands.

"I think there's something else in here," she said.

She unfolded the wallet and then undid the flap at one end and slipped her hand inside. At first there was nothing, but when she pushed her fingers all the way through, past the fold, she touched paper and pulled it out. It was an envelope folded in half, and inside it was a letter in Hawk's handwriting. Without a word, Swan handed it to Venetia.

There was nothing written on the envelope. The letter was a single page and dated September 13, 1986—two days before Heron's eleventh birthday. Seeing the expression change on Venetia's face, Swan got up and left the room, leaving Venetia to read alone.

Dear A. F.,

I hardly know how to begin this unhappy letter, which must mark our end. My feelings for you have not diminished—if anything, they grow stronger each time I am with you. Our friendship has been the most important, the most fulfilling, and the most exciting of my life. But it is wrong—and dangerous—and it must end before it goes too far and while I still have the strength to walk away from you. I am a married man, and my wife is a wonderful woman. When I married her, I made vows which at the time I meant with all my heart to keep. I am determined to be a good husband to her and a good father to my son—they deserve nothing less. I am not sure if it is decency or fear that has driven me to this decision. Perhaps it is a combination of the two. But please know that although I can never see you again, I will never forget you. You taught me what true love feels like, and for that I shall always be grateful.

Yours ever,
Hawk

WHEN SWAN RETURNED, she was carrying a tray loaded with two cups of coffee and a bottle of brandy.

"I wasn't sure if you might need something stronger than coffee."

Venetia handed her the letter, and while she read it, Venetia poured a small shot of brandy into each cup.

After a moment, Swan looked up. "Bloody hell! Talk about a dark horse! Did you have any idea?"

Venetia considered her answer. "No . . . and yes. I don't know."

"Well, that's covered all the options. Are you all right?"

"I'm really not sure, but if I'm absolutely honest, I'm not entirely surprised."

"You mean you suspected back then that he was having an affair?"

"Perhaps not then, but later, on reflection. Hawk had seemed distant for a while, staying over in London more often than usual. He told me it was work—a big case. I had no reason to doubt that he was telling the truth. I was worried that he might not be home for Heron's birthday—it was his eleventh. I remember because it was his last before he went to boarding school. He wanted a bicycle, and we bought him one and wrapped it up in brown paper."

"And was Hawk there?"

"Yes. We had a party for Heron and some of his friends, and I remember Hawk playing football with them in the garden."

Swan studied Venetia with a serious gaze. "You seem remarkably calm. Are you sure you're not in shock?"

She offered Venetia more brandy, and when Venetia shook her head, she topped up her own cup instead.

Venetia sighed. "Ours was never a very *passionate* marriage. It was based on friendship more than anything else. Hawk was always very caring and loving—in his own undemonstrative way. But he never seemed very interested in the physical side of things, particularly once Heron was born. Some men are like that, apparently—once you've had their child, they see you as a mother rather than a lover."

Swan looked unconvinced. "To be completely frank, Venetia, I never really understood why you married my brother in the first place. You were such a stunning creature—a dancer, for heaven's sake! I always thought that if Hawk *were* to marry anyone, it would be some nice, sensible, presentable young woman with good teeth, a solid bosom, and childbearing hips. Most likely the daughter or sister of one of his fellow barristers, who would steer the ship at home, so to speak, while Hawk concentrated on his career. I mean, I loved my big brother to bits, but I should have thought you were well out of his league. I can't believe that you never wanted passionate romance and mind-blowing sex?"

Venetia thought about all the nights she had lain awake next to her husband feeling frustrated, rejected, and lonely while she listened to him snore. Her eyes filled with tears, but she brushed them away angrily with the back of her hand. "I knew what I was getting when I married Hawk, and I had my reasons for accepting his proposal."

"Did you ever love him?"

Venetia smiled. "I grew to love many things about him. And yes, I did love him. But now, I think, only ever as a friend."

Swan shook her head in amazement. "Why do I get the feeling that there's so much more that you haven't told me?"

"Well, I did warn you it was a long story."

The door, which had been left ajar, slowly opened, and Colin wandered in and came and sat in front of Venetia.

"I know," she said, reaching out and stroking his head. "It's time for your walk. Come on, Swan." She pushed herself up out of her chair. "Walk with us."

"I'll come—but only if you tell me the rest of the story over lunch when we get back."

CHAPTER 47

The two women and the dog battled their way up the Embankment, buffeted by the rough, blustering mid-March weather. Three crews of schoolgirl rowers, cheeks wind-whipped scarlet and bare legs goose-bumped by the cold, sliced through the choppy water of the river in their boats. They were cheered on by their coach, who rode a bicycle along the towpath beside them, shouting instructions through a bullhorn. Venetia and Swan walked in silence. The wild weather made conversation difficult, but, in any case, each woman was lost in her own thoughts. Venetia was wondering if it was finally time to confide in someone and confess what had made her decide to marry Hawk all those years ago. If so, was her sister-in-law the most suitable confidante? And then there was the letter to A. F. As she had explained to Swan earlier, the fact that Hawk had apparently had an affair wasn't completely unexpected, but what had surprised her was the sincerity and tenderness of his words. She was touched by the loyalty expressed toward herself and Heron, but it was clear that both she and Hawk had remained married from a sense of duty and doing what was right on his part, and now, somehow, it all seemed like such a waste. In making that choice, Hawk had given up someone who may have been the love of his life, and Venetia had sacrificed the chance to be with hers. And why hadn't he sent the letter? Had the affair continued alongside their marriage because in the end he couldn't walk away from either? At least the knowledge of Hawk's infidelity might go some way to assuage the guilt that she had always felt for marrying him, knowing on her wedding day that she didn't love him in the way that a bride should love her groom, and that she probably never would.

Swan was mulling over what she had seen and been told that morning, trying to make connections between the principal players. She had never understood how Hawk and Venetia had ended up together and what on earth had possessed them to get married. She had always thought Hawk more suited to the life of an eternal bachelor, contenting himself with his existing family and friends. She couldn't recall Francis Taylor or Torin McGuire from the funeral or anywhere else, but she had come up with a pretty good idea of how Venetia might find them. As for A. F.—that could be tricky. It was a delicate matter and Swan had a theory, but she wasn't sure if she should share it with Venetia. She wondered why Hawk hadn't sent the letter and if he had wanted Venetia to discover it, but only after he was no longer around to face the consequences.

Colin was thinking about his lunch.

They struggled on for around twenty minutes more before admitting defeat and heading toward home. Having sniffed and peed up several trees, greeted a poodle, and barked at numerous squirrels, Colin was happy to go with them. Once back in the cozy warmth of the kitchen and tucking in to cheese on toast, the two women picked up the threads of their earlier conversation.

"I've thought of a way you might be able to trace Taylor and McGuire," Swan announced.

"That's marvelous. How?"

"You said you didn't have any contact details for either of them?"

"That's right."

"So how did they find out about the funeral?"

"Perhaps they heard about it from one of Hawk's other friends or colleagues."

"But you said they were different. They weren't like Hawk's other cronies, so it's unlikely that they knew them."

"I suppose . . . So, come on, Sherlock, what's the big idea?"

"Hawk's obituary and details of the funeral were published in *The Times*—I'm convinced that's how they found out. So why don't you post a message in its announcements column and ask Messrs. Taylor and McGuire to contact you?"

Venetia shook her head in disbelief that she hadn't thought of it herself. It was so simple! "You're a genius, Swan!"

"I know. I told you I could be a private detective. And now we have to try and uncover the identity of Hawk's mysterious inamorata."

"Or inamorato," Venetia added quietly.

Swan looked up and met Venetia's steady gaze. "You've thought that too?" she said. "I often wondered if Hawk might have walked on the Oscar Wilde side, but I never dared mention it to anyone in case I was wrong. Or maybe in case I was right. But if you even suspected that Hawk might have preferred men, why marry him?"

"Because when I first met him, I didn't. He was a little shy and awkward around me, but very keen. I was different back then—a social butterfly. My colleague and dance partner Brendan and I were the king and queen of the floor! I'm afraid we were frightful show-offs, but we were passionate about our dancing. We won so many trophies, and we were planning to go to Blackpool to compete in the Amateur Latin Championships. I just thought Hawk was a little in awe of me."

The sadness and regret at giving up on that life suddenly felt overwhelming, and Venetia paused to check her emotions.

"It wasn't until years after Heron was born that I began to suspect," she continued. "You see, for a long time I blamed myself for the lack of physical intimacy—sex—in our marriage. I assumed that Hawk didn't find me attractive."

Swan scoffed. "That's ridiculous! You were utterly gorgeous—you still are."

Venetia smiled gratefully.

"But I'm bald, Swan." Venetia pulled off her wig. "And I was bald when I married Hawk."

"Good God! Well, I didn't see that one coming. Great wig, by the way," Swan replied with commendable equanimity. "Did Hawk know before the wedding night?"

"Of course he did," Venetia replied with a rueful smile. "Hawk rescued me when my life was falling apart. But I didn't just feel ugly on the outside—I felt ugly on the inside too."

Swan reached forward and squeezed Venetia's hand. "What happened?"

CHAPTER 48

March 1972

It was Saturday night, and the ballroom was packed with people waiting for the music to start. It was one of the regular Latin nights that Venetia and Brendan had introduced at the beginning of the year, and they had proven to be very popular. The evening was a mixture of standard Latin dances and a disco with mainly Latin American music.

"You look sensational!" Brendan exclaimed as Venetia sashayed across the room toward him in a short, gold-sequined fringe dress that accentuated the sway of her hips.

"It's my racy rumba dress!" she replied, giving him a twirl. "Blackpool is only two months away now, so I'm going to start trialing my outfits. We don't want any dress disasters at the competition."

Venetia wasn't oblivious to the admiring looks that she was attracting from all around the room, but the only man whose approval she was interested in was Brendan's. As her dance partner, he knew that costumes were a vital part of their performance, particularly in a top-level competition, but she hoped that his appreciation of her outfit was rather more than just professional. They had grown closer than ever during their months of preparation for the Amateur Latin Championships—one of the competitions at the Blackpool Dance Festival—and Venetia felt sure that *something* would happen in Blackpool. She had high hopes that they would return home as a couple—in life, not just on the dance floor.

"Well, it looks perfect to me," Brendan told her. "But we'll see how it holds up on the dance floor. We ought to dance with some of the pupils first, but as soon as they play a rumba, I'm coming to get you!"

Venetia scanned the room, searching for the familiar faces of her pupils. Brendan nudged her in the ribs with his elbow.

"If you're looking for your admirer, he's standing at the bar."

Venetia glanced over and saw Clifford Sykes staring at her, a lazy smile playing across his lips. "I wouldn't call Clifford Sykes *my* admirer. He's more like the resident Casanova!"

"Not him! Farther down, by the wall."

Venetia looked again and saw Hawk Hamilton Hargreaves standing with Andrew, drinking what looked like an orange juice. He was dressed more casually than usual, although casual was a relative term when applied to Hawk. His shirt was still pristine and sharply pressed, but it was a pale lilac rather than the usual white or subtle check, and his tie was nowhere to be seen. Andrew had gone even further and was wearing jeans and a shirt made of a loud, multicolored tropical-fish-print fabric. Hawk raised his hand in an awkward little wave when he saw Venetia looking toward him. She flashed him a broad smile before turning back to Brendan and rolling her eyes.

"I suppose I'll have to dance with him—he is still a pupil. He's such a nice man, but he's so straight!"

"Never mind, sugar. At least you won't have to worry about his hands wandering where they shouldn't. He's a perfect gentleman."

"You're right there—unlike some!" Venetia replied. "But I've got no intention of dancing with Slithery Sykes tonight."

The music began, and the floor filled up with couples. Brendan was immediately engaged to dance by his most ardent pupil, Pauline, and Hawk was just as swiftly at Venetia's side. It was a cha-cha—the only Latin dance that Hawk had mastered so far. His feet followed the steps with dogged precision, but his body remained as stiff and straight as his shirt collar.

"I hope you don't mind me saying so, but you look beautiful tonight," he told her.

"How could any girl object to a compliment like that?" she replied. "You look very dashing yourself."

Hawk blushed but said nothing more. Venetia guessed that he was concentrating too hard on getting the steps right. At the end of the dance, he thanked her before another of her pupils claimed her for the samba.

The final dance before the disco was the rumba, and as soon as the music started, Venetia and Brendan took to the floor.

"Imagine it's Blackpool," Brendan whispered in Venetia's ear. "Let's show them how it's done!"

As the couple shimmied and swayed to the seductive rhythm of the music, the floor gradually cleared and everyone else became spectators, mesmerized by their performance. At the end of the dance, the applause was rapturous.

"Not quite perfect, but not at all bad!" Brendan said, as he led Venetia from the floor.

"We've still got a few weeks to work on it, and my dress survived intact!" Venetia replied. "Listen, Brendan, do you mind if I go early tonight? It's the disco now anyway, and Mum was at the hospital again yesterday."

Her mother's drawn looks and exhaustion at Christmas had turned out to be the result of something much more serious than overdoing it at work. But the oncologist had said that they had caught it early and that with surgery and chemotherapy, the prognosis was good. The surgery had gone well, but the chemotherapy was hard, and Venetia was keen to get home and see how her mother was feeling.

"Of course!" Brendan replied. "Give her my love and tell her how brilliantly we danced tonight."

Her mother was determined to be well enough to see Venetia and Brendan compete at Blackpool, and was always eager to hear how their preparation was progressing. Venetia kissed Brendan on the cheek and went downstairs to collect her coat from the cloakroom. At the front door, she checked her watch. It was a cold night, and she didn't want to be standing at the bus stop for too long. The bus was due in fifteen minutes. She heard Clifford Sykes talking to someone as footsteps descended the stairs, so she slipped outside, hoping to avoid him. But she was too late. She didn't look back when she heard the door open behind her, just carried on walking.

"Hey, gorgeous, where's the fire?"

Damn! She couldn't just ignore him.

"Sorry, Clifford, I've got to go. I'll miss my bus."

He caught up with her and took her arm. "I'll walk you to the bus stop," he said.

"There's no need—really."

Venetia tried to free herself, but Clifford held her firm.

"Now, now. I can't allow a defenseless young lady to walk the streets alone in the dark. What sort of a gentleman would that make me?" His words were slightly slurred, and he reeked of beer.

She forced herself to stay calm and smiled at him. All she wanted to do was get to the bus stop and catch her bus. "I'll be fine, Clifford—honestly. It's only round the corner."

He ignored her protests and, still holding her arm, continued walking with her—although at a much slower pace than she would have liked.

"I like your dress. It suits you," he said slowly, deliberately. He leaned in close to her face, and she could feel his warm, boozy breath on her cheek. "It's very sexy. Just like you—just like your dancing," he murmured into her ear. "Provocative." He elongated the word into a sinister whisper.

Venetia tried to focus on each step forward they took. Her heart was racing, and her mouth was dry, but she forced her legs to keep moving. They turned the corner onto the high street, and she could see the bus stop up ahead. She just needed to get there. Perhaps if she just played along with him and kept him talking and walking, she would be okay. Clifford pulled her closer and changed his grip so that he could slip one arm around her back. Venetia could feel the panic rising inside her. A young couple stumbled out of a pub just in front of them. The girl was laughing at her boyfriend, who was struggling to get his arm into his jacket.

"Please help me," Venetia tried to say, but the words in her head wouldn't form in her mouth, and then the couple was gone, and it was too late.

"It's a crying shame you've got to go home so early. Because I wanted you to dance with me like that. That *sexy* dancing." Clifford's hand slid down her back and stroked her buttocks.

Once again, Venetia tried to break free, but he held on to her arm and began walking again.

"Easy does it. There's no need to make a scene. But you can't kid me that you're Little Miss Innocent the way you wiggled your way around that dance floor tonight. You knew exactly what you were doing."

Suddenly Venetia was furious. "Yes, I did! It's called the rumba!"

Clifford laughed in her face. "The prick-tease, more like."

They were almost at the bus stop, and Venetia knew that the bus must be due at any moment. A wave of relief washed over her as she saw it approaching, but at that moment she was dragged from the pavement and down a dark passageway between two buildings. Before she could scream, Clifford clamped his hand over her mouth and forced her farther down into the shadows. He slammed her back against the wall and held her there with the weight of his body. She tried to bite his hand, but it was too tightly clamped over her face, and she could taste blood where her teeth had punctured her own lip. Her struggles to escape him were futile—he was much heavier and stronger than her and was pressed so tightly against her that she could feel his panting breath hot on her neck, the rise and fall of his chest on hers, and the hardness of his groin against her thigh. He thrust his free hand between her legs, viciously pinching the soft flesh when she tried so desperately to clamp them together. He found the waistband of her tights and knickers and yanked them downward.

"Now you're going to get what you were begging for," he sneered as he unzipped his fly.

She could hardly breathe, and in that moment, fixed by fear and on the very edge of consciousness, she looked up into the black sky and wondered if she was going to die. She could never recall afterward whether she had fainted, but the next thing she was aware of was Clifford lying on his back, blood streaming from his nose, and Hawk Hamilton Hargreaves standing over him.

"If you come near her again, I'll kill you," he spat, before kicking Clifford hard in the ribs.

He turned to Venetia and offered her a spotless white handkerchief. He mimed dabbing his lips, and she realized that her mouth was smeared with blood. He turned away while she adjusted her clothes and then wrapped his arm around her shoulders and guided her out of the passageway. Out on the street, he paused and looked at her face, his eyes full of concern.

"Are you all right? I mean, of course you're not all right, but can you walk?"

She nodded, and he led her gently away. When they reached the Wimpy a few doors down, he took her inside and bought them each a coffee.

"Would you like me to take you to the police station?" he asked her.

Venetia shook her head. She took a gulp of her coffee and winced. Her lip was swollen and bruised, and her head was pounding.

"Are you sure? You really should report this."

Venetia's eyes filled with tears. She thought about saying the words that would describe her shame and humiliation out loud to strangers.

She thought about the excruciating show-and-tell that they would put her through. She thought about them knowing what he had said and where he had touched her, and she couldn't bear it. It would be worse than what had already happened. She swallowed some more coffee.

"I can't," she whispered. "I just can't."

He didn't try to persuade her. She looked down at the sparkling fabric of her dress and picked at one of the sequins that had come loose in the struggle. The dress that she had loved and been so excited to wear seemed tawdry and cheap now.

"You won't tell anyone, will you?"

He shook his head. "Of course not."

"You promise?" Venetia insisted tearfully.

"I give you my word."

The coffee was beginning to clear Venetia's head a little, and a thought occurred to her. "Why were you there?"

"I followed you."

"But why?"

"Well, I followed that lowlife Sykes. I'd seen the way he'd been looking at you all night, and when you went downstairs and he followed you, I followed him. I just wanted to make sure you were okay. I wasn't sure if maybe you . . ." Hawk hesitated for a moment. "If perhaps you liked him. And I didn't want to interfere. By the time I got downstairs, you were already walking off with him arm in arm."

Venetia sucked on her bruised lip. How could she have been so stupid? She should have told Clifford to leave her alone right then, outside the ballroom, where there were people around who would have heard her. She should have shouted—screamed, if necessary—but instead she had gone along with him. It had been asking for trouble. And Hawk had seen her with him and assumed, as anyone else would have, that she was going willingly.

"He was drunk. I didn't want to make a fuss." It sounded so pathetic as soon the words were out of her mouth. "I've never liked him.

I suppose I thought that if I could just get to the bus stop, I could catch my bus and he'd go away." She shook her head in disbelief that she had been so naive.

"I almost didn't come after you once I'd seen you leaving together, but . . . I'm not sure what it was, but something didn't feel right. When I was in the army, we were taught to trust our instincts. I decided to follow you for a bit until I thought you were safe."

Venetia looked at him and smiled sadly, tears once again spilling down her face. "Thank you, Hawk."

He nodded. "Would you like me to take you home?"

CHAPTER 49

S wan sat at the table in stunned silence. For once, it seemed that she was lost for words. Venetia couldn't quite believe what she'd done. For all these years, she had told no one—not her parents, not Brendan, not one of her friends. She had buried those memories under the rubble of all the dreams that had been demolished that night, and she had turned her back on the wreckage and walked away to start a new life with Hawk. But she realized now that she had never really left anything behind. She had carried the shame, the fear, the humiliation, the guilt, and the regrets with her wherever she went, like stones in her pockets. She had given them power by keeping them secret—protected them from scrutiny and questioning, which may have diminished or even dismantled them. But now that she had found the courage to admit what had happened and risk being judged for her part in it, she would no longer be held back by the past. Finally, Swan spoke.

"Thank you," she said. "Thank you for trusting me enough to tell me. I have a thousand questions, but you've probably had enough for today."

Venetia shook her head. "It's fine—I'm on a roll now. It's such a relief to have it out in the open, to talk about it. Hawk and I never discussed it again after that night, and I never spoke about it to anyone else. I used to worry that Clifford Sykes might say something, but I think that after the beating Hawk gave him, he wouldn't have dared. He never showed his face at the ballroom again."

"And you didn't tell your parents?"

Venetia shook her head. "I couldn't burden Mum with it—she was so ill at the time. It was only about a month before she died when it happened. And I certainly wasn't going to tell Dad or my brother."

"So why not Brendan? You two were close, weren't you?"

"Very close. Oh, Swan, I think I was in love with him! And I'm pretty sure—at least I hoped—that he felt the same way about me. But nothing was ever said. And that's why I couldn't tell him. I was embarrassed and humiliated. I couldn't help feeling that it was partly my own fault—the dress, the dancing, the fact that I let Clifford walk with me instead of standing up for myself. I couldn't bear for Brendan to think of me in that passageway like *that* with Clifford."

"But you must know now that it wasn't your fault—not at all. Not in any way whatsoever. That loathsome bastard took advantage of you. He forced you with physical violence to do something that was completely abhorrent to you. He committed a criminal act!"

"But it was the 1970s. The police would have taken one look at what I was wearing, and once they knew that I had let him walk me to the bus stop and hadn't screamed or cried out for help, that would have been the end of it."

"But Hawk was a witness. He could have corroborated your story."

Venetia sighed. "Hawk was a witness to me walking arm in arm with Clifford, apparently willingly. He even told me at the time that he thought I might have liked Clifford. I don't know exactly what else he saw, but it probably wouldn't have been enough to guarantee a charge, let alone a conviction, despite the fact that he was a barrister. Don't forget that back then the concept of consent was very different."

"But you were hurt—you had injuries to support your story."

"I'm not sure that would have made much difference. Clifford would have come up with some story, and it would have been his word against mine. And besides, I couldn't face the physical examination they would have put me through—the horrific intimacy of it."

"Well, it's a bloody good job that Hawk gave him a thrashing. But what about Brendan? Did you get to Blackpool?"

Venetia shook her head. "I tried to carry on—as much for Mum's sake as for ours. It was her last wish for us to dance at the Winter Gardens, even if she couldn't be there to see it herself. We kept rehearsing for a few weeks, but my heart wasn't in it. I couldn't bear the sight of that dress, and Latin dancing is very . . . well, sexy, for want of a better word, and I just couldn't do it. Brendan assumed that it was because of Mum—she was deteriorating fast by then—and I let him think that. And through all of it, Hawk was there, quietly supporting me. What happened that night bound us together whether I wanted it to or not. Hawk had seen me at my most vulnerable. He had witnessed my abject fear and humiliation—my disgrace, as I saw it then. And despite that, he still wanted me. He was so kind, so considerate, and so capable. He was the most decent man I had ever met. He came to Mum's funeral, and after that, when my hair began to fall out, he took me to see a trichologist in Harley Street who told me that it was probably the result of shock or trauma and was unlikely to grow back. I was devastated. I saw it as some sort of punishment for what I had allowed to happen to me."

"But, darling Venetia, it wasn't your fault!"

"I know that now, but at the time I was a complete wreck—physically and mentally. Hawk said that it didn't matter, that I was still beautiful to him. And he made me believe it. He made me feel safe. And so I took the easy way out and married him. But I let Mum and Brendan down, two people that I truly loved, by not dancing at Blackpool. And although I didn't realize it at the time, I let myself down too. I allowed that unspeakable lowlife, Sykes, to rob me of my dreams."

Colin, who had been sleeping at Venetia's feet, got up at the sound of the front door opening.

"We're back!" called Kite.

"We're in here," Venetia replied.

Kite came into the kitchen followed by his father. He spotted the remains of their cheese on toast lunch on the table.

"I'm starving!" he announced.

Heron shook his head in disbelief. "You ate an entire pizza less than an hour ago! You can't possibly be hungry again."

"He's a growing boy," Swan replied. "His grandfather was exactly the same at his age. He was always in the larder stealing something."

"I'll put the kettle on." Venetia stood up. "I think there's some of that cake that Liberty made left in the tin."

"Where is Liberty?" asked Kite, feeding a crust of toast from Swan's plate to Colin.

"She's having a day off. She's gone to Cambridge." Venetia noted an expression of relief flit across her son's face.

"Can I take Dad to see my den in the ballroom attic next weekend?"

"Yes—I think it's about time I got to see this wreck of a building that you've bought."

"It isn't a wreck at all," Venetia replied evenly. "In fact, the repairs to the fire damage begin next week, and after that the renovations to the ballroom will begin in earnest. The church and drop-in center have remained open for business as usual, and Liberty estimates that the ballroom will be fit for use in just a couple of months."

Heron smiled. "Well, I'm not sure we should place too much store by that. Miss Bell is hardly a qualified project manager. But I'll be happy to have a look and deal with the contractors for you if you like. They'll be far less likely to take advantage if they know I'm in charge."

"What a complete pile of patronizing horse manure!" Swan banged the flat of her hand down on the table, making the crockery rattle and her great-nephew giggle. "Heaven only knows how this poor gaggle of gullible women have managed without you for so long! Well, let me enlighten you. We've been doing splendidly!"

"It's kind of you to offer, Heron. But Liberty's perfectly capable," Venetia added. "We've drawn up a business plan together, and with the rent from the church and the drop-in center, and the projected income from the ballroom, we'll be fine. We plan to rent the ballroom out for events and to freelance dance teachers as well as running our own classes. We may even make a small profit."

"And Nisha's going to teach some dancing too, aren't you?" Kite added. "She's already been practicing with me and Swan."

Heron looked horrified. "Seriously, Mother—at your age? It's not very . . ." He searched for an appropriate word but settled, unhappily for him, on "dignified."

"Dignified! Good God, Heron, we're not living in a Jane Austen novel!"

"Just as well," muttered Swan, not quite under her breath. "Because it would be *your* private life that would be causing a scandal, and not your mother's dance classes!"

"But really," Heron continued, ignoring his aunt, "are you up to it? Shouldn't you be taking it easy at—"

"My age?!" Venetia was exasperated. "Heron, I am seventy-four years old and fit as a flea! I'm not ready to sit by the fire crocheting antimacassars with a blanket over my knees! Dancing will keep me fit, and more than that, it will make me happy. Very happy. I gave it up once, but I shan't do it again. I'm going to dance, and this time, no one's going to stop me."

There was a brief silence, and then Swan applauded. "Brava, Venetia! Well said!"

Heron appeared to consider his mother's words for a moment, and then he slumped down into a chair and buried his head in his hands. Venetia stood behind him and placed her hand between his shoulder blades. He looked up and smiled. "I'm sorry. I can be such an idiot. But I just want you to be safe and happy."

So very like his father, thought Venetia.

"I know that," she replied. "And I do appreciate it. But it isn't your job. We are each of us responsible for our own happiness—and that is why I'm determined to dance. You need to concentrate on finding out what it is that will make *you* happy."

"Perhaps you can teach me to dance like you taught Dad?"

Kite let out an exaggerated sigh. "What would make me happy right now is some cake! And what's an antimacassar?"

CHAPTER 50

The widow of Hawk Hamilton Hargreaves, QC,
is keen to contact his former associates
Mr. Francis Taylor and Mr. Torin McGuire.
Please email vhamilton.hargreaves@ntlworld.com.

There it was in today's paper. Venetia had asked Liberty to arrange for it to be printed on three consecutive Saturdays. Now all she could do was wait. She was currently waiting for Heron and Kite to convene in the hall so that they could make their way to the ballroom. Liberty and Swan were trying a new hairdresser and then going out to lunch. They had invited Venetia to go with them, but she always felt a little uncomfortable in hair salons. Besides, she wanted to show Heron the ballroom herself. She wanted to try to make him understand that it wasn't simply an impulse buy, but a serious venture that would hopefully prove to be an asset to the local community, just as the drop-in center and church already were. Heron was on the phone in the kitchen, talking to Monica in clipped tones about the sale of their house. Kite galloped down the stairs followed by Colin, who was panting and wagging his tail excitedly.

"I've been teaching him to dance," explained Kite. "Like those collies you see on the TV dancing with their owners. Maybe we could teach classes for dogs at the ballroom too."

"Hmm," Venetia replied doubtfully. "I'll think about it."

THE DROP-IN CENTER was busy, and Venetia watched as her son cast a wary gaze around the room, assessing its occupants.

"Crow!" Kite launched himself toward the figure of a man sitting awkwardly with one leg stretched out in front of him in a plaster cast. Venetia followed, ushering Heron in the same direction. "Dad! This is Crow, the man I told you about. He's a complete hero!"

Venetia flinched inwardly. It wasn't a great time for Heron to be hearing his only son describe another man in such glowing terms and with such obvious affection, but she was pleased to see that Crow was not only out of the hospital but also well enough to accompany Evangeline to the drop-in center.

"This is my son and Kite's father, Heron," she said, praying that Heron would find something suitable to say. "It's lovely to see you looking so much better."

Heron offered his hand to Crow, a little stiffly. "How do you do? I understand I have rather a lot to thank you for—I'm very grateful."

Crow shook his hand warmly. "You have a fine boy. He almost beat me at chess the other day! And your mother is an amazing woman. Without her, Evangeline would have lost this place and these people"—he gestured around the room—"would have nowhere to go. You must be very proud of her."

"And without *you,* this whole place would have gone up in smoke!" Evangeline had appeared behind Crow and rested her hands lightly on his shoulders for a moment. Venetia recognized, with a little surprise, the evident affection in the gesture.

"And this handsome man must be the son that Venetia's told me so much about," Evangeline said, approaching a rather surprised-looking Heron and giving him a warm hug. She stepped back and held him at arm's length while she studied his face. "I can see where Kite gets that mischievous twinkle in his eyes," she told him with a wink.

Venetia could have kissed her. She had shared with Evangeline the news of Heron's divorce and how hard it had hit him, and here she was meeting him for the first time and knowing exactly what to say to make him stand up a little straighter and feel a little better about himself.

"Come on, Dad!" Kite grabbed hold of Heron's hand. "I want to show you my den."

Venetia followed them out of the room, and as they passed the church, Heron peered through the door, unable to contain his curiosity—or his cynicism.

"Is this the so-called church? What's all that junk on the window-sills? Are they having a rummage sale?"

"Dad! Don't be so rude! They're presents, not junk."

Heron shook his head in condescending dismissal, and Venetia realized at that moment that her son needed more than just sympathy and support—he needed a few home truths.

"Kite's right," she said firmly. "They are gifts from people Evangeline has helped. And whether it was with the assistance of God or ghosts hardly matters. Whatever you believe—or don't believe—the fact remains that a great deal of good is done here, both in the church and in the drop-in center. Evangeline and her helpers deserve respect rather than ridicule, and I expect better from you."

Heron was somewhat taken aback by this new incarnation of his mother but had the good grace to mutter an apology. As she led the way upstairs, Venetia noted with satisfaction that the smell of smoke had almost gone. Inside the ballroom, the only evidence that remained of the fire, apart from the faint smell, was the burnt section of the floor. The walls, ceiling, floor, and windows had all been cleaned, and the piano, under its heavy cover, had survived unscathed. The morning sun sparkled on the panes of glass in the windows and threw diagonal shafts of light into the room. On impulse, Venetia waltzed through them holding an invisible partner in her arms.

"You see?" she said to Heron. "It's going to be wonderful!"

"It's a good space," he conceded a little grudgingly. "And with a view like that, you can understand why they wanted to turn it into apartments."

"But they can't now because it's ours!" Kite was always quick to claim joint ownership. "And now you need to come and see my den."

Venetia went back downstairs to talk to Crow and Evangeline while Kite took his father upstairs to the attic. He showed him the space he had cleared, with its table and chairs and beanbag, and his collection of books and his makeshift snack cupboard.

"Would you like some crisps?" he asked, offering Heron a bag from his stash.

Heron accepted, not because he was hungry but because he felt it was the right thing to do, to accept his son's hospitality in a space that he was obviously so proud to call his own.

"And this is the chair where Crow used to sit and where he left the paper animals for me," said Kite, pointing to the chair that was still by the window.

"But why did he come here?" Heron was still slightly suspicious of Crow. He had, after all, been trespassing on private property, and what sort of man makes friends with a little boy by leaving him paper animals? Crow was a person so far removed from Heron's own reality that he couldn't begin to imagine what his life was like and how hard it might be. When Monica had announced that she was leaving him, Heron had had his mother to turn to for advice and support and his son as consolation. He still had the invaluable security of a comfortable home, a regular income, and people who loved him. He had no idea what it was like to feel truly alone.

"Evangeline says he came here to get some peace and quiet. The place where he lives isn't very nice." Kite flopped down onto the beanbag.

"So why didn't he come to the drop-in center when it was open? Then he wouldn't have been breaking the law," replied Heron testily.

Kite frowned and thought about his father's question for a minute. "He wasn't *really* breaking the law, because nobody minded. And sometimes it's nice to be on your own, isn't it? Sometimes it's easier than being with other people." Kite understood that feeling well, but he wasn't sure if his father did. The lack of privacy was one of the reasons that Kite had hated boarding at school. "Anyway, what do you think of my den?"

Heron couldn't help but smile at his son's obvious delight in his attic hideaway. "I think it's splendid," he said, pulling open his bag of crisps.

For a moment it was silent, save for the sound of munching, and then Kite spoke again. "Dad, I think you should say sorry to Liberty. She's really nice, and you were horrid to her."

Heron's cheeks reddened a little and he coughed. "Yes, I've been meaning to say something. I suppose I was a bit abrupt."

"No, Dad, you were really rude! And you said you were going to fire her—even though you can't because you're not her boss."

"Well, I was going to have a quiet word with her the next time I saw her, but I haven't seen her yet."

The expression on Kite's face reminded Heron of his father when somebody had contradicted him.

"I think that you should go and see her in her flat and say sorry properly. You should take her a bunch of flowers to show that you mean it."

"Flowers! I think an apology will suffice."

Kite shook his head. "You were really, really rude. You should definitely take flowers."

CHAPTER 51

Liberty was glad to be safely back in her flat before Venetia returned from the ballroom with Heron and Kite. She hadn't seen Heron since that first morning after his return from France, and she was happy to avoid him if she could. She and Swan had had a successful morning at the hairdresser, and Swan had been delighted with her new, chic style, which had the added bonus of concealing her hearing aids. They had lunched at the Bubble and Squeak, and now Swan had retired to her room to read. She had joined the town library and had borrowed a selection of particularly grisly crime novels.

Liberty was trying hard not to open her laptop and continue tinkering with her business plans for the ballroom. She was so excited about the renovation work, which was about to begin. The electrician and decorators were starting on Monday, having reassured her that it would be possible for them to work around each other. Mick from Swell and Noble had been in touch to say that the mirrors and chandeliers were ready and that the chairs would be completed by the end of the following week, by which time the new curtains should also be ready to hang. She had drawn up a spreadsheet showing the time slots that would be available for classes and functions at the ballroom. Liberty had agreed with Venetia that an incremental opening would be prudent, releasing more slots as they grew busier. If they grew busier. Venetia had decided to teach five ballroom classes a week herself, and something that she had described as music and movement for adults. Her plan was to run less formal, fun classes for "the young at heart" to promote mobility, flexibility, and mental well-being. She had told Liberty that she planned to work with Evangeline to try to encourage some of the people who came to the drop-in center to take part, and that she would hold a special class for them once a week that would be free of charge. To everyone's surprise, Swan had volunteered to assist.

Liberty wandered over to the window and looked out over the trees in the garden. The tips of their branches were spiked with green as new leaves were just beginning to emerge. It had all been going so well until that wretched woman had stuck her nose in! Liberty had set up Instagram and Facebook accounts for the ballroom and had begun sharing the progress of its restoration to generate interest and hopefully clients. Unfortunately, her posts had generated interest of an entirely unwelcome nature on Facebook from a woman named Lavinia Whizen, who was conducting a social media smear campaign against the ballroom. She was urging people to join her in her objections, alleging that the ballroom would create a noise nuisance in the evening, both with music and with crowds behaving rowdily outside, and increased traffic and car-parking congestion. It was unclear from her profile how close Mrs. Whizen's home was to the ballroom, but she gave the impression that it would affect her personally, so Liberty assumed that she must live nearby. It was all nonsense, of course, and Liberty had replied with what she had hoped were a few placatory lines. But Mrs. Whizen was not to be placated and was gaining an alarming number of passengers on her ballroom bandwagon, many of whom didn't live locally but were clearly willing to be indignant on her behalf. She claimed to have the sympathetic ear of her local councilor and had, that afternoon, added a post on Facebook suggesting a protest outside the building. Liberty had delayed telling Venetia about it, hoping that she would be able to deal with Mrs. Whizen herself, but that was looking increasingly unlikely. And there was always the fear that if a local councilor became involved, things could get tricky, even if it was only in terms of bad publicity. She had called Evangeline when she saw the latest post to ask if she had come across her before—had Lavinia Whizen perhaps objected to the drop-in center at any time? Evangeline hadn't answered her phone, so Liberty had left a message. She was just about to flip open her laptop and check Facebook again when there was a knock at the door. She smiled, relieved to have a distraction. It was probably Kite come to tell her about his latest visit to his den or to persuade her to play Clue.

She opened the door, and her smile dissolved into an expression of shocked surprise. It was Heron, looking acutely embarrassed and brandishing a bouquet of yellow roses.

"May I come in?"

Without saying anything, she opened the door wider to allow him in. He stepped inside and stood, looking strangely marooned in the middle of the room, clutching the flowers. He thrust them toward her.

"For you," he said.

Liberty took them gingerly. "Why?"

"I wanted to apologize . . ." he began.

"Well, there's nothing stopping you," Liberty replied curtly before she could check herself.

What is it with men? she thought. *They treat you like dirt and then think if they turn up with flowers or wine or chocolates, all will be forgiven.* That was what Graham had done all the time. Let her down and then assumed that he could worm his way back into her bed with some glib apology and generic gift. Not that she'd been to bed with Heron, obviously. That was never going to happen. But the principle was the same. Heron looked startled and then embarrassed—and increasingly uncomfortable. His fingers plucked at the collar of his shirt, and a sheen of perspiration glistened on his top lip. Suddenly, Liberty was ashamed of herself. This person in front of her was not Graham. He was a pompous and socially inept man who was going through a painful divorce and was perhaps genuinely, if a little clumsily, trying to apologize for his bad behavior.

"I'm sorry," she said flatly. "That was rude. Please do carry on."

Heron cleared his throat. "Miss Bell, I'd like to apologize—no, I *do* apologize—for the way that I spoke to you and for threatening to fire you—"

"Which you can't because you're not my employer." Liberty wasn't going to let him off too lightly.

"Quite. I was angry and upset, which I realize is no excuse . . ."

"Quite."

"But I am genuinely sorry, and Kite told me that you like yellow roses."

Liberty couldn't help but smile. She wondered if Kite had brokered this whole apology. Still, at least Heron had seen it through. Perhaps she should give him the benefit of the doubt—if only for Kite's sake.

"Thank you. I do, very much, and these are beautiful. And please call me Liberty, Miss Bell makes me sound like a schoolteacher." She took the flowers over to the sink and ran some water into a vase. "I'm sorry to hear about your divorce. It must be very difficult for you."

Heron was silent, and when Liberty looked up from what she was doing, she was horrified to see that his eyes were full of tears.

"Come and sit down," she told him firmly, pulling out one of the chairs from beneath the table. She took an open bottle of wine from the fridge and poured them each a glass. "Here," she said, pushing one across the table toward him.

He rubbed angrily at his eyes with the back of his hand. "No, no," he said, shaking his head. "I'm fine. I'm just being pathetic. I need to get a grip. Besides, it's too early for a drink. It's only just gone four."

Liberty raised her eyebrows and defiantly took a large swig from her glass, and then she smiled at him. A gentle and kind, but slightly mischievous, smile—daring him to join her.

AN HOUR LATER they had opened a second bottle of wine, and Heron was looking slightly happier and a lot more relaxed. He had told Liberty a little about Monica's affair with Maurice, and, tentatively at first, they had exchanged anecdotes about their disappointing love lives. Liberty had stopped short of admitting that Graham had been married. It was likely to offend Heron's sense of propriety. And now that she thought about it, perhaps he would be right to be offended. For Heron was in the same position as Graham's wife had been. Liberty had never thought much about Graham's wife, but sitting here opposite Heron, she realized how selfish she had been. She had always thought of herself as the victim in her relationship with Graham, but now she realized that his wife had far more claim to that title than she had ever had. And if Graham treated his wife with so little respect, why would he have treated Liberty any better once the novelty had worn off? It was a sobering thought that she had been the architect of her own sad fate, but strangely reassuring too. It meant that she could make her own life better without waiting for someone else to do it for her. In fact, she already had.

"How did you like Kite's den?" she asked Heron.

He smiled broadly. "Kite's so thrilled with it, and it is a wonderful place, but I do worry about him sometimes. At his age I was always playing sports and having a whale of a time with my mates, but he appears to prefer his own company or the company of adults."

"He has his school friend, Ravi, and I shouldn't worry about him preferring the company of adults. He's perfectly capable of choosing his own friends wisely—and, of course, he and Colin are almost inseparable. I don't know much about kids, but I get the impression that Kite is growing into himself, if that makes any sense. He's not like most boys and he knows that, but I don't think that bothers him so much anymore."

"He does seem much happier now that he's not boarding, and he obviously loves living here. I honestly thought he would enjoy being a boarder—I did. And I suppose I hoped that it might bring him out of himself, give him more confidence. It seems I couldn't have been more wrong. But living here has done the trick."

"Your mother certainly has a way of bringing out the best in people. She makes you feel as though anything is possible. And over the last few months she's been unstoppable. She has the energy of a woman half her age! It's as though the ballroom has reignited something inside her." Liberty smiled. "I know that sounds a bit bonkers, but that's the best way I can describe it."

Heron had to concede that his mother was a very different person now from the widow he had left behind when he'd gone to France. Her new self-assurance had taken him by surprise, but more than that, she had a joie de vivre that he hadn't seen in her before. He hoped that it was the ballroom rather than the death of his father that had brought about this change. He had always believed that his parents' marriage had been a happy one, and he would hate to discover that he had been deluded. The thought made him fidgety, and he got up and wandered around the room, inspecting the contents of Liberty's bookshelves and her collection of records. He spotted the photograph album that Liberty's mother had left her and picked it up.

"May I?" he asked.

Liberty nodded. "My mother left it to me in her will. It may or may not contain some sort of message."

Heron's eyes lit up, and for the first time, Liberty saw a real resemblance to Kite.

"I love cracking codes and puzzles and the like!"

As he flicked through the pages, his brow descended into a puzzled frown.

"It's an unusual selection. The pictures could be completely random or carefully chosen."

He sat down again at the table and began to look through the photographs more closely. In the first, Liberty was a toddler eating something from a bowl. She didn't look as though she was enjoying it very much.

"I don't suppose you can remember what it was?"

Liberty shook her head. She had been a fussy eater as a child, and her mother had always struggled to persuade her to try anything new. The next photo was the one taken before the fateful dance class.

"I didn't want to go, and when I got there, I wouldn't join in." She spared him the embarrassing details. She explained that the next one was taken with her friends before a Take That concert.

"You don't look very happy. Didn't you want to go there either?"

"I did—I really, really did. I was just nervous. I remember I was up so late the night before, trying to decide what to wear. I was desperate to look as cool as my friends."

She could tell by the expression on Heron's face that this notion was completely lost on him. They moved on to the next photo—one of Liberty in a bridesmaid's dress—and once again she wasn't smiling.

"This was at my cousin's wedding. I had to read a poem at the service, and I got my words mixed up. It was so embarrassing."

There was a picture of Liberty standing next to a friend's dog and another of her sitting next to her father in a roller coaster at Blackpool. She looked horribly uncomfortable in both. She had always been wary around dogs.

Heron pointed at the Blackpool photo. "I take it you don't like roller coasters?"

Liberty gave a rueful smile. "I love them. But I always used to worry that something would go wrong and that the cars would come flying off the tracks and crash to the ground. It didn't stop me riding them, but it always spoiled it a little bit."

The day she went off to university for the first time was captured: Liberty looking nervous and flanked by suitcases next to her father's car. The last two in the album were the only photos in which Liberty looked truly happy. In the penultimate one she was pictured in her old bedroom, sitting on the floor next to her record player. She was pulling a record from its paper sleeve, ready to play it, and she was grinning broadly.

"Do you still have all your vinyl from back then?" Heron asked.

"Pretty much. There have been a few casualties during moves over the years, but I still have most of them." She wondered if she still had the single in the photograph. The cover looked familiar, but she couldn't remember for the life of her what the record had been.

The final picture was of Liberty and her parents outside the Brighton beach hut.

"Well, at least the album has a happy ending! That's a lovely photo."

"Yes, but what about the others?" Liberty replied. "They're all reminders of times when I was anxious or unhappy—or maybe occasions when Mum felt that I had let her down, like the dance class and the wedding."

"Or perhaps that's just how you see it. You could argue that they're simply photos of things that your mother wanted to remember— milestones in her daughter's life captured as she was growing up. God knows, my mother has plenty of pictures of me looking grumpy, but I'm pretty sure that wasn't why she took them."

There was a knock on the door, and without waiting for an answer, Kite burst in. He scanned the room, taking in the bottle of wine and glasses on the table.

"You've been ages, Dad!" he said with a meaningful smirk. "We're having takeaway from the Purple Elephant, and Nisha said to ask if you wanted anything?" He paused for a moment before adding with comedic emphasis, "Both of you!"

CHAPTER 52

The email had arrived in Venetia's inbox the day after her notice had appeared in *The Times* for the second week. It was from Francis Taylor, brief but unexpectedly friendly, considering that he was a stranger to her.

Dear Venetia,

I hope that you are well.

I saw your notice in *The Times* concerning Francis Taylor and Torin McGuire, and I am responding on behalf of us both. I am Francis, and we met briefly at Hawk's funeral. If there is anything I can help you with, then I should be more than happy to speak to you or to meet with you in person. I live in Brighton, but it would be no trouble for me to come to Bedford, or you could come here for a day at the seaside if you would prefer!

I look forward to hearing from you.

With very best wishes,
Francis

Venetia had decided that a face-to-face meeting would be better. She couldn't know for certain what Francis might be able to reveal about her husband, but if her suspicions were correct, it wasn't the sort of thing that would be easy to discuss on the telephone.

"I've got you a coffee." Swan arrived at her side and handed her a lidded cup. "Shall we make our way to the platform? Our train should be here soon."

Venetia had debated whether to go to Brighton alone, but Swan had offered to accompany her, and she had accepted. It would be nice to have some moral support from the one person who understood the possible ramifications of the meeting, and Swan's presence gave her a cover story—a "girls' day out" at the seaside. Kite had been disappointed that he couldn't go too, as it was a school day, but Venetia had told him that they would go again in the summer holidays. She didn't want anyone else to know her real reason for going to Brighton—particularly Heron. Whatever she discovered, she was determined that Heron's memories of his father should remain unaltered. Until recently, she would have told Liberty the truth about why she was going to Brighton. After all, Liberty had made great efforts to find Francis Taylor and Torin McGuire. But although Venetia had told Liberty about the email, she merely said that she had been able to thank them for attending the funeral at last.

The reason for Venetia's reticence was the rather surprising friendship that was developing between Liberty and Heron. Since the evening of the Purple Elephant takeaway, Heron had taking to calling in at the house more frequently during the week, and the previous Saturday, Liberty had joined Heron and Kite on a kite-flying expedition, followed by a brownie-making session in Venetia's kitchen. Venetia had returned home from a walk with Colin to be greeted by the sound of laughter coming from the kitchen and an appraising smile from Swan as she passed her in the hallway on the way up to her room.

It was midmorning, and the train was mercifully uncrowded. Venetia sat staring out the window while Swan grappled with the crossword, occasionally asking Venetia for assistance. As they passed through Blackfriars, where the Thames glittered in the bright spring sunshine beside and beneath them, Swan folded her newspaper and looked straight at Venetia.

"Now, you must tell me what you would like me to do. If you want me to stay with you while you speak with Mr. Taylor, I will. But if you'd prefer me to make myself scarce and come back at an agreed time, then I'm sure I'll be able to find something to keep me amused. I may buy some chips and wander down the pier!"

Venetia leaned over and touched Swan's hand. "Thank you for coming with me today—I'm really grateful. And no, I don't want you to make yourself scarce—that is, unless you're afraid you might hear something you don't want to about Hawk."

Swan shook her head. "Hawk was my brother, and I shall always love him. There may be things I don't know about him, but what I do know, and what I've always known, is that he was a good man, and I very much doubt that anything Mr. Taylor says will change my mind. But what about you? Are you worried about what you might find out?"

"I don't think I am. As you say, Hawk was a good man—perhaps in some respects too good for his own good."

They got a cab from Brighton station to the agreed meeting place, the Victoria Bar at the Grand. At the entrance to the hotel, one of the tartan-trousered porters raised his bowler hat to them and opened the door. Venetia recognized the man seated on a plush gold sofa in the bar area as soon as she saw him. His pale green eyes met hers, and he stood up, offering both hands in greeting, which she clasped briefly in her own. His smile was warm and reassuring, and Venetia felt herself relax a little.

"This is my sister-in-law Swan—Hawk's sister. She was at his funeral, but I don't think you met."

"Probably just as well—I was drunk," Swan added with her customary bluntness.

They sat down and ordered coffee, much to Swan's disappointment. The bar had a tempting cocktail menu.

"It's lovely to see you again," Francis began, "but I must admit I'm intrigued as to why you wanted to talk to me. How are you getting on? It must be hard being alone after so many years of marriage."

Venetia looked down at the wedding ring she still wore and twisted it around on her finger. "Actually, I'm not alone," she said brightly. "Swan has come to live with me, my grandson is currently staying with us, I have a resident PA, and I rescued a German shepherd from a drugs factory. In truth, the house hasn't been so full of life in years."

"And she's bought a ballroom," Swan couldn't resist interjecting. Over recent weeks she had become as enthusiastic about the ballroom as Kite was, and equally keen to be involved.

Francis smiled. "A ballroom! That's quite something. Didn't you used to be a dancer?"

"That's how I met Hawk," Venetia replied. "I was his dance teacher."

Francis nodded. "I remember now. Hawk told me."

There was a brief silence during which Swan caught Venetia's eye and gave her an encouraging nod, as if to say, "Get on with it."

Venetia took a sip of her coffee to steel herself and then set down her cup. "Francis—if I may call you that—I wanted to ask you some questions about Hawk. I found a book in his study with an inscription and a letter to someone—someone I've never heard of. It was a very . . . intimate letter, and although Hawk never sent it, he didn't destroy it, which makes me think that he wanted me to find it, but only after he was dead.

"I always felt throughout our marriage that there was a compartment in Hawk's life that he kept from me, and the book and the letter—I think they may belong to it. I wondered if you could shed any light on them?"

"What was the book?" Francis asked in a quiet voice.

Venetia took the copy of *The Lion, the Witch and the Wardrobe* from her handbag and handed it to him. He traced his fingers over the cover before opening it and reading the words written on the title page.

"Do you know who A. F. is?" Venetia asked.

Francis sighed and closed the book but continued to hold it carefully between his hands. "Are you sure you want to know? It was all so long ago. I hadn't seen Hawk for years. Might it be better to leave the past in the past?"

Venetia shook her head. "I need to know. But this isn't about recriminations—quite the opposite, in fact. It's about reconciliation. There are things I need to know before I can move on and make the most of the future." She paused for a moment, trying to find the right words. "I loved Hawk, but I was never in love with him. I molded myself into exactly the kind of wife he wanted, and I gave him a son who became the center of his world. I tried to give him everything I possibly could because I felt it was what he deserved for marrying me. For so long I felt guilty about the reasons I agreed to be his wife."

Venetia paused again and looked directly at Francis before continuing.

"In the beginning, I was convinced that Hawk was head over heels in love with me. But later, there were times when I questioned this and wondered if he had merely convinced himself that he was, because it was what he wanted. Whether we had each, for our own reasons, settled for a union that offered safety, security, and a loving friendship at the expense of passion and romance. Please understand, Francis, I have no complaints. Hawk was the best husband to me that he could be. But it would really help me to move on and perhaps let go of my guilt if I'm right."

Francis appeared to consider Venetia's words carefully before finally replying. "You are a very perceptive woman, Venetia. Hawk was lucky to have you in his life."

"Believe me, I was just as lucky to have him in mine."

"Do you mind me asking why you did agree to marry him?"

Swan reached over and squeezed her arm. "You don't have to answer that," she said.

Venetia knew she must. If she was expecting Francis to be honest with her, she had to return the favor.

"I was sexually assaulted. Hawk witnessed the attack and intervened. He rescued me."

"And beat the crap out of the bastard who did it," Swan muttered under her breath.

"Then my mother died, my hair fell out, and my life fell apart. I'd been training for months with my dance partner for a big competition in Blackpool, but I lost my nerve and couldn't face dancing anymore. Through all that, Hawk was there for me. He made me feel safe and loved, and at the time, they were the two things I wanted most."

Francis nodded. "I'm so sorry." He was still holding the book.

"But can you help?" Patience wasn't one of Swan's virtues.

"Yes, I can." He paused for a moment, as though gathering himself. "I gave this book to Hawk as a birthday present. I am A. F."

Venetia felt her face flush as she thought about the letter from Hawk's wallet that she had also brought with her. "How did you know him?" she asked, trying to keep her voice steady.

"I ran a secondhand bookshop in London near to Hawk's chambers, and one day he came in looking for a copy of *The Diary of a Nobody* for his brother." Francis sighed. "Even after all these years I can still remember tiny details about that day. It was raining and business was slow. I'd brought potato and leek soup from home for my lunch, and Hawk was wearing a navy-blue-and-silver-striped bow tie. The attraction between us was obvious and instant, but as we stood and talked, it was clear that it made Hawk uncomfortable. He bought the book and left, and I didn't expect to see him again. I was sorry, but in a way relieved. I'd met men before who lived and passed as straight but couldn't resist the occasional clandestine foray into gay sex. For most of them, it was like trying to keep a hungry lion satisfied with scraps. It merely stoked the craving. It was a dangerous way to live, and someone always got hurt. But I was wrong about Hawk. He did come back, and there was something very moving about the way he persevered through his discomfort."

Venetia recalled the way that Hawk had persisted with his dance lessons.

"We became friends, and although I wanted more—and so too, I believed, did Hawk—I didn't push things any further. I was prepared to wait and see what happened. Gradually, I introduced him to my friends, including Torin, and took him to some of the quieter pubs and clubs that we frequented, but he was always conflicted and riddled with guilt." Francis smiled sadly. "That was why I wrote the inscription in the book. I saw his pain and I wanted to make it go away. I wanted him to allow himself to be honest—to be the man he was instead of the man he thought he should be. I wanted him to stop living in fear and have some fun." He looked at Venetia. "I'm sorry—I know how terrible that sounds given that he was married to you at the time. But you see, I was in love with him."

Venetia shook her head. "Don't be sorry. I'm glad that Hawk experienced love with another man at least once in his life. Because the whole time he was married to me, he was denying who he really was and depriving himself of a relationship that might have made him truly happy."

"But what about you? Wasn't it the same for you? By keeping you safe, Hawk also stopped you from facing your fears and reclaiming the life that was taken from you by your attacker."

It was true, Venetia thought. They had each been a refuge for the other. Their marriage had been a place to hide from the lives they had really wanted but had been too afraid to live. Now with the ballroom, at least she had a second chance. An opportunity to live a life more like the one she had envisaged for herself when she was young.

"We were coconspirators in our marriage," she admitted. "And now I'm trying to make amends. But what happened to you and Hawk?"

Francis's expression grew serious. "Would anyone like a drink?"

HAVING ORDERED LUNCH and moved on to wine—much to Swan's relief—Francis continued with his story.

"It was late summer in 1986, and we'd been seeing each other for about a year. Our relationship had progressed beyond friendship, but . . ." Francis hesitated, clearly searching for a tactful way to express himself. "But it was never *fully* physical. Hawk came to the bookshop one day to meet me for lunch, and just as he arrived, the phone rang. It was Torin. He could barely speak, and I could hear him crying—sobbing on the other end of the phone. Scot, one of our friends, had just died of an AIDS-related illness. We hadn't seen him for a while, and it transpired that as soon as he knew he was ill he had gone home to his parents' house in Bristol. His mother had written to Torin with details of the arrangements for Scot's funeral. He was only twenty-three."

They sat in silence for a moment, each with their own memories of the genesis of what had then been a terrifying, stigmatizing, and catastrophic virus. Venetia recalled the press coverage of Princess Diana shaking hands with an AIDS patient without wearing gloves. She had had no idea at the time how deeply it must have affected Hawk.

"We went for lunch, but neither of us could eat anything," Francis continued. "Scot made it real, you see. It was no longer something that was happening in the newspapers and on television; it was happening to us in real life. Real death. It could kill us—specifically us, because of who we were."

Venetia recalled the lines in Hawk's letter:

Our friendship has been the most important, the most fulfilling,
and the most exciting of my life. But it is wrong—and dangerous—
and it must end before it goes too far and while I still have the strength
to walk away from you.

"Hawk walked me back to the shop and then walked away. I never
saw him again. I rang him at work, but he wouldn't take my call, so I
wrote to him, but he didn't reply. After that, I respected his decision
that our relationship was over. It broke my heart. But I think perhaps
that it was love only for me and more of a friendship for Hawk. I don't
think that he could allow himself to love another man."

"But why did you sign yourself A. F. in the book?" Swan asked.
"They aren't your initials."

Francis smiled. "For a gay man, Hawk could be so straitlaced! My
friends all called me Frankie back then, but Hawk hated it. He said it
was too camp. He would only ever call me by my full name. He said
that I would always be Francis to him. Always Francis—A. F."

Their food arrived and the waiter topped up their wineglasses.

"It's such a waste!" Venetia exclaimed suddenly, unable to keep
her frustration to herself. "All those years of living in fear and pre-
tending to be people we weren't. I do hope that you had a second
chance for love, Francis."

"I did, actually. After years of Torin and I being just friends, it
became something else. He's my husband, and we're very happy."

When they had finished lunch, Venetia suggested that she and
Swan go for a walk along the pier. "Would you like to join us?" she
asked Francis.

"I'd love to, but I need to get back to the shop. You see, I haven't
quite managed to retire yet, and Torin and I have a little bookshop
in the Lanes. You must pay us a visit next time you're in Brighton."

"We shall! And you must come and see my ballroom. Thank you
so much again for your honesty. Now that I know the truth, I think I

can finally let go of what belongs in the past." She raised her glass in a toast: "Here's to second chances!"

As they got up to leave, Venetia took Francis's arm for a moment.

"You were wrong about one thing," she said, and handed him the letter. "I don't know why Hawk didn't send it. But I do know that he would never have written it if he hadn't meant every word. He *did* love you."

CHAPTER 53

Liberty stopped in at her flat to pick up her laptop before heading off to the ballroom. The house was empty; Venetia, Swan, and Colin would be there already. The grand opening was just a few weeks away, and they were having a meeting that afternoon to finalize some of the details and discuss future plans. Liberty had been to lunch with Mr. Court, and she had decided that it would be the last time. He had been friendly enough, but it all seemed so pointless. He still wouldn't tell her anything about the mysterious inheritance or the conditions of her mother's will that Liberty had been trying to fulfill in order to earn it. Well, she'd had enough. And besides, she didn't need it, whatever it was. She had a job she loved and was surrounded by people she really cared about. She felt as though she had finally found her place with Venetia, Swan, and Kite. She even liked the dog now. And then there was Heron. It was early days, but much to her surprise she was becoming quite fond of him, and they were spending more and more time together. He had even offered to speak to Mr. Court on her behalf. She'd been grateful but had declined. There was only one thing that continued to worry her. She had spoken to Evangeline about Lavinia Whizen and her malicious posts on Facebook, and Evangeline had told her not to worry about it—she would deal with it. Liberty had taken her at her word, grateful to hand over the problem to someone else. But now that the launch was so close, she wished that she had checked with Evangeline that she had indeed been able to silence the wretched woman and her hangers-on.

The meeting was taking place in the drop-in center. Venetia had made it clear to Evangeline that she had no wish to interfere in the day-to-day running of the center or the church, but that they would need to coordinate their timetables to ensure that they were never in conflict with each other. For example, they wouldn't want a particularly noisy dance class taking place in the ballroom at the same time that a church service was being conducted. A generous legacy from a former member of the church meant that the rent payments for the church and the center were guaranteed for the next three years. The aim was that the combined revenue from all three ventures would at least cover the running costs of the building, including the salary of a part-time caretaker—a job that was earmarked for Crow—and, depending on the success of the ballroom, perhaps in the future a general manager.

When Liberty arrived, Venetia, Swan, Evangeline, Crow, and Norma were discussing new activities planned for the drop-in center. Currently for teas, coffees, and lunches, a voluntary donation system was in place, which meant that those who could afford to pay subsidized those who couldn't. Evangeline had suggested that they extend this to cover the proposed new book club and library, as well as arts and crafts classes.

"We can ask for donations to get the library started, and then people can bring in books they have read and swap them for ones they haven't," Evangeline explained.

"And those who haven't got any books and can't afford to buy them can borrow them anyway," Crow added.

"Crow's a big reader," Evangeline said, "and he came up with the idea of a monthly book club. He's also agreed to run some arts and crafts classes."

"Evangeline can be a very persuasive woman," Crow said with a smile.

"Well, we can't let talent like that go to waste! You make the most amazing paper animals, so I'm sure you've got other artistic strings to your bow," Evangeline replied with a wink.

Venetia wasn't at all surprised that Evangeline had managed to get Crow so involved. Although nothing had been said, she was pretty sure that they were now a couple, and she was very happy for them.

"And that lovely son of yours," Evangeline continued, addressing Venetia, "I was wondering if he might consider doing a free legal clinic for a couple of hours, maybe once a month? I know that some of our ladies and gentlemen would really benefit from some expert advice that they often don't know how to access and certainly couldn't afford to pay for."

"That's a marvelous idea," Venetia replied, while wondering how likely it was that Heron would agree to it.

"Perhaps we should get Liberty to ask him," Swan suggested.

A few months ago, Liberty would have been embarrassed at Swan's innuendo, but now she just smiled tolerantly. "Would you like to hear my update on the ballroom?" she asked, flipping open her laptop. "As you know, the renovations are complete."

"And it looks beautiful." Evangeline clapped her hands together.

"You're not the only one who thinks so," continued Liberty. "As a result of the showings I've done this week, I've secured regular bookings for ten sessions a week so far, including Irish dancing, belly dancing, bhangra, and, of course, ballroom. I've invited all the teachers of these classes to attend the launch, along with a number of others who've expressed an interest. I'm still pursuing a license to sell alcohol on the premises and the necessary permissions to hold evening events in the ballroom, which would be a significant source of income, but it's looking promising—particularly as there are no residential properties close or adjacent to the building."

"And we shut up that witch woman Lavinia Whizen!" Evangeline added gleefully.

Everyone's face except for Liberty's was blank.

"I hadn't actually said anything to Venetia—" Liberty began.

"Ha! That nasty woman was trying to sabotage us on Facebook with her ridiculous objections, but I called her bluff!"

Evangeline went on to explain about Lavinia Whizen's Facebook posts and how, when Liberty had told her about them, she had recognized the woman's surname. It turned out that she was the wife of the previous buyer, who had dropped out when planning permission for the luxury apartments had been denied and the prospect of making an enormous profit disappeared. It seemed that her objections to the ballroom were simply the result of extremely sour grapes and nothing better to do with her time than incite unrest on social media. When Evangeline had confronted her with the embarrassing truth, she had swiftly backed off. She didn't even live in Bedford.

Venetia could hardly take it all in. They were almost there. What had seemed like a completely madcap idea only months ago was about to become reality.

"When are the formal invitations to the launch going out?" she asked Liberty.

"I just need you to approve the guest list and then they're good to go," Liberty replied.

"Well, if that's everything, I have just one final announcement to make." Venetia smiled at the expectant faces around the table. "The ballroom needs a name, and I think that Kite has come up with the perfect suggestion. He got the idea from the last model you made him, Crow, and it couldn't be more fitting. Its name will be the Phoenix Ballroom!"

There were murmurs of approval followed by an enthusiastic round of applause.

"Well, I think we should all have tea to celebrate!" Evangeline declared. "And I've made a pineapple upside-down cake specially to go with it!"

While the others got up from the table and went in search of tea,

Venetia slipped away and went upstairs to the ballroom. Showers of light fragments danced across the wooden floor as the afternoon sun reflected off the chandeliers. She walked over to the record player that had been retrieved from the attic and selected a record from the pile that stood beside it. The disc dropped onto the deck with a satisfying click, and the familiar melody of "A Kiss to Build a Dream On" echoed around the room. Venetia began to dance. Even after all these years the steps came as easily to her as walking. As she turned, she caught sight of a figure standing in the doorway.

"It would appear that you're in need of a partner."

Venetia froze. She hadn't heard that voice for so long, but she would recognize it anywhere. He walked toward her, a little uncertain, but then he smiled, and tears filled Venetia's eyes. He threw open his arms and drew her in close, resting his chin on the top of her head.

THEY SAT IN the quiet of the church and drank tea while Brendan told her why he had come.

"I saw the posts about the renovations on Instagram. I couldn't believe that it was you who had bought it. I had to come and see for myself."

Venetia couldn't stop staring at him. She couldn't quite register that he was really there. She had so much to ask, so much to tell him. So much to explain.

She began with something safe. "How are you? Where are you living these days?"

"I'm back in Bedford now—well, a village close by. When my wife died a couple of years back, I wanted to be closer to my sister, so I sold our place in London and came home."

"And do you have children?"

Brendan smiled. "Two. A boy and a girl—and six grandchildren. Although I don't feel old enough to be a grandad! And what about you?"

"I have a son and a grandson, Kite."

"And what about Hawk?" The tone of his voice involuntarily hardened just a little.

"He died—last year."

"I'm sorry."

"Oh God, Brendan, so am I. For so many things. I can't tell you how much I've missed you."

This time it was Brendan's eyes that filled with tears. He shook his head. "Why, Venetia? What in God's name made you do it? I loved you. You must have known that! But you shut me out completely, and you have no idea how much that hurt. You gave up everything we'd worked so hard for. I know it must have been difficult when you lost your mum, but it was her last wish. She wanted you to live your life—to dance at Blackpool. All this time I've chased it round and round in my head, trying to understand—" He broke off and took a breath, trying to calm his anger. "And then you married that man. A good, decent man, I'm sure—but you didn't love him! Tell me I'm wrong if I am—but I know you weren't in love with him."

Venetia reached over and took his hand. "You aren't wrong," she said. She lifted his hand to her lips and gently kissed it. "I have a son and a grandson to protect, and they must never hear of this. But I think it's about time I told you the truth."

CHAPTER 54

Venetia gazed out at the river from her bedroom window. The swans were there again. They were facing each other beak to beak, their arched necks forming the shape of a heart. She recalled that evening after Hawk's funeral when she had stood in this same spot, poised on the precipice of a new life, wondering if she would have the courage to jump. And here she was, just nine months later, reincarnated. She was about to take to the dance floor again in her own ballroom. She smiled to herself and wondered what Hawk would make of it. She hoped he would be glad for her. Her widow's weeds were a distant memory now; instead she was dressed in a pale pink gown printed with gray-and-white storks—very art deco, she had thought when she had first seen it. It was the evening of the launch party, and Venetia wanted to look her best.

LIBERTY CHECKED HER to-do list one more time before leaving her flat. She was nervous and excited. She had bought a new dress for the occasion—it was midnight blue, fitted, and with a side split that reached the bottom of her thigh. She had dithered in the shop, wondering if it was too daring, but had then thought, *What the hell!* and bought it anyway. And then she'd gone the whole nine yards and had her hair and nails done too. She and Swan had spent a couple of hours at the salon that afternoon, and Liberty had fretted the whole time that she ought to be at the ballroom, even though she knew that everything was prepared for the party because she had checked it all herself several times already. She slipped on her coat and checked her reflection in the mirror by the door. She smiled at herself. "Well done, Liberty!" she told her reflection. "I'm proud of you." And she was. The ballroom was about to open, and she knew that she had played a major part in making it happen.

"AT LEAST THERE are proper sandwiches—even if they are tiny!" Kite declared approvingly to Venetia when they arrived at the ballroom, surveying the buffet that Liberty had ordered from the caterers. Kite had also dressed for the occasion and was wearing another of Hawk's bow ties. Evangeline had wanted to prepare the food herself, but Venetia had forbidden it, insisting that she take the night off to enjoy the party. Kite made a mental note to take some sandwiches home. He would wrap them up in a paper napkin and slip them into his coat pocket when no one was looking. He had been most put out that dogs weren't invited to the party, but Venetia had said that it would be too noisy and crowded for them and that they wouldn't enjoy it. Kite was pretty sure that they would've enjoyed the sandwiches.

Venetia stood by the door greeting guests with Liberty, who had been introducing her to each of the dance teachers as they arrived. Heron poured drinks at the bar, Kite hovered by the buffet, and Evangeline, unable to resist helping, walked around the room with a tray of canapés and sandwiches. Crow was manning the record player and Brendan was with him, selecting music for the dancing that was planned for later in the evening. As part of the renovations, a new sound system had been installed, but for this evening Venetia had wanted to use the record player that she and Brendan had used when they were practicing for competitions.

"Good evening, Tommy." Venetia welcomed a man she barely recognized. The once filthy, bearded, and bedraggled ex-soldier had undergone his own transformation. Clean-shaven and dressed in a secondhand but nonetheless very smart suit, he was here as Swan's guest. When she spotted him, she glided over and took his arm. She was dressed in a long gown of peacock blue with a matching kimono and a black feather boa.

"You look very nice," Tommy muttered to her, "but don't expect me to dance."

"You look very dapper yourself, soldier," she replied. "And trust me—you will definitely be dancing."

Through Evangeline, Swan had found a hostel for homeless men, and she had badgered them relentlessly until they had offered Tommy a place. The only problem had been that they wouldn't take dogs, which was how Hedgehog had become a live-in companion for Colin Firth, much to Kite's delight. The next phase of Swan's mission was to help Tommy find a job, which was going to be easier now that he had a permanent address.

Mr. Court had not been on Liberty's list and was the last person she was expecting to see walk through the door. He greeted her with a smile. "What a beautiful dress," he said. "You look lovely."

She met his compliment with a frown. "Mr. Court—what are you doing here?"

"Your friend invited me," he replied, looking a little flustered. "The lady who came to lunch with you that first time."

"He's quite right—I did." Once again Swan had appeared through the throng. She offered Mr. Court her arm. "Do come with me, Mr. Court. Let's get you a drink."

Venetia wondered what on earth Swan was up to, but before she could speculate any further, her next guests were at the door, and they had been at the top of her list.

"Francis! I'm so glad you could come. And, Torin, it's lovely to see you again. Liberty, these are the elusive funeral guests that you tried so hard to find."

Venetia abandoned her post at the door to show them the ballroom.

"It's stunning, Venetia!" Francis gasped. "I wasn't expecting any-thing as grand as this!"

Venetia beamed with pride. She introduced them to Brendan and Crow and Evangeline. "And this is my grandson, Kite," she said, tak-ing them over to the table where the food was laid out and where Kite was still loitering. "Kite, this is Francis and Torin—they were old friends of your grandpa."

"I remember you!" Kite announced triumphantly. "You were at Grandpa's funeral party where the food was so rubbish. It's much better here—we've got proper sandwiches."

"And it looks as though you've been sampling them already," Venetia said with a smile.

"I've been testing them," he said, his face serious. "You wouldn't want anyone to get food poisoning, would you?"

"It's a tough job, but someone's got to do it!" Heron appeared at his son's side and ruffled his hair affectionately. Kite wriggled free with a laugh.

"Can I offer you gentlemen a drink?" Heron asked. "You'll be needing champagne to toast my brilliant mother when she makes her speech."

Venetia helped herself to a glass and took a large swallow. "Bril-liant"! Venetia would tuck that word of praise away and treasure it. She couldn't recall the last time that Heron had paid her a compliment.

"You remember my son, Heron. You met him briefly at the funeral. Francis and Torin were friends of your father's many years ago."

Francis offered Heron his hand, assessing him with his pale green eyes. "It's good to see you again. You have the look of him," he said. Venetia caught the wistful expression that drifted across his face before he banished it with a smile. "And you're right about your mother. She is a brilliant woman to have achieved all of this," he added, gesturing around the ballroom.

Once all the guests had arrived, Venetia stepped onto the small stage that had been erected at one end of the room. She looked out over the sea of smiling faces and took a moment to savor the myriad emotions that were making her deliciously light-headed. Perhaps the strongest of them all was gratitude. The ballroom had been abandoned, its magic buried beneath years of neglect. But Venetia had rescued it, and in return, it had given her a second chance to dance. A second chance at life and maybe even love. It had given her the opportunity to wipe the slate clean and write a new story. But not just for her; the magic had rippled outward to touch others too. Crow and Evangeline, Tommy and Swan, Kite and Liberty. Their lives had all changed for the better since she had bought the ballroom. And perhaps now, Heron could also make a fresh start.

Someone banged a spoon on a glass, the crowd hushed, and Venetia took a deep breath. Her speech was full of thanks—to everyone for coming, Liberty for all her hard work, Evangeline for her support, Crow for his heroics, Swan for her sound advice, and Kite for his food-poison-prevention services.

"I should also like to thank my son, Heron, for helping me to find my wonderful assistant—and new friend—Liberty. And although at the time he was keen to appoint another candidate, I think it's safe to say he's learned the error of his ways."

Venetia smiled at Heron, whose cheeks were now pink, to let him know that she was only teasing.

"I have, of course, to thank my late husband for leaving me in a position to buy the ballroom in the first place, but I know that it is money well spent. Together, under one roof, the ballroom, the drop-in center, and the church can support one another and provide what will hopefully prove to be an invaluable asset to our local community— something that I know my late husband would applaud."

As Venetia spoke these words, Francis caught her eye and nodded.

"Some of you may not know that many years ago, I worked here in this very ballroom as a dance teacher and even had dreams of owning my own dance school. Back then, I had a very special dance partner who shared my plans for the future, but our lives traveled in different directions and our dance school remained a dream. Until now."

Some spontaneous cheering and applause erupted, but Venetia wasn't quite finished, and she held up her hands to silence the crowd.

"I'm delighted to announce that my former colleague and dance partner has agreed, with only a little arm-twisting, to reprise his role not only as my partner but also as a teacher here with immediate effect."

She turned to Brendan with a dazzling smile and took his hand.

"Brendan, let's dance!"

As Venetia and Brendan made their way onto the dance floor, the crowd parted to allow them through. There was an expectant hush as they took up their starting position, and then Crow lowered the needle and the music of Pérez Prado began to play. Their samba was still magnificent!

Swan greeted Venetia at the end of the dance when she and Brendan came over to get another drink. "Brava! And this gentleman is every bit as good as you said he was," she added, winking at Brendan. She'd already had three glasses of champagne.

"Thank you," Venetia replied, giving Swan an affectionate hug. "But now tell me," she continued, "what are you up to?"

Swan shrugged with feigned innocence. "I have no idea what you're talking about."

Venetia narrowed her eyes. "Mr. Court. What's he doing here?"

"Yes, what's he doing here?" Liberty overheard the question as she came over to refill her glass and was now waiting for an answer.

"I thought he should see the ballroom," Swan replied. "I thought he should see what an amazing job you've done. You must have done more than enough to pass whatever ridiculous test he's been told to set you. I've been trying to ply him with champagne all evening, but he's only had half a glass because he's driving."

"Thank you, Swan. It's really kind of you to try, but honestly, I don't care anymore. I'm perfectly happy as I am." Liberty raised her glass to Swan and took a swig. Her broad smile corroborated her words.

None of them except Swan realized that Mr. Court was standing chatting in a group of people right behind them and had heard everything.

The next dance was a waltz. When the music began, Venetia and Brendan returned to the floor, Swan strong-armed Tommy up from his seat to join them, and Kite climbed onto the stage to showcase his solo moves. Even Crow temporarily abandoned his post at the record player and was dancing cheek to cheek with Evangeline. In resetting the bones in Crow's leg after he had fallen down the stairs, the surgeon had managed to rectify some of the problems caused by his old injury, and Crow's limp was barely noticeable these days. Heron came and found Liberty, who was standing by the door.

"Would you like to dance with me?"

Liberty shook her head. "I don't dance. I can't. I've got two left feet."

Heron took her hand, emboldened by the champagne. "Come on—please! I'm no Fred Astaire, but this one's pretty slow. We can just shuffle around a bit, and if we bump into anyone, you can blame me."

The eager expression on his face reminded her of Kite when he was trying to persuade her to make macaroni and cheese for supper or let him have chips for breakfast.

What the hell, she thought. Surely even she could shuffle. She allowed herself to be led onto the dance floor, and Mr. Court watched with a smile as Heron took her very politely into his arms.

Eventually the party began to wind down and people started saying their goodbyes. Francis and Torin left to catch a late train back to Brighton, and Venetia promised to visit soon with Swan to see the bookshop. It seemed that the evening had been a great success and had resulted in a good many prospective bookings for the ballroom. Before leaving, Mr. Court thanked Swan for his invitation and then asked Liberty if he could have a word with her in private.

"It won't take a moment," he said, taking her to one side. "I just wanted to say that your mother would be proud of you. But more important, she would be happy for you."

He handed her a small padded envelope.

"This is for you," he said. "Have fun."

CHAPTER 55

The beach hut was nestled in the sand dunes on a quiet beach in Norfolk. It was painted in soft pastel shades, and a set of steps led up to a small veranda. The sign above the door read "Liberty Starlight" in gold lettering. Liberty sat in a deck chair on the veranda, staring out across the seemingly boundless sands toward the distant sea, where she could just about make out a group of figures splashing in the waves at the water's edge. She checked her watch. It was nearly lunchtime, and no doubt they would all be starving when they came back. Kite had brought Ravi with him and had begged to bring the dogs as well. As she watched them playing, Liberty was glad that she had agreed.

The envelope Mr. Court had handed her at the end of the party had contained a key and a set of directions. Puzzled, Liberty had rung Mr. Court the following day.

"Does this mean I've passed?" she had asked him.

"It was never like that," he had replied. "Your mother simply wanted two things for you. She told me that she wanted you to live up to your name—Liberty. She wanted you to feel free, and most important, she wanted you to be happy."

"And you think now that I am?"

"From how much you've changed since your mother died and what I saw at the party last night—yes, I do."

"Am I allowed to know where the money from the house went now?"

Liberty heard the smile in his voice. "Your mother left everything to the church and the drop-in center. Funny how things turn out, isn't it?"

"And what about the key?" she had asked. "What's it for?"

"I think it would be more fun if you found out for yourself."

The next weekend, Liberty, Heron, and Kite had set off on a magical mystery tour that had ended up here on the beach. Liberty had turned the key in the lock and walked into her very own beach hut. The inside was picture-perfect, with a camping stove and fridge, a table and two chairs, a small sofa, and a trunk full of beach paraphernalia. The walls were swagged with bunting and fairy lights, and from the ceiling hung a tealight chandelier. Her mother had left an envelope for her on the table.

"Come on, young man," Heron had said to Kite. "Let's leave Liberty in peace for a bit. I'll race you to the sea!"

Liberty had been grateful for his thoughtfulness. Inside the envelope there had been a card with a picture of a winged unicorn on the front. Very much her mother's taste, she had thought.

My darling girl—Liberty!

Enjoy the beach hut. I remember how you always loved the one in Brighton. I'm afraid I couldn't afford one there this time, but hopefully this won't disappoint. If you're here, it means that your life has changed and I can rest in peace, although I'm hoping it's a bit more party-party than peace where I'm going! I knew I had to do something drastic to shake you out of your safe but dull existence, and I thought that if I left you with nothing—pushed you off the edge, so to speak, with no safety net—then maybe you'd learn to fly. The photos in the album were reminders of all the times when you were scared to try, scared to fail—when you had no faith in yourself. I always did—I always believed in you. You are worth so much more

than you think you are. The last two photos were the biggest clues,
though. The beach hut is obvious now, but did you get the one of you
in your bedroom holding the record? You drove me crazy playing it
over and over again.

Don't worry, be happy.

Love you always,
Mum

Of course! That was what had kept nagging at her about the photo.
She had recognized the record sleeve in the photograph but had never
got around to checking her collection to see if she still had it. "Don't
Worry, Be Happy" by Bobby McFerrin. A mother's last wish for her
daughter, and one that Liberty fully intended to embrace.

THE WIND WHISKED grains of sand across the surface of the beach,
but here in the dunes it was warm and sheltered. The only sounds
were the hum of insects and the whisper of marram grass. They came
to the beach hut on weekends as often as they could, and Heron had
even suggested that they book a cottage here during the school holidays for a couple of weeks—just Liberty, Heron, and Kite. Over the
past months Heron had lost a little weight, and his cheeks were more
rosy than florid. Happiness was making him healthier. His commu-
nications with Monica had become much less acrimonious, and between them they had agreed on arrangements that would enable her
to spend time with Kite on a regular basis. The house that they had
shared had been sold, and Heron had moved back into his childhood
home.

It was supposed to be temporary until he could find somewhere for
himself and Kite, but it seemed Venetia's house had worked its magic
on him as it had on Kite and Swan and Colin Firth and Hedgehog,
and Heron now had no plans to leave. It was a home that appeared to

have gathered in its own family, and Liberty was so happy to be one of them. She shaded her eyes from the sun and scanned the horizon. The figures were moving toward her now, and as they grew closer, she could hear excited barks and boyish laughter. They all piled onto the veranda, showering Liberty with sand and droplets of salty water. Colin and Hedgehog gulped fresh water from a shared bowl, and Kite and Ravi collapsed in a heap on the sofa. They rolled their eyes in exaggerated revulsion as Heron bent down and planted a kiss on Liberty's cheek.

"Darling," he said, "I'm absolutely starving!"

CHAPTER 56

Their gondola glided through the rippling waters of the Grand Canal, expertly piloted by Leonardo. He was, he had informed them as he had helped them onto his gleaming boat, a proud Venetian and third-generation gondolier.

"Oh, Venetia, look!" Swan pointed to an exquisite domed building swathed in skeins of morning mist. "It's the Santa Maria della Salute!"

It had been six months since the ballroom had opened and it was thriving. The classes that Venetia taught with Brendan were almost always full, and Liberty had finally secured a license to serve alcohol, so they were now taking bookings for events. Venetia had decided that it was time to make good her promise to accompany Swan to Venice. They had drunk creamy espressos from tiny cups in Saint Mark's Square and visited the basilica and the Doge's Palace. They had seen *La traviata* at La Fenice and drunk champagne during the interval. They had stood outside Ca' Foscari University and wondered what had happened to Tommaso, and Swan had shed a tear. And she had then declared that he was probably fat and bald by now, with a gaggle of grandchildren, but that she hoped he was happy.

"Not that there's anything wrong with being bald," Swan had added, looking to Venetia for reassurance that she hadn't offended her.

"Some of the best people are bald!" Venetia had replied, unfazed.

"Does Brendan know?"

Venetia had nodded.

"Does he mind?"

Venetia had shaken her head.

"Good man!"

It was November, and the sun was no more than a faint promise of light hiding behind leaden clouds, but the city was more beautiful than either of them could have imagined. They passed the graceful frontage of Palazzina Selva and the Royal Gardens, and as they gazed in wonder, Swan asked Leonardo if he would take them to the Bridge of Sighs.

"Ah, yes! The Ponte dei Sospiri. Of course, signora. It's still early so it shouldn't be too busy."

They turned onto the Rio del Palazzo, and as they slipped under the Ponte della Paglia, the sun finally emerged, and the ornate arch of the Bridge of Sighs rose up before them. It's said that if you kiss your lover beneath the bridge at the exact moment of sunset when the bells of Saint Mark's Campanile can be heard across the city, then your love will be eternal. It was ten thirty in the morning, the sun had only just made an appearance, and the man she loved was hundreds of miles away, but Venetia was the happiest she had been in her entire life. As they passed beneath the Bridge of Sighs, Swan trailed her hand briefly through the chilly water.

"It's strange, isn't it, how a bridge with such a dark history is now considered to be one of the most romantic places in Venice," she pondered aloud.

"But it's rather wonderful too," Venetia replied, thinking about the diamond engagement ring that Brendan had recently placed on her finger, and her house back in England that was now full of life and love and laughter. She looked up at Swan and smiled. "It's rather wonderful that the past doesn't have to define us. That having a dark history doesn't mean that we can't have a bright future."

Swan rose unsteadily to her feet, causing the gondola to rock, and took a deep breath and flung her arms open wide.

"*Il futuro!*" she called, her voice echoing in the misty morning air. *The future!*

ACKNOWLEDGMENTS

Well, here we are—my fifth book—and some days I still have to pinch myself. My first thanks go to my wonderful readers, because without you I'd have crashed and burned by now (and, yes, that is a *Top Gun* quote). Thank you so much for buying, borrowing, reading, reviewing, and recommending my books. Thank you for all your feedback and support and for the pictures of your animal companions. You'll never know how grateful I am and how much you brighten my days with all your messages.

My heartfelt thanks also go to all the book bloggers, reviewers, booksellers, and librarians who help readers find my books. I really appreciate the brilliant job you do.

As always, I am indebted to a whole army of people who have turned *The Phoenix Ballroom* into a real book. The first mention must be my truly awesome agent and friend, Lisa Highton. Thank you, Lisa, for your steadfast faith in this book from the start and for your knowledge, guidance, and unfailing humor. Working with you is always a privilege and a joy. Thank you also for your patience and tolerance of my idiosyncrasies and for putting up with my insisting that every time we saw a crow it was a sign. It was (just saying). Huge thanks to all the team at Jenny Brown Associates for welcoming me on board and for all your hard work on my behalf.

I am so excited to have found a new home for my stories at Corvus/Atlantic UK. I'm truly grateful to Sarah Hodgson for her belief in this story and for her sensitive and insightful editing, and to the lovely people at Corvus and Atlantic Books—especially Dave Woodhouse, Felice McKeown, and Kirsty Doole, for all their hard work, support, and enthusiasm and for the conjuring of such a magical cover. It is an absolute pleasure to be working with you. Thank you also to Amber Burlinson for her scrupulous copyediting.

I am very fortunate to have so many wonderful readers in the United States, thanks to Rachel Kahan, my amazing editor at William Morrow, and the team at HarperCollins. Huge thanks to Rachel for championing my books from the beginning and for continuing to bring my stories to readers in the US.

Thank you too to all the publishers in translation who have supported my work and taken my writing to so many places that I hope to visit someday.

Writing can be a solitary business, so I'd like to thank fellow authors Matt Cain, Celia Anderson, Annie Lyons, Kit Fielding, Chris Barrington, Ronald Frame, and Peter Budek for their much-appreciated friendship and support.

Special thanks to Laura Macdougall for taking a chance on me at the start and giving me the opportunity to make my dream of becoming an author come true.

Thank you, as always, to my mum and dad for bringing me up surrounded by books and teaching me the joy of reading.

And last but not least, we get to the dogs and the husband. Thank you, Squadron Leader Timothy Bear and Mr. Zachariah Popov, for choosing me as your human and for your unconditional love. Paul—ditto.

ABOUT THE AUTHOR

RUTH HOGAN is the author of *The Keeper of Lost Things* and *Queenie Malone's Paradise Hotel*, which have been bestsellers around the world. She lives in Bedford, England, with her husband and a pack of much-loved rescue dogs.